PE

NEW BOY

William Sutcliffe was born in 1971 in London. While at university he spent two years writing and performing with the Cambridge Footlights. Since then he has been working as a TV researcher. *New Boy* is his first novel.

WILLIAM SUTCLIFFE

NEW BOY

PENGUIN BOOKS

PENGUIN BOOKS

Published by the Penguin Group
Penguin Books Ltd, 27 Wrights Lane, London w8 5TZ, England
Penguin Books USA Inc., 375 Hudson Street, New York, New York 10014, USA
Penguin Books Australia Ltd, Ringwood, Victoria, Australia
Penguin Books Canada Ltd, 10 Alcorn Avenue, Toronto, Ontario, Canada M4V 3B2
Penguin Books (NZ) Ltd, 182–190 Wairau Road, Auckland 10, New Zealand

Penguin Books Ltd, Registered Offices: Harmondsworth, Middlesex, England

First published 1996
5 7 9 10 8 6

Set in 10.5/12.5 Monotype Sabon
Typeset by Datix International Limited, Bungay, Suffolk
Printed in England by Clays Ltd, St Ives plc

For Mum, Dad, Adam and Georgie

CONTENTS

THE NEW BOY

CHAPTER ONE

Along with the rest of the staff, the chaplain at my school failed to notice that the place had long since been taken over by Jews and Asians. He was the kind of chirpy Englishman who Christians think of as 'a character' but we Jews prefer to call 'a wanker'.

His sermons, which everyone had to sit through on a Friday, came from an endless, dreary repertoire of anecdotes of his parish days in some county or other that wasn't London, all involving the same pitiful cast of quaint English grannies. Neither the setting nor the characters meant anything to his audience, most of whom had barely been outside the M25, and whose grannies weren't quaint and tended to live abroad. The headmaster would do his runaway-vibrator-up-the-arse routine – fat red face shuddering itself into a purple frenzy of mirth, while the rest of us picked our noses and stared at the ceiling.

It is not surprising, then, that during the optional Wednesday service, everyone who could claim even a toe-full of non-English blood would head for the chaos of the Jewish assemblies in the classroom block. Each year-group was assigned two adjacent classrooms, and a different assembly would be given in each room by a pair or trio of sixth formers, who were supposed to deal with a different aspect of Judaism each week. This enormous operation was monitored by a harassed-looking Dr Kuper from the physics department who trotted between the ten rooms, poking his head round each door to check that the matters under discussion were of a religious nature.

Some of the duller assemblies would be spent persuading Dr Kuper that the welfare of Tottenham FC was of key significance to the place of the modern Jew in contemporary London. 'But sir! Hoddle's useless. He's lost it. And Clive Allen is a waste of space unless he gets decent service from the midfield.

It is essential for Jewish self-respect that we bring up a ball player of Mabbutt's quality from the reserves.'

If the sixth former taking the assembly was a good talker, however, Dr Kuper didn't have to be persuaded of anything. Any subject under the sun could be discussed, with one eye on the door, the slightest movement of which would bring about an instant and seamless leap into theological matters. By the time I was in the sixth form, I loved giving these talks more than anything. As long as you could make them laugh, the younger boys would worship you, and you could pass yourself off as a man of infinite experience.

I used to read the first few chapters from biographies of the rich and famous and adopt their childhood sex-lives as my own. Kirk Douglas had a particularly good story involving a married woman, a ladder and a pair of curling tongs, which I had used several times in my suavest you'll-never-guess-what-happened-to-me-this-weekend manner. This reading was essential research, because the good-looking amongst the thirteen-year-olds tended to be more sexually experienced than me.

The main topic of conversation was always, invariably, sex.

The worst mistake was to start the assembly by asking them to shut up, because they never would. You needed an arresting opening. So I would start by quietly drawing a diagram on the blackboard. Curiosity then brought the noise level down.

'Can anyone tell me what these are? These two curves. Anyone?'

Stillness. Tension.

'They are known as outer labia. Now you've probably all seen a pair of them somewhere or other before, and wondered what purpose they serve. Technically speaking, are they or are they not part of the vagina proper?'

Silence. Awe. Adoration.

'Well, this is a matter of some contention amongst experienced lovers. It is usually agreed upon that they are, if you like, the entranceway to the vagina. To ask whether or not it is actually part thereof is rather like asking whether or not a door is

4

outside or inside a house. The question is purely semantic. The key fact to remember is that however useful a door is for getting into a house, it must not be mistaken for the house itself. There are far more interesting things inside, concealed from the casual observer. Always remember – a courteous guest does not spend long admiring the paintwork on his hostess's porch, he heads straight for the living room, compliments her on the family portraits and warms his hands at the hearth. This little dot here represents the hearth – the fireplace – the focus of social activity. It is always further from the doorway than you expect, but it *must* be found quickly, before you (or your hostess) cools down.'

Wonder. Respect. I am a God.

'Now – your invitation will often specify certain dress codes. Formal: condommed, or informal: *au naturel*. It is worth noting that a hostess of a social gathering will often specify formal dress simply as a matter of course. It is more important to gauge her character than to read the invitation. Often, one impresses by turning up to a black tie party dressed in jeans and a T-shirt, so to speak. Try wherever possible to get away without wearing a condom. The experience is far better: more daring, more exciting, warmer, wetter. They only ask you to wear one as a test of your skill and enthusiasm – rather like asking a concert pianist to perform with gloves on. If you are asked to put one on –' enter Dr Kuper. '– either at home or in the synagogue, you should do so without the slightest hesitation. It is worn on the top of the head as a sign of devotion and respect to God, often clipped to the hair to stop it blowing away in the wind. It is very embarrassing to have it fall off at the wrong moment. While the devout wear one all the time, most of us only put one on during worship. These days they come in a number of amusing shapes and sizes, but I always find that the fancy ones never fit properly. Women, as you all know, are never required to wear one, though the orthodox sometimes shave off the hair and cover up with a wig.' Dr Kuper looks puzzled by the laughter at the last comment, so I ask him a question. 'I think it's an important part of Jewish identity to be seen wearing one as often as possible. I wish I had the courage to wear one to school. What do you think, Dr Kuper?'

'Well, Mark, I used to wear one as a child, but I stopped as soon as my parents let me. I found it caused embarrassment. People would comment, and I got stared at, so I just stopped. I prefer to have my head as nature intended it.'

He is interrupted by peals of laughter, which he chooses to ignore. 'Well done, Mark. Good assembly,' he says. Then he leaves.

CHAPTER TWO

We were only allowed to start taking Jewish assemblies from the start of the sixth form, and it was at my third one, long before I had my crowd-control technique sorted out, that I found myself behaving strangely. The beginning of the sixth form was a difficult time for me, and it was extremely important that I established myself quickly as a cool person. I had spent my first five years at the school marooned in the social backwaters of the unsporty homework-doers, and in the first few weeks of the sixth form, for the first time since we had arrived, social status was up for grabs again. This was down to the fact that we were now allowed to wear our own clothes (it had to be a jacket and tie, but at least it wasn't school uniform), so the new divide between the fashionable and the unfashionable created opportunities for crossing the previously unbridgeable gulf between the elect (the Lads) and the rejects (the Spods). Also, it was just beginning – *just* beginning – to be cool to be clever. That was where my opportunities lay. If I wanted to leave school with any self-respect whatsoever, I had to let everyone know as quickly as possible just how fucking clever I was.

This effort to reinvent my personality, combined with the fact my life had been turned over by the arrival of Barry – a new boy in my year – put me in a state of permanent nervous tension. My brain was in overdrive. I think this is why I went a little too far in one Jewish assembly. I *had* to do well. I *had* to be clever.

I was taking the fifth form, who were notorious for being the hardest group to control, and was trying to spin out some bullshit nicked from Burt Reynolds' fifteenth birthday party. It wasn't really working, and I could tell that the group were getting bored and were about to start taking the piss out of me. So I turned on a boy called Robert Levin – it was just a way to get myself out of a potentially embarrassing situation, really.

Levin wasn't the usual victim type – he wasn't small, he wasn't ugly, he wasn't a Christian – in fact he was a pleasant, friendly kind of guy. It just so happened that five years earlier he had tossed off Jeremy Jacobs in a jacuzzi. No one actually knew whether or not the story was true, but everyone had heard it, and it was constantly told and retold around the school. Even if you didn't know anyone in the fifth form, you would have heard of Robert Levin, and you would know that he had tossed off Jeremy Jacobs in a jacuzzi.

The story was so catchy, so neatly alliterative that it was almost certainly a malicious fabrication, but it was widespread enough to have acquired the unchallengeable status of a School Myth. The fact that Jeremy Jacobs had left the school years ago, before the rumour emerged, made the story even more convenient, since everyone's sexual insecurities could be focused on one person.

Every conceivable torment had been visited on Robert Levin, ranging from the most basic daily taunting, through to notes about killing gays being left in his schoolbag. Given that his life at the school must have been one of absolute misery, he dealt with it pretty well. I remember, the first time I ever met him, I asked him casually (as everyone did) whether or not it was true about him and Jeremy Jacobs, and he just shrugged it off. He didn't even get cross with me – he just ignored it.

So, when I felt the assembly slipping away from me, and I saw Levin in the corner of the room, without looking at him I gradually changed the subject to masturbation and jacuzzis. Suddenly everyone was listening again. I held their attention, because I didn't allude to anything directly, I just subtly slid between the two topics – first I talked about how friends occasionally jerk each other off, and about what this means, then I mentioned how bathroom decor said a lot about one's sexual tastes, and how convenient jacuzzis are for masturbation. Then I just started chatting about how it was a shame Jeremy Jacobs had left the school because his parents had a lovely jacuzzi that he could have told us all about, and on and on I went, with everyone in the room laughing. I don't mean to brag, but I was being very funny – and not in a coarse way, because I was alluding to things very subtly. I didn't even look at Levin, and I never mentioned his name. It was hilarious. I was being very, *very* funny. It was one of those moments of complete power. I had that audience absolutely at my command.

Having said that, I have to admit that a lot of people were laughing too hard. They weren't really laughing with me, more at Robert Levin – and in a nasty way. This pissed me off, because I wasn't being cruel. I was just being funny.

Levin, obviously, wasn't amused. He didn't look angry, though. He must have been annoyed, but it really didn't show. His face was completely blank. He just stared at me, almost as if he was listening attentively to what I was saying, and trying to remember it.

At the end of the assembly, after I had stopped talking, while everyone else filed out of the room, he stayed in the same position, still sitting down, still looking at me. It felt as if he was waiting for me to finish, even though I already had. The way he looked at me, in the empty classroom, with voices echoing into the room from the corridor, stopped me from leaving. He was making me wait for something.

He stood up, walked to the door, and gently closed it. The room went quiet. When his eyes moved from the door-handle back to my face, I felt a collapsing sensation in my chest.

Still he didn't speak.

It was up to me to say something first.

'Don't take it the wrong way,' I said. 'It was only a joke.' He didn't move. He didn't even seem that angry – his body looked completely calm – but there was something frightening in the air. I noticed for the first time that he was bigger than me.

'Look, I wasn't laughing *at* you,' I said. 'I was just having a joke. I was only protecting myself – they were all about to turn on me. Some of them were laughing *at* you, but not me. That's what I meant. I'm as pissed off as you are that they took it the wrong way. I've got nothing against you. They're the wankers. They're the ones you should be angry with.'

When he spoke, he spoke very quietly.

'But it's you I'm angry with,' he said.

He said it so softly that I opened my mouth to say, 'What?', but closed it again. I had heard.

I felt the collapsing sensation again.

'You don't *look* very angry,' I said, and forced out a laugh.

Then some lower school boys came in for a lesson, and Levin left.

I should have punched him.

During a school career you're bound to humiliate the odd person out of pure malice here and there. It's not as if having an enemy for life ever did anyone any harm, and I certainly didn't give a toss that some little squit in the fifth form now hated me. The problem was just that the episode left a nasty taste in my mouth. I'm not the kind of person who mopes around feeling guilty about every little social slip-up, but whenever I remembered what I had done, I couldn't help feeling that in some personal way I had . . . well . . . betrayed myself.

It all got confused in my head with these thoughts I was having about Barry, the new boy.

CHAPTER THREE

Barry had joined the school three weeks earlier, at the start of the sixth form. There was a tradition at the school that any new boy would be ignored by everyone except the Christians for roughly a year. While this operated perfectly well for all the other new sixth formers, it didn't work on Barry because he managed to ignore everyone else before they got a chance to get in first and start ignoring him. It wasn't even as if he was being actively aloof, he just gave the impression that he had no interest in acquiring friends. Given that he also happened to be six foot two, was built like a God and had the face of a movie star, it is easy to see how he managed to intimidate every boy in the school without even trying.

His unrevealing expression preyed on everyone's paranoia about their own bodies. Just standing next to him, you began to feel ugly, short, hairy and awkward. People felt his eyes burning on their spotty chin, their shiny nose, their greasy hair or too-short legs. Everyone was afraid of him.

But we couldn't stop looking at him. At least, I couldn't stop looking at him. I'm not into self-analysis, but I have to admit that Barry was doing strange things to my mind. I kept looking for him in crowds. When the door opened in the sixth-form common-room, I couldn't stop myself spinning round to see if it was him. In the dining room, I wouldn't sit next to him, but I would wander with my tray until I had at least seen where he was eating before I took my place. I was – sort of – obsessed with him.

The only time I managed to stop thinking about him was in the gaps when I found time to worry about myself.

What the fuck was happening to me? Why couldn't I take my eyes off him?

And I couldn't help feeling that I wasn't the only worried

one. Wherever Barry went, I could detect a little change in the social temperature. Sometimes it got hotter, sometimes it got colder, but once his presence had been noticed it never stayed the same. It was almost identical to what happened when there were girls wandering around the school.

Even the School Animal – the boy who could fit eighteen two-pence coins under his foreskin and regularly proved it – even he seemed slightly cowed in the presence of Barry. He quietened down a bit. And he certainly didn't get his dick out and start asking around for coppers. Somehow, Barry put people on their best behaviour.

Everyone noticed him, that much was obvious. What I needed to know was whether or not I was noticing him more than everyone else. It sort of felt as if I was.

Do you see what I mean?

It was a very worrying time for me.

Let's face it – Barry was sex on legs. And I . . . well, I wasn't.

I have a huge hooked nose, I am perpetually covered in stubble whether I shave or not, my hair is wiry and my eyebrows look like two moustaches. I am an anti-Semite's dream. The Ku Klux Klan would pay a fortune for pictures of my face to stick up all over American classrooms to frighten little girls.

Don't get me wrong, though. By the time I met Barry I wasn't one of those adolescent turds who's too paranoid about their appearance to notice that there's a world beyond the pus on the end of their nose. Quite the opposite. I had gone through that phase, and was just beginning to reach a point where I was comfortable with the way I looked. I felt distinguished. And I liked the fact that stupid people recoiled from me, because I wouldn't want to talk to stupid people anyway.

Everyone knows that a man doesn't need to be good-looking to be attractive. So, being ugly was an advantage since it would force me to make the extra effort to get noticed. Ideally I wouldn't have had myself *quite* so hideous, but still . . . I could live with it.

Stupid people recoiled from Barry, too. I thought I might be able to use this shared experience to somehow make myself his . . . ally. That's a good way of putting it. I'm not the kind of jerk who runs around trying to make friends with people, but I just thought that Barry would be a useful person to have as an ally.

CHAPTER FOUR

Getting to know Barry wasn't easy. The mere thought of starting a conversation with him put an apple in my throat. When I once actually spoke to him, I had to force the words past several basketballs lodged throughout my respiratory system. As a result it came out three times louder than I intended, and Barry's first impression of me was, 'COULD I BORROW A PENCIL, PLEASE!!!'

This pissed me off. It was a very bad start. For several weeks I had nightmares in which beautiful women stripped off and offered their bodies to me while I kept my clothes on and asked them questions about pencils.

Throughout my pencil-impotence nightmare phase I hovered around Barry at school, hoping to find some other opening to start a conversation which might compensate for my bad first impression. Once I successfully managed a 'No, Room 63 is that way,' which came out quivery, but at a natural volume, though I didn't feel that this exactly burned my existence as a person very deep into Barry's consciousness.

Then, one weekend, I was wandering around London when I saw him drowning in the Thames. I stripped off all my clothes, leapt into the river, tore his ankle free from the reeds which were dragging him down and hauled him to the shore, where I revived him with the kiss of life.

Or maybe that was just a dream.

What actually happened was that Barry was on a geology field trip when he stumbled on a kerbstone and fell into the road, knocking himself unconscious on the tarmac directly in the path of a juggernaut with the driver asleep at the wheel and severed brake-cables. Luckily I happened to be passing by, but since Barry was an exceptionally diligent geologist, he had filled his pockets with too many rocks for me to be able to drag him from the road, so I had to sprint uphill, leap onto the moving juggernaut, wrestle the slumbering trucker from the wheel and steer us into a nearby marsh from which I swam to safety just in time to revive Barry with the kiss of life.

This is how I became his friend.

Yes?

OK, OK, so I'm not exactly being literal here. If you want the truth truth, as in pissboringgrowabraincan'tyouthinkofanythingbetter truth, the fact of the matter is that Barry and I took the same school bus, so, bit by bit, I managed to familiarize myself with him.

There.

Crap, isn't it?

Actually, now I think of it, it's a bit more interesting than that, since the politics of where you sat on the school bus was an intricate subject, heavily complicated by the fact that the coach was shared with members of the adjacent girls' school. In Barry's first week, when he arrived and sat in the third row from the front, this was a revolution. It represented a fundamental undermining of years of tacit negotiation and not-very-tacit fights. He was the kind of person who could have gone straight to the back seat, but probably should have undergone a couple of weeks in the second or third row from the back, then he just turned up and sat in the third row from the front! It was unbelievable!

Once, when a first year sat next to him, a) he gave him the window seat, and b) they had a conversation. I couldn't believe it! I couldn't fucking believe it! It just wasn't right.

The standard, accepted, handed-down-through-generations seating plan for the coach was as follows:

Front Front:	Teachers.
Back Front:	Sad cases, Christians, uncool 1st–3rd forms, ugly girls.
Front Middle:	Cool 1st–3rd forms, uncool 4th–6th forms.
Back Middle:	Cool 4th and 5th forms (heirs to the back seat), 6th-form scientists who think white

	shoes make them cool, stray obnoxious maso-chistic 1st–3rd form Jews who enjoy getting beaten up.
Front Back:	Sexy girls.
Back Seat:	Cool 6th-form boys.

The differentiation between front middle and back middle was vague, to say the least, so as you can imagine, the 4th and 5th forms were a key period for establishing the five people who would eventually graduate to the back seat. It is worth noting that one's school status did not necessarily correspond to one's coach status, partly due to the presence of girls, but mainly due to the gradual erosion of conventional snap judgements through the course of twice daily exposure in an enclosed space for seven years. People who would normally not acknowledge one another's existence in the school corridors were eventually, after three or four years, forced to come up with some kind of mutual greeting for when they caught each other's eye getting on and off the coach. This could be anything from a smile or a nod, to a 'hello' or a punch in the face, but it was at least some little gesture of mutual recognition.

My fourth and fifth years were dominated by an ongoing conflict with the coach prefect of the time, a fascist army-boy called Michael Carter. This conflict was mainly contrived by me, since I knew that I had to provoke him in some way if I wanted to get bullied, which I desperately needed to happen in order to show that I could stand up for myself – which was necessary in order to graduate from front middle to back middle, putting me in a position where I would be able to move to the back seat when the sixth form came along. Obvious, really.

Provoking Michael Carter was easy. If he got on the coach and started talking to Petra (the chief sexy girl of the period), I would kneel on my seat, face the back of the coach, and ask him polite but curious questions.

'Michael, why are you talking to Petra when you know she doesn't fancy you? Michael, why are you doing that? You know she doesn't fancy you, so why are you talking to her? Why,

Michael? Tell me. I'm only curious so that I can learn from your vast sexual experience.' He would usually tell me to shut up and face the front, in which case I would say, 'Are you asking me to do that so that you can make a stand in front of Petra? Is that why you're asking me to sit down and face the front? Is it just to show that you're an authoritative person? Do you think that will make her fancy you? Does that tend to work, in your vast sexual experience, Michael? Tell me, I want to learn.'

I would continue in this vein until he came and hit me.

If he got on the coach and didn't start talking to Petra I would turn round and say, 'Michael, why aren't you talking to Petra today? Why aren't you talking to her? Is it because you've finally realized that she doesn't fancy you? Is that why? Is that why you aren't talking to her? Don't you think you should keep on trying, Michael? You never know – she might start fancying you if you keep on trying. Is it because you're not wearing your army uniform today, Michael? Is that why you're not talking to Petra? Is it because you know you look much sexier in your army uniform? Is that why? Tell me, Michael – I want to learn from your vast sexual experience.'

I would continue in this vein until he came and hit me.

The longer I managed to wind him up, the harder he hit me, but it was definitely worth it. Thanks to my relationship with Michael Carter, by the end of the fifth form I was at the very back of the middle, almost at the front of the back. (This put me extremely near Petra, who I secretly thought fancied me – but that's another story.)

As a result of all this, by the time I was in the lower sixth, just as Barry arrived at the school, I was at last taking my place on the back seat. I was one of those people whose coach status was considerably above their school status, and if it hadn't been for the fortunate coincidence of Barry getting the same bus as me, I don't think I would have stood a chance of ever getting close to him.

A few weeks into the sixth form, once I felt he must have at least become aware of my face as something vaguely recognizable,

I walked up to him at the coach-stop and started talking to him. I was psyched up – I was calm – I was ready for anything – so I just went for it.

'Cold, isn't it?' I said.

'Yes,' he said.

'Coach is a bit late,' I said.

'Yes,' he said.

'Mind you, it is November,' I said.

'What,' he said, 'is the coach often late in November?'

'No, I meant the cold,' I said.

'Right,' he said.

'I meant it's often cold in November,' I said.

'It is. It is,' he said.

'Listen,' I said, 'why don't you sit on the back seat? It's better.'

'All right,' he said.

YES! YES! YES! YYYYYYYYYEEEEEEEEEEAAAAA AAAAHHHHHHHH! YESYESYES! YES! YES! YES!

My brain was having an orgasm. I couldn't believe it!

That's it really. That's the truth truth. That's how our friendship started.

CHAPTER FIVE

Wednesday afternoon. Rugby. Mr Dean, resplendent in red tracksuit trousers, orange socks, *England U23 Women's Hockey Training Weekend – Wycombe '83* sweatshirt and green referee's whistle that never works, lines us up on the touch line. He regales us yet again with the story of the Wycombe '83 training weekend – the usual dedicated-sportswomen-you're-just-a-bunch-of-pansies routine. Although we've heard it fifty times before we're still not convinced, and school wisdom says that he got the sweatshirt at an Oxfam shop.

Then we pick teams: first the good players, then the fat bad players, then me, then the thin bad players, then the wimps and the Christians.

Lecture over, teams picked, everyone in position. Mr Dean raises the green whistle to his lips. No one looks vaguely ready to start, because we all know what is going to happen.

'Come on lads – look lively!'

We all pretend to look lively. He blows the whistle. No sound comes out. This happens every Wednesday, but no one ever reminds him that the green whistle doesn't work because we all want him to look like an arsehole, which indeed he does.

'Damn – whistle's buggered. I knew it. Who wants to run back and fetch my whistle?'

All the smokers volunteer, and Unstead is chosen. He jogs off, picking up fags and lighter from his tracksuit on the touchline. We all know he won't come back but can't be bothered to say anything. To pass the time Mr Dean gives us a stamina test.

We all fail the stamina test. A couple of Christians vomit meekly behind the try-line.

Cohen feeds Mr Dean a line about how he'd rather be watching TV, so we all get to settle for another lecture in place of the planned endurance measurement.

Mr Dean realizes that Unstead isn't coming back. We all pretend to be worried, and try and convince Mr Dean that some terrible accident must have occurred. The rest of the smokers volunteer to go and ring for an ambulance. Mr Dean informs us that he wasn't born yesterday and tells us that Unstead is for the high jump. I tell him that I would like to join the school athletics team too, and Mr Dean threatens me with '. . . something' (because he can't think of anything).

We are positioned for the start of the game, and are told that the game will be refereed using Mr Dean's wolf whistle. He puts his fingers in his mouth, we 'look lively', he blows. He tries three or four times blasting out in a red-faced fury an inaudible whoosh of air. I offer to teach him how to wolf whistle. He gives me a suspicious look, unable to tell whether I am being helpful or facetious, in the end guessing correctly and threatening me with '. . . something'.

He attempts to salvage his dignity by doing an ordinary whistle, but with his fingers resting on his chin. Bored with humiliating Mr Dean, our captain kicks off, and the game somehow starts itself.

The quietness of the referee's whistle is a perfect excuse for ignoring it when you hear a blow, and pretending to hear one when none was given. Mr Dean soon loses all control of the game, but rather than descending into chaos, an admirable spirit of cooperation reigns between the teams, with both sides aiding each other wherever possible to misunderstand any command given by the referee. All thirty players on the pitch work together in harmony to masquerade a desire to win, while in fact concentrating exclusively on the attempt to give Mr Dean a nervous breakdown.

For example, a perfectly organized line-out is executed near the blues' try-line while Mr Dean stands a hundred yards away under the stripes' goal-posts shouting, 'SCRUM! SCRUM! OVER HERE! SCRUM OVER HERE! ARE YOU LISTENING? COME BACK! THAT LINE-OUT IS VOID. THERE IS NO LINE-OUT. WHAT ARE YOU DOING? COME BACK! THAT IS NOT A LEGITIMATE PLAY.

YOU'RE GIVING UP GROUND, BLUES. ALL RIGHT, ALL RIGHT, WAIT FOR ME!'

His voice is weak but audible. He has been there for several minutes. We take the line-out.

Later, Atkins breaks free, sprints the entire length of the pitch then stops two yards short of a try, swearing blind that he heard a whistle. Mr Dean doesn't know what to do so he orders a drop-ball, which is from football rules not rugby, but no one tells him.

One scrum lasts ten minutes because no one pushes. After nine minutes, Mr Dean threatens that everyone involved in the scrum will have a detention unless someone starts to push. The blues' hooker shouts from the middle of the scrum that it's not fair on him because the props are so big that his feet aren't touching the ground and he'd really like to push but can't and his parents will cut his pocket money if he gets another detention before Christmas and it's not fair.

The blues then start to wheel the scrum, and the stripes seem to cooperate. The scrum goes round and round several times, with the ball resting immobile in the centre. It is about to enter its eighth full revolution when Mr Dean blows for half time.

There is a hitch in starting the second half over the changing of ends for the teams, when everyone decides to disagree about which ends we had in the first half. Amazingly, Mr Dean joins in the argument and ends up losing.

The first ten minutes of the second half is conducted exclusively in slow motion, causing Mr Dean to leave the pitch close to tears. We feel a little guilty for a minute or two, but generally no one can recall a better games afternoon. The atmosphere in the changing-rooms, however, just isn't the same without Mr Dean marching up and down, shouting 'Get stripped! Get stripped! Showers are compulsory. Get stripped!' We realize that he must be exceptionally upset if he is missing out on this little thrill.

In the past, my school has been criticized for churning out ruthless, self-seeking, out-and-out Thatcherites, and while this is difficult to deny, it is worth remarking that the above episode does bear witness to the fact that we weren't immune to the spirit of cooperation, as long as suitable circumstances arose. You could go to the most laid-back, hippy-clappy Steiner school in the country, and I would be amazed if you would find such an admirable example of young people working together in self-motivated harmony towards a common goal.

Besides, any school which *wasn't* turning out ruthless, self-seeking Thatcherites in 1986 was quite blatantly out of step with the times, and my school seemed to have adapted to the eighties better than any other. When I started there in 1981, the school motto, 'Serve and Obey', which was sewn into my blazer pocket, had a stately, historical ring to it. By the time I was in the sixth form, however, the ethos of the times had altered the meaning of the phrase. As the fees went up and the school built new libraries and sports centres, the implication of the motto shifted from 'I will serve and obey you' to 'You will serve and obey me because my parents have got lots of cash and they're buying me an education so I'm gonna be really rich so watch out'.

They didn't quite have space for the revised motto on our blazer pockets, but it was there, all right – in the way we walked – in the way we talked louder than people from other schools. People got the message.

CHAPTER SIX

In the changing-room after the game, I was changing just opposite Barry (surprise, surprise). He came in some time after me since he had been training with the school rugby squad, and while I dressed, I just couldn't stop my eyes from straying towards him as he took his clothes off.

What a body! *What* a body!

And when he walked to the shower – not the hunched scamper of most naked men – just an ordinary walk – I simply could not take my eyes off his backside. What an arse! What a *fantastic* arse!

I didn't want to touch it or anything. I certainly didn't want to put my cock up it. I just, for some reason, couldn't stop myself looking at it. Now I'm no homophobe – don't get me wrong – but I'm also not a fucking bender. I'm not. I didn't get an erection or anything when I was looking at Barry. I just . . . I just felt a certain manly admiration for his beauty. I think maybe I was jealous of his power to attract women. The reason why I couldn't stop thinking about him or staring at him was that I wanted to look like him so that I could have sex with lots of women. That's what it was.

It didn't matter much, anyway, because I decided not to let myself think about it. And it certainly didn't matter to Barry because my pretty little friend was basically very slow on the uptake about most things, and he didn't have a clue about what was going on in my head.

In fact, that's another thing I was jealous about. I would have given anything to have a mind like his. Nothing seemed to bother him. He didn't worry about anything. He just did things. Nothing ever preyed on his mind. Anything he didn't understand he forgot about in seconds. No whingeing and analysing and agonizing and moping – he just forgot. It was incredible.

Or maybe all Gentiles could do this. Whatever it was, Barry just didn't seem very in touch with his own emotions.

Gradually, as we spent more time together on the coach, talking for an hour every day, we got to know each other better and better. I managed to dampen down the obsessive side of my feelings for him, and the tension between us began to dwindle. As our conversations became less tentative, I stopped feeling in awe of him, and before long, we became just like ordinary friends.

I still fantasized about him. And I still worried that there was something a little unnatural going on. I still thought that maybe I had been born with faulty hormones. But even if my brain frequently embarked on free-fall nose-dives of sexual paranoia, on the surface I behaved perfectly naturally towards Barry, and no one ever noticed anything odd about me.

While everyone else kept their distance from Barry, I was the one person who made the effort to get to know him – and I was amazed that he responded. I couldn't figure out why anyone as incredible-looking as him would take any interest in an ugly sod like me, but he did. If I had been him, I would have been out with a different woman every night – shagging my way through the beds of North London.

Why he wasn't, I just couldn't figure out, and I didn't get the chance to ask him, because we simply never discussed sex. Or masturbation – we never discussed that either. Given that almost all my previous school relationships were based on solid, wide-ranging and frequent debates about masturbation, this was odd.

Maybe I was afraid to raise the subject. Maybe I just felt that sex and Barry were incompatible, highly flammable thoughts. Or maybe *he* didn't like talking about it, either. Perhaps he didn't want to show off. He must have been aware that my sex life was non-existent – maybe he never mentioned it because he didn't want to make me feel bad. It was odd.

How we found other subjects to discuss I shall never know.

CHAPTER SEVEN

Towards the end of the term came our first sixth-form parents' evening. For me, these were always a highlight of the academic year. I *loved* them. Ever since the fourth form, we had been expected to come with our parents, turning the evening into an orgy of social embarrassment. It was an extravaganza of excruciating moments – social and intellectual paranoia stripped bare. Fantastic!

It was also a key opportunity to see who had fit mothers. Jeremy Dorlin's mum never ceased to amaze, and Robert Konigsberg, another ugly boy, also provided a pleasant surprise in the form of a mother who was said to have the best post-forty arse in the whole of Edgware. All the Christians, of course, had ugly mothers, except for Peter Pillow, the vicar's son, whose mother had the subtle allure of a diffident but shaggable nun.

Richard Cone, who had spent the entire term in brown corduroy trousers and a blue checked shirt with seventies collar tucked into a high-necked navy jumper under a grey tweed jacket, proved to have a father worthy of note when he, too, turned up in brown corduroy trousers and a blue checked shirt with seventies collar tucked into a high-necked navy jumper under a grey tweed jacket.

Most of the Asian mums turned up in their best saris and swept elegantly around the colourless corridors looking utterly out of place yet occasionally relatively horny, with the odd fit daughter in tow. All the Edgware Jewish mothers (apart from Mrs Konigsberg) looked frightful, dressed uniformly in high heels, stone-washed jeans and fur jackets with shoulder-length hair curled and dyed red. They wore so much make-up that they had to pout all evening to stop it falling off in chunks. The Stanmore Jewish mothers tended to go for the drab but over-dressed combo, leaving only the Hampstead and Golders Green set to dress with any style.

The Jews dotted along the Metropolitan Line, including my own family, tended to settle for the bland but inoffensive option.

Most of the maternal horn was in zone two of the London Underground, with the odd smattering around zone three. Zone four and outwards were an absolute write-off.

The fathers fell into two groups: brown and white. Other than that they were indistinguishable, and could only be told apart by the cars they drove. Sexiness of car also tended to follow the London Underground zone correlation, with Hampstead notching up the odd Porsche while Watford and Barnet spluttered into the car park often boasting little more than a Cortina or Renault 12. This group, the 'we're making enormous sacrifices for our son's education' set, were always good for a laugh, and invariably looked stressed to the point of anguish as they hurried from interview to interview, frantically discussing their child's performance. Edgware was again a source of horrific statistical anomalies, with families doing their best to turn up in more than one sports car, roaring into the car park in a penis-red cortège of vulgarity.

The Christian fathers were easier to tell apart than their children or wives, tending to divide neatly in two: either Volvo (classy) or BMW (yob made good).

Graham Hammond came up trumps when he failed to bring a father, arriving in a Volkswagen Beetle driven by his mother who wore dungarees and told a teacher who asked after Mr Hammond to fuck off. Maybe that was why Graham had spent every lunch time for the last two months crying in the school toilets.

Perretta's dad (who was in charge of the Wimpy franchise throughout Scandinavia) reputedly threatened to punch Mr Barber (who thought piano-key ties were trendy) for having called his son thick three weeks previously.

I was even more excited than usual at this particular parents' evening, thanks to the thought that I was going to meet Barry's parents. Who on earth could produce someone like him?

Unfortunately, when I did come across them, our parents proceeded to have such a cringingly embarrassing conversation that my eyes were closed for most of it, and I never really got a proper look. Barry's mother was quite good-looking but nothing special, and Barry's father I can't remember at all. If I'd known that he was going to die a few months later, I would have paid far more attention.

It was Barry's mum who opened the bout: 'Is this your Mark?' she said. 'According to Barry they've become best friends jolly quickly.' This was a serious body-blow to open with, and I could see Barry reeling in the corner.

'Yes,' replied my mum, 'Mark hardly talks to us these days, but when he finally opens his mouth, he has only the nicest things to say about Barry.' Then she stroked my arm – a powerful strike which almost sent me crashing to my knees.

'Thank you for being so nice to Barry,' countered his mum. Fuck! She was talking to me! 'He's been finding it very hard starting at a new school, and you've made the world of difference. Hasn't he, Barry?' That was it – the KO. Barry was out for the count.

Then, just as I thought I was in the clear, my mum piped up. 'Mark's always been like that. He doesn't like to admit it, but he's always been the one who was kind to the new boy. I remember back in primary school, when Joseph Bloom, the boy with a skin complaint – he was crumbly all over – when Joseph Bloom gave out invitations to his eighth birthday party and everyone tore them up, Mark was the only one who folded it up politely and put it in his pocket. The party was cancelled, of course, so Mark didn't have to go and he got the best of both worlds. It's basic kindness, that's what it is.'

Fuck me! What a combination! I was done for – out cold. Would I ever walk again?

(It is worth paying tribute here to the fascinating contrast of fighting styles which makes for a good bout. English: 'My son's a bit of an idiot and needs help wherever possible' versus the traditional Jewish 'My son's a genius and has always done everything right throughout his life.' In my opinion, the English style is at an advantage as long as it can get a quick KO, but if the Jew can last the first few rounds, then the longer bout will almost certainly be hers.)

Since, like me, my parents considered the evening to be principally a social occasion, the academic side was never much of a problem. My parents hardly listened to the teachers and spent most of the interviews nervously flicking through my form list, trying to figure out who they were going to bump into in the corridor next. Besides, my schoolwork was always good anyway. As we drove home, my dad did give me one piece of advice, though.

'Never become a teacher,' he said.

CHAPTER EIGHT

I could lie about my parents, or I could tell you the truth. To be completely honest with you, I really ought to lie. In fact, I already have done. My father didn't really say 'never become a teacher' on the way home. He didn't say anything. Or at least he didn't say anything I can remember. I wasn't listening, anyway. I was sitting in the back inventing what he would be saying if he was someone more interesting.

Look – it will be far better for all of us if you agree to let me lie about this. I'm far more practised at it. It's infinitely more interesting. I've got several pairs of pre-prepared fantasy parents, and you can take your pick. If you want something sexy/sporty, I've got a nice Kevin Keegan and Bo Derek set-up. If you fancy something a bit more kinky, I've got an enigmatic blue-collar/high-brow one of Sid James and Germaine Greer, or if you want something exotic you can go for my single-mother-on-the-game-who-I-have-to-pimp-for-to-make-ends-meet scenario. If you want tragedy, you can have my blind wheelchair-bound widower father with optional war wounds (this one comes free with a heart-rending anecdote in which the school bully laughs at me and beats me up when he finds a Braille shopping list in my schoolbag).

Or if you insist on realism, I even have the stock suburban fiction fall-back of a two-CSE housewife mother and boring accountant father who somehow breed me, the boy genius who is deeply misunderstood and sulks in his bedroom analysing *The Smiths* lyrics and making his skin shiny with too much spot cream.

But unfortunately the truth is far worse than all of these. My parents are both graduates, both liberal, both successful in their jobs without being too ambitious or pushy. They are both laid-back about smoking, drugs and sex, and neither of them particularly bothers to tell me what to do. Can you believe it? Isn't it awful! Can you think of a more comprehensive and evil way to completely fuck up your son? The tossers are playing games with my mind. Their attitude as good as puts me off tobacco, narcotics and copulation – all of which deals a near fatal blow to my social life. They have deliberately contrived a set-up in which the only way I can rebel is by conforming, which is clearly no fucking good whatsoever. And worst of all, they are helpful and understanding about how difficult it must be for me.

There.

Um . . .

Actually that one's a fantasy, too. I was hoping I might be able to fob you off with a bit of sub-Adrian Mole child psychology, spiced up with the odd 'fuck' to make it sound like me. But no.

I'm finding this chapter very difficult.

Look – I can't describe them. They're my parents. They're just there. They cook my food, buy my clothes and get on my tits. Just like everyone else's parents. That's it, really.

Honestly.

I just don't think about them. They're only my parents, for fuck's sake.

And in case you were wondering, my mother didn't really say all of that stuff at the parents' evening. She said something along those lines, but I've spiced it up to make it interesting. What she said was actually quite boring. I wasn't really very embarrassed, either.

People talk a lot of crap about how their father beats them up and throws them out of the house, but they love him anyway because he's their father. I don't believe a word of it. My father has never laid a finger on me, he hardly ever shouts at me, and I still don't think I can be bothered to love him. And the same goes for my mum. There's the old breast-feeding/Oedipus bond – but other than that I don't really think there's much there.

In fact, I'm deeply suspicious of anyone who goes on about loving their parents. The whole idea just doesn't hang together.

It's not that I hate my parents, or actively don't love them. It's just that my definition of love has to include, somewhere along the line, a certain desire to spend at least a minimal amount of time with the loved one. And let's face it, the idea of not seeing my parents for a week is hardly the most depressing thought I have ever had. In fact, the idea of not seeing them for a year doesn't exactly bring water pricking to my eyeballs.

To be honest, the idea of not seeing them *ever* registers a dramatic failure to provoke any emotional response at all. This is where it gets a bit worrying. I've got nothing against them – as far as parents go, they're really pretty OK – but if I fantasize about them dying and leaving a big house and loads of life insurance money for me and my brother to live off in enormous luxury for the rest of our lives, I can't quite tell whether this is a happy fantasy or a sad one.

It's on the borderline somewhere.

But let's face facts, I'm not exactly close to tears when I think about it. And I'd be pretty stupid if I didn't admit to myself that this doesn't cross-reference too well with the old 'love thy parents' idea.

This is why I don't see how anyone who is even remotely well-off can feel any love for their parents whatsoever. I think they're all liars.

And compared to everyone else at school, my family's not rich at all. If my dad owned the Wimpy franchise for the whole of Scandinavia, I'd want him dead like a shot.

CHAPTER NINE

Listen. I want to explain myself here. About Barry and me. I know what you're thinking. You're thinking, 'That Mark – he's a poof.'

And I take your point. Granted – I have been shamelessly eyeing up a person whose gender bears remarkable similarities to my own. Granted. I can't deny it. And ... well ... I'm not going to try and convince you that it's normal for a hetero-sexual guy to lust after other men – that would be defeating the object of the whole heterosexual thing – but I would just like to say that I still consider myself a damn sight straighter than most of the other boys at my school. I'm not saying that everyone else was gay. All I mean is that casting an appreciative eye over the odd well-turned buttock is nothing compared to what the rugby team got up to with each other. And this isn't the old 'oooeeerrr we all know what goes on in a scrum' slur. This is what they used to do off the field. For fun.

At morning break in the sixth-form common-room, there was a game they used to play which was the highlight of the rugby team's week. It was known as a 'bundle', and the rules were as follows:

It is all started by a small tussle between two boys, of the type which occurs in any conversation. Then, a spectator to this minor fracas kicks off the game proper by shouting, 'BUNDLE!' and jumping on top of them. It is then the duty of every healthy red-blooded male in the room to shout 'BUU-UUNNNNDLLLLLLLE!' and join the heap of writhing, squealing boys, leaping on with as much force as possible.

The largest of these bundles contains up to thirty boys, causing severe injury to those at the bottom. It was an act of bravery to start the game because it meant that you would end up underneath, but altruism prevailed and certain boys fre-quently gave themselves up to the pleasure of others.

This game was common throughout the school, but only really took off in the upper four years (the post-pubescents), and was most popular of all amongst the loudest, cockiest, noisiest, biggest boys in the sixth form – the social kings – the Rugby First XV. The top dog – the king of kings – was the School Animal (the guy who could fit eighteen two-pence coins under his foreskin).

Now these guys were all straight. I'm sure of it. They used to beat up skinny Christians for being gay just to prove it. It's just that if the rugby team had ever got around to looking up the word 'homoerotic' in a dictionary, they might have had second thoughts about the way they chose to have fun together.

So you can see how in an all-boys' school, at an age when one's pubes still have that freshly grown sheen, it isn't easy to gauge which team you bat for. If no one is having any sex, and 90 per cent of the school population regularly indulge in mutual humping, it becomes very difficult to tell what is normal. This is why, despite the fact that odd things were happening with regard to Barry, I still felt pretty sure that I was a solid mid-to-low-order batsman for the hetties.

More than once, a bundle was so vigorous that it broke the sofa.

This mystified the teacher in charge. Mr Wright, the head of sixth form, thought he was trendy, so instead of being angry he tended to be 'disappointed'.

'I just don't understand. How did you do it? I'm very disappointed. There are boys in comprehensive schools who would give their right arm to have a sofa like that in their sixth-form common-room.'

'That proves that they're thick, then, doesn't it,' shouted Joel Schneider.

'That is the kind of comment that . . . it just makes me sick. *You*, Schneider, are thick. You are very thick.'

'That doesn't matter though, sir. I'm rich. Much richer than you, sir.'

'I feel sorry for you, Schneider.'

'Likewise, sir. Here's ten quid. Take it. Go and drown your sorrows.'

Mr Wright was the kind of person who became a teacher because he was an idealist, moved to a private school because he wanted to earn a bit more money, then had the piss taken out of him for the rest of his life. He hated the rich Jews for being rich Jews, and they always wound him up for it and won. There was nothing they liked more than being hated for being rich, simply because it gave them an extra opportunity to point out just how rich they were. As an added bonus, Mr Wright was pleasingly slow on the uptake.

'Look. Shut up. Put your money away. I was asking who broke the sofa. I want to know who is responsible. I know that it was a group of you, and you *will* tell me just what the hell you were doing.'

I was always tempted to grass: 'It was those thirty boys over there, sir. The school 1st and 2nd rugby XV. Every morning break they jump on the sofa and simulate buggery together, sir.' I never quite got up the courage, though.

Mr Wright's speech usually tailed away with a would-you-do-that-at-home routine, while Joel Schneider explained that the problem wouldn't arise because good quality sofas don't break so easily, and if he wanted to be put in touch with someone who would do a good deal on some top quality leather-look . . .

Right next door to the school, separated by what was known as the Berlin Wall, was a girls' school partnered to our own. Other than on the coaches and at the coach park, there was no contact allowed between the pupils of the two schools. Not one single class was mixed, and there was reputedly a school rule which stated that a distance of one metre had to be kept between visitors to the partner school. The most famous infringement of this rule was when the daughter of Alvin Stardust's drummer was caught in the cricket pavilion giving a blowjob to the son of Golders Green's best optician.

Apart from this freak episode (for which the girl was expelled and the boy given two weeks' suspension and a clap on the back), little interest was shown by the boys in the girls. The general consensus was that they were all ugly. A small group would hang around the girls' school gate at lunch-time, but they were thought to be a bit gay. Most people preferred to play football, while the Christians and the eunuchs did their homework in the library.

People talked about sex a lot, but it was always in terms of movie stars, musicians or television presenters. When females of our own age actually presented themselves, we tended to shrink away, muttering diffident rejoinders such as 'Fuck off you slag,' and 'Don't touch me you dog.' Not that anyone ever had tried to touch us, but it was worth saying, just in case.

The only people who were polite to girls were the boys who lived in Edgware and Stanmore. This was because they all had a ready-made social life outside school involving a regular round of discos at their local synagogues, and had all been having frequent and varied sex with endless streams of beautiful girls since the age of thirteen. Their parents were so keen for their children to marry a Jew that they didn't care how early they ran around getting each other pregnant. The rest of us at the school were pant-shakingly jealous of their social life, but it was too painful a subject to talk about.

I still remember the day, back in the second form, when Marc Avener announced loudly to Daniel Balint in morning registration that his girlfriend's periods had just started. To me, this was like saying that he had spent the weekend on the moon. I couldn't believe it. What a lucky bastard!

As we were getting to the end of the Autumn term of the lower sixth, I began to detect a certain thaw, an element of détente in relations between the two schools. There was more mixing at the coach park, with even a certain degree of touching, and the odd . . . dare I say it . . . the odd . . . no, I can't (you must) I can't (you must) . . . the odd . . . kiss! (Phew!)

In a dramatic reversal, it suddenly meant that you were gay if you *didn't* talk to girls. At a mixed school, this shift of opinion would have happened at the age of eleven. I found it hard enough aged seventeen.

And yet I had *still* never had a conversation with Barry about sex. I was burning with curiosity. I wanted to hear lurid tales about week-long shagfests in Swiss chalets. I wanted to hear about celebrity rubber fetish parties. I wanted to learn about technique. Even if it would be a while before I could put it into practice, I felt sure that he would teach me *everything*.

One day, on the coach home, I came out with it. I asked.

CHAPTER TEN

'WHAT! YOU'RE A WHAT?'

'A virgin.'

'A WHAT? . . . A WHAT?'

'A virgin.'

'A WHAT?'

'A VIRGIN, YOU ARSEHOLE, A VIRGIN!'

'Fuck. I'm stunned. I can't believe it.'

'Why? Aren't you?'

'Of course I am, you twat. Look at my face.'

'What about your face?'

'It's ugly, that's what. It is not a shaggable face.'

'You're not ugly,' he said. 'You're just a bit hairy, that's all.'

'Believe me, this is a books face. It is not a sex face. Now this,' I pulled at his cheeks, 'THIS, is a sex face.'

'You reckon?'

'You moron. What a fucking waste. What a waste of a face.'

'I'd like to have sex at some stage . . .'

'At some stage?'

'When I've found the right woman, I mean.'

'What do you mean the right woman?'

'Someone I want to spend time with – you know.'

'Oh my God.' I was in shock. I didn't know what to say. Who would have thought that Barry, of all people, would be like that. What a poof!

'Why are you a virgin?' I asked.

'What do you mean, why?'

'Why? – WHY? WHY ARE YOU A VIRGIN, YOU BAS-TARD? TELL ME!' I was beginning to get angry. The world had ceased to make sense. I tried to breathe deeply and slowly. 'Listen,' I said, as patiently as I could, 'I am a virgin because I am ugly. No one wants to have sex with me due to the un-pleasing arrangement of my facial features. I am undesirable.

But you . . . You are so . . . Why are you . . . What have you been doing – what the fuck have you been doing? WHY? ARE YOU A MORON? LISTEN, YOU WANKER – WHAT THE FUCK HAVE YOU BEEN DOING WITH YOUR LIFE?'

I was being a little irrational.

'You're weird, Mark.'

'I'm sorry. I just don't understand. It's an emotional subject for me.'

'Do you really want a reason?'

'OF COURSE I DO, YOU SHITHEAD.'

'All right, all right. Let me think.' He thought. It was a slow process. 'Nope. I can't think of a reason. I just haven't got round to it, I suppose.'

'How can you . . . What do you mean? That's not possible.'

'Given the chance, I suppose I wouldn't mind. You know – just doing it once and getting it over with, so I'm not in too much of a hurry when I'm looking for the right person afterwards.'

'You are sick. You have a diseased mind. You are pumped full of the crappest, most outdated Hollywood sexual clichés. It's sad.'

'No I'm not. I don't watch films.'

'What? You don't watch films?'

'Not really.'

'What about on TV? You must watch them on TV.'

'Not much. I don't really watch telly.'

'You don't? You don't watch telly? Do you read books?'

'Nooo – don't be silly.'

'Magazines?'

'Nope.'

'Music? Gigs?'

'Nope.'

'Jesus Christ! What do you do with your life?'

'Dunno. This and that. You know. I keep busy.'

'You are extraordinary. It's unbelievable. What the hell do you DO?'

There was no answer.

'Listen,' I offered, 'would you like to have sex?'

'Fuck off!'

'Not with me, you arsehole. With a girl. With a horny girl.'

'Dunno.'

'Don't give me that. Would you like to? Yes or no.'

'Well I suppose so. Theoretically.'

'I'm not talking theory, Barry, I mean practically – real life – doing it – with another human being.'

'Well . . . Yes. But who's going to want to sleep with me?'

'Jesus! Everyone. Everyone wants to sleep with you, Barry.'

'Don't be ridiculous!'

'Listen to me, Barry. I am being deadly serious. Every single girl in the girls' school, without exception, plus every single member of the girls' school staff, half the boys' school staff (male and female) and most of the members of the boys' school are ALL, EVERY SINGLE ONE OF US, DESPERATE TO JUMP INTO BED WITH YOU AND SCREW YOUR FUCKING BRAINS OUT!'

This took him a while to digest. 'Don't be silly. That's not possible . . . Really? . . . No, it's ridiculous . . . Is it true? . . . Is that really what you think? . . . No . . . you're stupid . . . Do they want to? . . . With me? . . . I mean am I? . . . I'm not . . . Am I? . . . Do they? . . . Do they really? – The girls, I mean.'

'Yes you are. Yes they do.'

'Shit. Really?'

'Yes – of course, really! Do I look like I'm joking? This is not funny at all. You're stunted. Mentally stunted. And I asked you a question, you tosser. Do you, or do you not, want to have sex with someone from the girls' school?'

'God! . . . This is . . . What are you, a pimp or something?'

'Yes. For the time being, I am a pimp. I will find a girl, she will come to you. The pair of you will have sex. No money will change hands.'

'That's not possible.'

'It *is* possible, you idiot.'

'Naaaa.'

'Believe me. It is. All you have to do is say yes, and I'll sort it out.'

'Fucking hell!'

'You just have to say yes or no.'

'Shit.'

'Well?'

'Fuck.'

'Well?'

'Are you asking me to say yes or no?'

'Yes.'

'Either yes –'

'Or no.'

'Right.'

'Right.'

'O K then,' he said. 'My answer is . . . um . . . yes . . . I think . . . but I still don't believe you . . . I mean it won't happen . . . Will it? . . . It won't . . . But yes, anyway.'

CHAPTER ELEVEN

The following morning, I put word out to the girls' school that Barry was a virgin, and that evening he slept with the best-looking girl in North West London.

Within a couple of weeks he was a changed man. Having discovered that sex was easier to get hold of than fruit Polos, he became quite a fan of it as a cheap and pleasurable way of passing the time. Having previously never put any effort into anything, he suddenly found himself chasing after people, making late-night phone calls, and dashing out for emergency supplies of condoms. He became a different person. He was rejuvenated. Or, more precisely, he was juvenated – entering on his adolescence at the last minute, just before time ran out and he became an adult.

At the end of the day, I would usually walk with him from the classrooms to the school coach park. Roughly fifty metres from the buses, the paths from the two schools converged. In the thrilling days of Barry's sexual awakening, these walks were always eventful. The minute we came into view, every female head turned. This wasn't unusual, but the new development was that rather than being looked at with blanket dewy-eyed awe, one or two faces would register a flicker of recognition. The eyes would then glaze over for a few seconds, before the girl in question would either faint or burst into tears. The walk lasted around two minutes and felt like a surreal game of human skittles, with us as the bowling ball, and the snot-green uniformed girls as the pins. As each one went down, I would ask Barry who it was.

'Oh, just some girl, who . . .'

'Yeah, I met that one at the . . .'

'She's just someone that I . . .'

No two stories were ever alike. It was extraordinary. Of course, this should have been my big opportunity. I should have been running to the side of these skittled women, lifting them off the ground and gently talking them through Barry's nasty misogynist character and on to the subject of my own kind, loving nature. A poor substitute for Barry's beauty, but 'now that you have seen the dangers of the beautiful, you will want a man with a heart, a man you can trust.'

However, this didn't happen. I never got up the courage to approach a single one of his lovers. I wanted to. I just didn't.

CHAPTER TWELVE

I was actually quite pissed off when the Christmas holidays came around, because for once things were beginning to get a bit exciting at school. I didn't have any work that I could be bothered to do, and it was too cold to go away anywhere, so I basically just sat around for four weeks picking my nose. Metaphorically, that is. I didn't literally sit with fingers up my nose for four consecutive weeks. What I mean is that I didn't do very much. Actually, now I think about it, I *did* spend a significant proportion of that time picking my nose – about a quarter, I reckon – but that's not the point I was trying to make. What I mean is, I had very little to do during my Christmas holiday.

I had almost asked Barry for his phone number on the last day of term, but at the last minute I had chickened out. I could have got his number from the phone book, but I didn't do it because it would have felt too weird ringing him at home. I don't know why, but I just couldn't phone him – it would have been embarrassing.

My brother, Dan, came home from university for a few days, and it was such a relief to have someone around to deflect parental attention that I could have kissed him. He's a good bloke, my brother. Bit strange, generally very OTT, but fundamentally a very kind person. Normally I hate kind people, but Dan seems to do it in the right way – like, if he's helping you with something, he'll take the piss at the same time so you don't feel patronized.

He didn't come back from Cambridge very often, and seeing him again after almost a year, he was different from how I remembered him. He seemed more confident, happier, and for the first time in his life he was wearing vaguely decent clothes. I mean his taste was still appalling, but for once he actually seemed to be trying. I went so far as to ask after his grey polyester too-short trousers with button-down pockets on the thigh and unfortunate yoghurt stains in the groin area, and he told me he had thrown them away – a grave loss to our country's cultural heritage.

Also – this is going to sound wrong, but – well, seeing him set my mind at rest, because it made me think that if anyone in my family is a whoopsie, then it's definitely not me. Any squiffy genes flying around the family tree seem to have gone straight for him.

Obviously, he's not actually gay – I mean, he is my brother – but when I see the way he walks, and the way he hugs everyone, I just breathe a sigh of relief because it makes me feel comparatively normal.

Christmas Day plumbed new, hitherto uncharted, unin-habitable-to-marine-life depths of awfulness. I just can't inflict it on you. Put it this way: we ended up playing charades. Can you believe it? 1986 draws to a close, ushering in another year for ever-more spectacular discoveries in the age of the information revolution, and I sit on a sofa with my fucking family, pretending to laugh at some lunatic socially dysfunctional cousin failing to mime the word *Ghostbusters*.

If John Logie Baird had known that people would still be playing charades in 1986, I don't think he would have bothered. He probably would have turned his attention to psychiatry, and we might have been blessed with the frontal lobotomy a few years earlier.

The day after Boxing Day, I took Dan for a tour of St Anne's Shopping Centre, which had just opened in Harrow. We also paid homage to the new 'Sally: Statue of a Skipping Girl' which had been erected in the town centre, presumably in order to serve as a focus for community activity.

'Ahh,' I sighed, 'at last, Harrow's position on the world's cultural map is assured.'

'Indeed, indeed,' said Dan.

'I'm finding it hard to hold in my tears of joy, Dan.'

'Let them out Mark, let them out. It's what the artist would have wanted.'

Sobs wracked my body as I placed my head on Sally's foot.

'Is it the two small holes which have been Black-and-Deckered into the eyeballs which move you so, dear brother?'

'Indeed, indeed. They communicate so clearly the artist's idea of the glee that a child can find in simple things.'

A wave of tacit awe engulfed us one more time.

'Dan?'

'Yes?'

'Do you know what I would like to do more than anything in the whole world?'

'No, dear brother, no.'

'I would like to smear a turd in Sally's face.'

'Next time, dear Mark, next time we will bring a turd in a bag.'

'It's what the artist would have wanted.'

'Quite.'

We wandered around Harrow for the next hour or so, taking the piss out of every single thing we could see, but gradually Dan seemed to drift off. When I asked him what was wrong, he started saying that he had come home for a reason.

When I asked him what the reason was, he just went quiet. The atmosphere became very serious all of a sudden, and I got the feeling that he was just about to speak, when we bumped into an old friend from primary school. She shouted at us from the other side of the street, and the minute she crossed to talk to us, the atmosphere evaporated.

Dan seemed relieved that she had turned up, and even though we hadn't seen her for more than three years, he flung his arms around her and kissed her on both cheeks, which I found very embarrassing. Poor Dan – I love him dearly, but he's got no social skills, that boy.

I gave her one peck, from a safe distance, even though I've always secretly fancied her.

Anyway, the three of us went for a coffee, and by the time we had finished, it was too late to get back to the original conversation. When Dan went back to Cambridge a couple of days later, he still hadn't told me what he was going to say.

CHAPTER THIRTEEN

By the start of the Lent term, it had become evident that schoolgirls were too easy for Barry, so I suggested that he take on a more serious challenge. Barry told me that he now found an ejaculation during the lunch hour an essential prerequisite for mental health, so we set about choosing someone who worked within the school grounds.

We made a list of every possibility, with comments:

Kitchen staff	Ugly, thick.
Cleaning ladies	Ugly, dirty.
Mrs Webb – Physics teacher	Ugly, inhuman.
French teachers:	
Mrs Thomas	Ugly, no tits.
Mrs Mumford	Not too ugly.
Miss Gall	Unspeakably ugly.
Headmaster's wife	Ugly, old.
Assistant Librarian	Ugly, boring.

Following our extensive research, there was clearly only one option. Barry set off after Mrs Mumford.

A few years ago, a boy in my French class had been given a detention by Mrs Mumford for staring at her breasts during class. 'Excessive attention to irrelevant detail' was the offence that she entered on the detention card. Ever since then, despite her catatonically dull teaching style and consistent failure to respond to any kind of humour, she had been accorded some respect from the boys of the school: partly for the beauty of her breasts, but mainly for that one witticism which showed the faintest glimmer of humanity underneath her otherwise impenetrable shell of professionalism. 'Maybe,' we all thought, 'she isn't anything like the bland, overworked housewife she pretends to be. Underneath it all, maybe she's a witty, horny, laugh-a-minute, good-time chick.' Her previous image as the most humourless woman in the world was shattered.

That one joke, written out in small, regular handwriting on a detention card which was only ever read by two people (the tit-starer and the detention master) changed the way everyone thought about her. It made her an enigma. It was as if she had walked over an air vent, and her long, brown pleated skirt had been blown upwards to reveal stockings, suspenders and leather silk-gusseted panties.

Ever since the story about the detention card had got round, boys often got dangerously horny in her classes. It was rumoured that in her classroom, not all the gooey lumps under the desks were chewing gum.

The art of seduction is an extremely delicate one. Unless, that is, you happen to be gifted with exceptional sex appeal, in which case it's a piece of piss. This was fortunate for Barry and myself, since our combined experience of seduction was, to say the least, minimal. The plan we settled on was this:

We find out where Mrs Mumford parks, then, every day for a week, after the final bell, Barry leans sexily against a nearby wall, ogling her as she gets into her car to drive home. Then, for two days he doesn't turn up. On the following day, just as she's beginning to wonder where he's got to, he hobbles up to her, tells her that he's injured his foot and asks for a lift to Stanmore (which is where she lives). Then, on a secluded spot on the A41 Barry suddenly shouts, 'Stop! Stop the car! I'm carsick.'

She stops the car at the next lay-by. Barry breathes deeply, as if in pain. Then, without a word, he gets out of the passenger seat, and moves into the back of the car. 'Please,' he says, 'please, my head is in agony. Oh, the pain! Will you massage my temples?'

Mrs Mumford then gets into the back of the car and massages Barry's temples. A few minutes later, Barry says that he feels a bit better and offers to massage her temples. He then asks if her breasts are at all sore and offers to massage them, too.

The next step is that as soon as he can tell that she's getting excited, he lets go of her tits and shouts, 'Oh, shit! My lower abdomen injury is playing up again. Will you massage it for me?'

After that, he ought to be home and wet.

This, I realize, is maybe not the most sophisticated of plans, and knowing how bad an actor Barry is, it is remarkable that he even got a lift from her in the first place, let alone that he ended up shagging her right on cue in a lay-by of the A41.

It just goes to show what a beautiful face and perfect physique can do for your love life.

CHAPTER FOURTEEN

I have a little confession to make. I have not, strictly speaking, been 100 per cent literal, here. I'm not lying or anything – don't worry – I'm just . . . filling in a few gaps – trying my humble best to compensate for certain holes in my knowledge of events.

Besides, no one knew *exactly* what happened because Barry wouldn't let on. But they definitely snogged. *Definitely*. At the very least. And one person saw them in a pub together near Barnet.

Although I made up the car story bit, word got round, so it might as well have been true – everyone believed it.

Well, not *everyone*. For the time being, it only had the status of sixth-form myth. A bit like the one about the medical school party where they found a penis at the bottom of the punch bowl, it was one of those stories that you heard, said 'Naaaah-bollocks' to, then found yourself repeating ten minutes later as the God-given truth.

And yes – OK, OK, I admit it – all that stuff about skittling girls on the way to the coach park – maybe it was a tiny weeny bit exaggerated. But Barry *did* sleep with lots of girls – that much is absolutely 100 per cent true – I swear.

The trouble with the Barry and Mrs Mumford lay-by lay story was that there wasn't *quite* enough evidence, so by the time it was eighth or ninth hand, it began to sound a little thin. As soon as there was something a bit more solid, though, it would be all over the school in minutes.

You mustn't think I was trying to spread rumours. I'm not a malicious person, and I never have been. If you think I was jealous of the fact that Barry was living through a period of incessant sensual bliss while I slogged sexlessly through my A-levels, you have got completely the wrong end of the stick. He was my friend, and I was happy for him. I'm not the jealous type. I wouldn't know how to feel bitter if I tried. I wasn't bitter. Not me, not bitter. No, not me. Not bitter. I didn't want the story to spread. I just told a couple of people for fun – I didn't even expect them to believe me – then they went around repeating it all over the place. I was genuinely angry with them.

CHAPTER FIFTEEN

Barry wasn't my only friend. I still had my old group of mates who I had been friends with ever since the first form: mainly laid-back Metropolitan Line Jews, with the odd Asian and Chinese thrown in here and there, spiced up by one or two rich Hampsteadites. Half way through the sixth form we were still doing the same things we had always done: wandering around the grounds chatting at lunch time, and seeing each other in the West End every Saturday night for a film and a few games in the amusement arcades. The lunch time crowd had about seven people, but every Saturday it dwindled to the same three: Dave, Gaung-Bai, and me.

It wasn't particularly exciting, but it was pretty much normal for a person of my age with a stunted sex life.

When we first started going out, it had actually been quite cool. I still remember a Monday afternoon during half-term of the third form when the three of us went on a mission to get into our first '18' film. We were so frightened by the prospect of the woman selling the tickets, and so amazed when she let us in, that we failed to take into account the fact that the film might be even more frightening than the box office. We were in the huge Odeon Marble Arch, and being a Monday afternoon, we were almost the only people there. This was pretty spooky by itself, but in a mood of bravado we headed for the front row of the cinema, where the enormous screen towered above us.

From this position, even the credits were scary. The movie was *The Fly*, and when Jeff Goldblum with red flaky skin and no hair leaped through the wall of the operating theatre in the middle of his girlfriend's maggot abortion nightmare, all three of us leaped from our seats and tried to run out of the cinema. We watched rest of the film from right at the back, severely traumatized, trembling our way through a clinically dangerous adrenaline hit.

While this might have been a pretty hip thing to be doing aged thirteen, by the time we were seventeen it had somehow lost its chic. Still, we always had a laugh, so it didn't seem to matter too much. Besides, I had almost got up to level nine on *Nemesis* in the 'Loads 'O Fun' on Old Compton Street, and I had vowed to myself that when I finally topped the *Nemesis* Hall of Fame I would be in a position to tell the manager that the apostrophe ought to be on the other side of his 'O'.

(I actually think the manager probably knew, but didn't want his amusement arcade to sound like an Irish pub.)

This contentedly pre-pubescent existence started falling apart a few weeks into my sixth form when Dave ditched the crazy social whirl of Soho slot machines to take up clubbing with Neil Kothari.

It is bad enough having one of your closest friends dumping you and leaving your social life in tatters, but Neil Kothari was a boy I loathed. He was *such* a prick. Until the fourth form he had been known as Anil and had been one of the weedy, humble types, then suddenly he had taken up body-building, changed his name, and started hanging out with the school rugby team. The way he managed to work himself into their confidence was by getting the same coach as the School Animal and accompanying him to the nearest corner shop, where Neil would buy a few sweets and then shout 'Fwooaaarrr it smells in here! What's that fucking smell? Can you smell anything? Is that a fucking Paki smell? Fwooaaarrr!'

The irony of Neil's own racial origins was apparently lost on the School Animal, and after a week of regular visits to the newsagents of Kingsbury, Neil was firmly established as a 'good bloke', and became an honorary rugby-boy – one of the first ever Asians to join their ranks.

My mate Dave, on the other hand, was not quite there, and was still struggling to enter good bloke territory. However, he had reasonably good contacts with Neil from the days when he used to be Indian, and by becoming the school's first hip-hop expert, he managed to work his way back into Neil's confidence. Together with another guy called Eric (whose hair was already thinning at the age of sixteen and who was shortly to be kicked out of the school for being caught with a Collins Gem on his lap during an O-level German listening comprehension), they started spending every lunch-time in the Jennings' house-rooms practising Grandmaster Flash lyrics, reading books about 'subway art' and trying to spin on their heads.

I find it difficult to recall a sadder sight than two under-developed Jews and an ex-Asian sitting in a green-belt public school classroom with floor polish in their hair, pretending to be ghetto black kids. Still, this is what became of my friend Dave. Throughout the fifth form he managed to sustain the double life of rapper-gangster by day, suburban-white-boy-who-can't-think-of-anything-better-to-do-than-going-to-the-cinema-and-playing-electronic-games by night, but around the start of the sixth form he finally ditched me and became a full-time black man.

Three seventeen-year-old boys at the cinema every Saturday is bleak. Two is positively humiliating. The second half of the first term of my sixth form is, to this day, the social low point of my life. I don't expect to match it until I am well into my eighties.

And where was Barry in all this? Well – at this point I had still never spent any time with him outside school. He didn't fit in with my other friends. In fact, other than me, he didn't seem to fit in with anyone at the school. He just seemed separate. Something about him was either more mature or more immature than everyone else. I honestly couldn't tell which.

It didn't make any difference to me, though. We always got on incredibly well. It was never profound, and it was never even particularly silly – we were just on the same plane. Which is strange, because if he was so different from everyone else, and I thought that I was the same as everyone else, then where did that leave me when I discovered that I was just like him? Maybe neither of us fitted in . . .

Or am I being paranoid again?

The strange thing is that the more our relationship became a one-to-one thing, the less sexual it got.

You don't believe me, do you?

It's true, I swear. Things were only weird when we were just beginning to get to know each other. I had always been worried that people would notice how much I stared at him. But if you're alone with someone, it's natural to look at them – and once it became natural to look at Barry, I stopped needing to look at him *too much*, which is what had been causing all the problems in the first place. So the more time we spent alone together, the more the sexual tensions began to lift.

We still never saw each other outside school, though. But from our talks on the coach every morning and evening, we gradually developed a real knowledge of each other.

To be honest, I did most of the talking, so Barry probably learnt a lot more about me than I did about him. In fact, now I think of it, I hardly learnt anything about Barry at all. He was very secretive. But we talked a lot anyway, and it felt as if we knew everything about each other. Except for all the stuff I obviously couldn't tell him, that is. And since he didn't give away much, either . . . Oh, I don't know – we just became close friends. Trust me – it happened.

The nice thing was that all the egomania and competitiveness which spoilt so many of my other school friendships never entered into the conversations I had with Barry. There was something about the way Barry spoke to you that made you feel as if you could ask any question, however stupid, and he wouldn't laugh at you or judge you – he'd just do his best to give you a straight answer. This was rather special in a school where you couldn't ask the time without getting a put-down for an answer.

As a result, my friendship with Barry was very useful to me, because I felt I could at last debase myself and get around to asking all the questions which I spent most of my time straining to prove that I already knew the answers to.

The most obvious topic of all hit it big between us in January and February 1987:

'Barry?'

'Yes?'

'What's sex like?'

'Um . . . God . . . er . . . It's nice.'

'How nice?'

'Um . . . very nice.'

'Shit. I thought so . . . Is it easy?'

'What, easy to learn, or easy to do once you know how?'

'Fuck! Good point. Fuck! I'd never thought of that. Er . . . both, I suppose.'

'Well – it all depends really. First time's a bit tricky, but after that it's really no hassle at all. And once you know how . . . well, as long as you find the other person attractive, you can't go wrong, really.'

'Right, I see. That's amazing. I see. And is there any practice you can do to make the first time a bit easier?'

'Like what?'

'Well – I mean I've heard that a milk bottle filled with chopped liver is exactly the same as a vagina. Is that true?'

'I don't know, I've never put my dick in a milk bottle filled with chopped liver.'

'Oh, I have. It's very nice.'

'What! You've fucked a milk bottle filled with chopped liver?'

'Yes. Well, sort of.'

'What do you mean, sort of?'

'Well – I couldn't come. That's why I'm a bit worried. It made me think that maybe I wouldn't be able to come in a woman, either.'

'I see. I wouldn't worry too much. Women are much nicer than milk bottles, I assure you.'

'Fuck! Yes, you're right. I'm so stupid. You're right. I shouldn't worry too much. Jesus, I'm such a worrier.'

'Maybe if you're worried that you don't find women attractive, you should think about having sex with a man.'

'WHAT?! WHAT?! FUCK OFF! . . . FUCK OFF! . . . FUCKING HELL . . . FUCK . . . FUCK OFF! . . . What are you talking about? I didn't say that! Fuck off! That's not what I said at all, you fucking weirdo.'

'All right, all right. Calm down. It's nothing to get so excited about. I just mentioned it, that's all.'

'Well don't.'

'Jesus – there's no need be so homophobic.'

'I'm not homophobic. I'm just not a fucking arse-bandit, that's all.'

'You are so screwed up. You've got such a problem.'

'I have not got a problem. You're the one who brought up the subject. You're the one we should be worried about.'

'Worried?'

'Yeah – worried, Barry. You mentioned it – where did you get the idea from anyway?'

'From my uncle.'

'What?'

'From my uncle. He's gay.'

'Fuck! You know one.'

'Yes I do. And he's a very nice man.'

'Errrrr, yuk – it's in your genes.'

'Oh Mark, please. Don't be such an arsehole.'

'No, don't you be such an arsehole.'

'You're the arsehole.'

'No – you're the arsehole.'

'You're the fucking arsehole.'

It wasn't usually like that. I think you must have caught us on a bad day.

CHAPTER SIXTEEN

One of the first major moves made in the '87 East/West détente was a sixth-form boat party put together by the newly formed 'social committee'. The party was organized by Joel Schneider, who showed admirable business acumen by single-handedly operating the ticket selling, for which he also generously offered to do the accounting. Somewhere along the line a few hundred pounds vanished, but the accountant swore to the unimpeachable behaviour of the ticket seller and vice versa, so the money was never recovered.

A boat on the Thames was hired for the night to chug up and down the river, and every single-sixth former from both schools with two hormones to rub together was on board, having paid Joel Schneider five pounds for the privilege.

Parties on boats are torture. You can't arrive late, you can't leave early – the whole experience feels like a Sartre play.

When I stepped out of Embankment Station, on the pavement opposite stood a gang of boys, most of whom I had never seen out of school uniform, and some girls who I dimly recognized. Most of them seemed to be pissed already, and something in my stomach told me that this was going to be one of the most unpleasant evenings of my life. I was tempted to run away, to get straight back on the train home, but I had already been seen. Someone shouted a 'hello' at me from across the street. I shouted back, crossed the road, and was done for. The next five hours of my life would be spent with these people.

We shuffled on board the boat, and started drinking.

By the time we reached Waterloo Bridge, everyone was pissed.

The music was so loud that within five minutes my ears gave out. After ten minutes they started actively objecting, screeching at me from both sides of my head.

My hearing was only the first of my senses to be obliterated by the party, the other four following suit with alarming rapidity.

The boat consisted of an upper and a lower deck, both enclosed, with only a small porch-like area at the back open to the outside. For the first few hours, the party had two neat planes of symmetry, with loud music on the upper deck, heavy drinking on the lower deck, gentlemen on the port side, and females a-starboard. Before long I had joined the queue for a vomit from the outside deck, with both toilets already blocked by and awash with sick.

The air was thick with that most basic building block of teenage angst: the virginity millstone syndrome. The more you are afflicted by it, the more you have to drink before being able to talk to the opposite sex, rendering you too drunk to think of anything to say by the time you get up the courage to open a conversation, hence defeating the object of even trying to talk to them anyway, and so on in a vicious circle. The millstone grows, the drinking gets heavier, the gender divide widens, masturbation becomes a necessity rather than a pleasure, etc., etc. Hence, communal angst reaches fever pitch, and teenage parties become orgies of alcohol-drowned neurosis.

Only when the lower deck of the boat was lightly greased with vomit did the port/starboard divide melt away, as boys and girls staggered paralytically into one another's tongues. The snoggers clung to each other and swayed around the dance floor, chewing each other's faces. The benches at the side of the decks were soon covered by sprawling pairs of fingerers and hand-jobbers. In the red semi-darkness, one could just make out hands tearing away at underwear they didn't quite understand, grappling with genitals they barely recognized: the boys thrashing about amateurishly inside lacy knickers, while reluctant girls tickled ineffectually at angry purple helmets.

I could feel myself sobering up, but I felt too sick to drink any more, and the gradual return of my mental faculties sent me diving into depression. Why wasn't anyone lunging at me and trying to suck my teeth out? Why was no one slobbering noisily over my unwashed cock? Why didn't anyone want me to knead their cunt? What was wrong with me? There was no one there I felt I could talk to, no one I liked, and no one I wanted to snog.

Barry hadn't turned up. I was alone.

I staggered around the boat, desperate to have some kind of conversation. After a while I bumped into someone else who was clearly in the same situation. I looked in his face and saw a reflection of my own loneliness. I tried hard to think of something to say. I could see him trying, too. After a long wait, he came up with something.

'Are you drunk?' he said.

'Pardon?'

'Are you pissed?'

'Oh! . . . Yes,' I lied.

There was a long pause. We both chuckled weakly. There was another pause.

'Me too,' he said.

'Right.'

The third extended pause pronounced a death sentence on our efforts. We both could have spoken fluently for five minutes about how unhappy we were, but it was too noisy for that. It wasn't the place, either. The conversation was over. I was still alone.

'I'm going to get another drink,' I said.

'OK.'

'Bye.'

'Bye.'

Now I had to go and get another drink. I waded to the bar through the ever-thickening carpet of vomit, forced down a Bloody Mary (which tasted of petrol, but sounded as if it must be dangerously strong), and lunged at the least ugly girl I could see.

I misjudged a little and we clashed teeth painfully, but neither of us acknowledged it. We were snogging. The relief was enormous. At last – the evening's paranoia was over.

This thought lasted less than a second. A worse self-doubt than ever now loomed, with 'why won't anyone snog me?' replaced by 'why don't I enjoy this?' The new one was far worse.

I was bored, I didn't know what she looked like, my jaw was getting cramp, and the boat wouldn't be docking for another two hours. From where I stood, those two hours looked like a long, long time.

I thought we had been at it for around half an hour when I took my first breather. I used the pretext of clearing her saliva from my chin to check my watch, and was stunned to discover that only ten minutes had passed since I had thrown myself at her. Not even a quarter of an hour and we were bored of each other already. 'Jesus Christ!' I thought. 'How do people stay married for forty years?'

There was still much more time to kill. If I could give her a fingering, I thought, at least that would salvage something useful from the evening. Throughout my bravado in Jewish assemblies I always felt like something of a sham, with all my knowledge gleaned from diagrams and novels. On an academic level I knew the vagina intimately, but my practical experience on the 3-D model was extremely limited. In fact, barring one afternoon twelve years ago in a paddling-pool with my cousin, I had never even clapped eyes on one.

I wrestled with her clothes trying to figure out whether her pants were inside or outside her tights, and was badly hindered by her attempts to push my arms away. I knew from books that this was standard practice, but found her strength and persistence rather surprising. I responded with all my might, and before long we were engaged in a full-scale arm wrestle. When her arm gave way, mine was carried upwards with surprising momentum and I punched her in the vagina.

Not just a baby punch, either – this was a full-scale uppercut – impeccably placed and timed, planting itself firmly right slap bang on her vag.

I may not have been the world expert on sexual mores, but I knew enough about the basic etiquette to realize that this was extremely rude. One does not just go around casually thumping other people's genitals. At least, not without asking permission first.

Amazingly, she wasn't screaming with pain. She just looked shocked.

'Fuck!' I thought. 'Vaginas must be a lot tougher than testicles! That's a blessing, at least.'

Rather than spending these precious seconds marvelling at the resilience of the female sexual organs, I really ought to have used them concocting some kind of apology, because before I had opened my mouth to say anything, she left.

I thought of chasing after her to explain that it had been an accident, but it was all too embarrassing. I just wanted to forget that it had happened. I wanted to forget that she existed. I wanted to forget that *I* existed.

What I really wanted was to crawl into a large opaque bag and hide for ten years.

This line of philosophical speculation was interrupted by a yelp from my stomach which sent me hurtling to the window to puke up the Bloody Mary. It tasted marginally better on the way out.

There was still an hour and a half to go.

I went upstairs and tried to dance, but the dance floor was too full. People were just bobbing up and down on the spot, wiping sweat from body to body. It was too hot and loud to think.

I went onto the open air deck, where some boys were smoking a joint. I had my first ever puff, which made me feel nauseous and randy at the same time – a gross combination. I thought of going to the toilet for a wank, but when I remembered that it was full of sick, my stomach contracted. I rushed for the river and puked over the side of the boat, banging my erection painfully on the railing.

I looked for a chair. There was only one, wedged between a snogging couple and a fingering one, so I sat there.

I closed my eyes. When I did this I felt as if the room was swaying, and my stomach protested. If I didn't want to puke again, I had to keep my eyes open.

I sat still and tried to shut out the world. I tried to concentrate on my churning stomach – it was the least unpleasant thing available to my senses. I stroked the arm of my suede jacket. That, too, wasn't terrible. There was nothing to taste, smell, hear or see, but if I just kept touching the suede I might be able to blot the others out. I tried to look out of the window for a star, but they were invisible behind the London streetlights. I just had to concentrate on the sleeve of my jacket.

There was one hour and twenty-five minutes to go. Whoever was controlling the speed of my watch was being cruel.

I had to go home.

I had to go home.

Ihadtogohome.

IhadtogohomeIhadtogohomeIhadtogohomeIhadtogohome.

CHAPTER SEVENTEEN

When the party finally ended and I could get the train back to Harrow, I was so happy that I decided to postpone suicide for at least a week.

Despite the fact that I never enjoyed one single moment of any of my sixth-form parties, I attended them all.

Let me just run that by you once more. Number of parties: a lot. Total number of moments at parties: a much bigger lot. Total number of moments at parties containing an element of pleasure: zero.

This is not an ideal social equation, but I put up with it none the less, mainly because I had no choice. Dave was now black, and Guang-Bai had snogged a fantastically beautiful Chinese girl at the boat party who he went out with for the next five years, conducting the relationship exclusively in the Cantonese language, and in the process offering me vast, hitherto unexplored plains of meaning for the term 'gooseberry'.

Barry, by the way, turned up at one party, told me he thought it was shit, left after half an hour, and never went to another one again.

Despite the zero pleasure-rating of these parties, there was something which drew me to them more than the mere lack of an alternative to do anything else. I always went with a spirit of conquest, discovery and adventure in my heart. Not in the sense that I expected to unearth new people or discover hidden things about myself. My voyage of discovery was strictly biological. Enjoyment was not the point. I went, like everyone else, purely in order to piece together the jigsaw of what it was that . . . that made the opposite sex squidgey in some places and not in others.

Ideally, I would also have learnt how to talk to them, but this was aiming a bit high.

Despite my below average sex-appeal, I found that by the time everyone was drunk, and all the good-looking people had paired off, I would usually manage to find myself someone to experiment on.

One of the worst parties came towards the end of term, at which I witnessed the School Animal rinsing his cock in a mouthwash bottle which he then replaced in the bathroom cupboard. While I was heartily in favour of the mouthwash trick (after all, it was Neil Kothari's house), what depressed me was that one of my first full-length conversations with a member of the girls' school had culminated in her letting slip that my nickname on the other side of the Berlin Wall was 'Bruno'. I made the disastrous error of forcing her to tell me what it meant, and rather than discovering that it was an affectionate reference to my voice sounding like Bruno Brookes, or my brain resembling Bruno Bettelheim's, it actually emerged after half an hour of guessing that I was named after Frank Bruno in honour of my now legendary vaginal thump.

Everyone, yes everyone, knew about it.

Everyone.

This did not bode well for the short-term future of my sex life.

Not well, at all.

CHAPTER EIGHTEEN

'Barry?'

'Yes?'

'Why don't you go to parties?'

'Dunno.'

'You must have a reason.'

'Ummm . . . I think it's probably because they're shit.'

'Right.'

'Why? Do *you* like them?'

'No. I think they're shit,' I said.

'Why do you go, then?'

'Dunno.'

'You must have a reason. There must be something which makes you want to go.'

'No. I don't need a reason – I just go.'

'Oh.'

'I hate them, though,' I said. 'I really hate them.'

'Because they're shit?'

'Yeah. Because they're shit. Because they're really shit. Fuck, they really are shit. They are *so* shit. Fuck! *SO SHIT!* Fuck! Now I think about it . . . Fuck. They're so shit. So bad. Just *SO, SO SHIT! FUCK!*'

'You're very articulate when you have a spiritual revelation. Has anyone ever told you that before?'

'They're so shit.'

'Why do you go, then, you twat?'

'I don't know. I just don't know. Why do I go? Barry – tell me – why the fuck do I go?'

'Snogs?'

'Yes. In theory, yes. But I don't really get many. And I don't even enjoy them when I do.'

'Shit. Maybe I should put you in touch with my uncle.'

'Very funny. Maybe you should.'

'Look, Mark. Don't be such a prick. Of course you don't enjoy licking the tonsils of some complete stranger when you're both pissed and you don't even like each other. It's repulsive.'

'Is it?'

'Of course it fucking is.'

'So I'm not meant to enjoy it?'

'Well – you are *meant* to enjoy it. That does tend to be the idea behind these things. But if you don't enjoy it, you shouldn't do it.'

'Don't be an arsehole. I can't just give up on women two weeks short of my eighteenth birthday. It's a bit early for that.'

'I'm not saying you should give up on women. I'm just saying you should give up on adolescent groping.'

'What *else* is there for me to do. I'm an adolescent, and I only know how to grope.'

'You can wait.'

'For what?'

'Until you meet someone you like.'

'Until I meet someone I like! Are you serious? That won't happen for ages. I'll have to wait 'till university.'

'*If* you go to university.'

'Of course I'll fucking go to university. I'm not a moron.'

'Besides,' he said, 'snogs are shit. No one enjoys snogs.'

'What?'

'At least I never did. It's not fun.'

'WHAT?'

'It isn't. It's boring.'

'What are you talking about? I can't believe it! You can't say that. Everyone snogs. Not just teenagers – everyone. In films they do it all the time.'

'That's different.'

'What, because it's made up?'

'No – because it's foreplay. Or at least that's what it represents. Kissing and squeezing and all that stuff is just foreplay. You do it before you have sex. It's what you do to get each other excited.'

'But . . . but . . . people do it on its own. Adults, I mean. You don't *have* to have sex, do you?'

'You don't *have* to. People usually do, but you don't have to.'

'Jesus! Are you telling me that there is no point in me laying one single finger on a woman unless she gives me a signed contract in advance stating a solemn and legally binding promise to take it all the way to a full-blown shag?'

'No no no. Don't be stupid. All I am saying is – foreplay on its own with someone you love is nice – foreplay followed by sex with someone you love is great – foreplay followed by sex with someone you don't love is OK – foreplay without sex with someone you don't even like when you're pissed in a room full of other people with neither party willing to remove any clothing is a fucking disastrously unpleasurable experience.'

'Fuck! I can't believe it! What is this? You were a virgin two months ago!'

'I'm a quick learner.'

'Jesus. How did you? . . . Where did you? . . . Fuck! You're so right! I can't believe it. I'm such an idiot. Shit! What do I do now? What the fuck do I do now?'

'Dunno. Whatever you want.'

'Shit!'

'Listen,' said Barry. 'This weekend, why don't we go to the cinema together, or something.'

'Really? Do you really want to? I mean . . . shall we? I mean yes. Yes. Let's.'

'All right, calm down.'

'Right. Yes. What do you want to see?'

'*The Fly II*'s just come out,' he said.

'Naah. Horror's not really my scene. Bit boring. How about *Four Adventures of Reinette and Mirabelle* at the Everyman?'

'God – you *are* gay.'

CHAPTER NINETEEN

One boy, by the name of Piers Ward, was a puzzle. He had the regulation floppy hair, corduroy trousers and Barbour jacket of a boy from a *proper* public school, but for some reason spent seven years languishing in the cultural melting pot. He was without doubt the most unpopular boy in the school, but he didn't appear to mind in the slightest. He seemed to view the universal repulsion with which he was greeted as proof of his superiority. Similarly, he reacted to his ineptness at sport as if he was too clever for the merely physical, and to his failure in the classroom as if he was too important to have to try and be clever. He gave the impression that he was born with such self-confidence that any failure, however resounding, in whatever field, couldn't make the slightest impression on his opinion of himself. It was as if there was some scale of achievement, so important that the rest of us weren't even aware of it, at which he excelled – something of which we couldn't even conceive, in which he played a starring role.

His private arena of brilliance was, of course, breeding, about which we Jews had not a clue. Everyone laughed at him when he applied for a place at Cambridge, but it seemed that Trinity College somehow had access to his secret achievements, lowering their standard entry offer for him, promising to accept him not for three As, but for a B and two Cs. He just succeeded in getting his place, and went on to achieve great success, becoming president of the Cambridge Union Society where he was acclaimed as a public speaker for his ability to stand by an argument in the face of universal ridicule. He is now on his way to a promising career in politics.

No one quite knew what he was doing at my school, though. There were a number of rumours about why he wasn't getting a proper education, the wildest of which was that it was a punishment from his parents for trying to steal an Estate in Kent.

In terms of history, prestigious alumni and beautiful grounds, there was certainly nothing wrong with my school. It could even have aspired to the ranks of the real public schools suitable for the likes of Piers, had it not been for the . . . had the school not become . . . had it not been taken over by . . . I think you know what I am getting at.

The fees were high, the academic results were good, but it was generally felt amongst people with breeding that my school somehow attracted 'the wrong sort of person'. The school had . . . maybe . . . lost its way.

One couldn't help feeling that this sentiment was shared by certain members of staff.

There was nothing racist about this. Oh, no. Yids, Pakis, Spics and Coons are all very well in their place. They just don't know when to stop, that's all. The way they acted once they were let into the school just proves that whatever you teach them, they'll never become proper Englishmen. They complain about the food, they cheat at sport, and they expect to go home in the evenings. You'd think they'd be grateful to have been allowed in. But oh, no – the minute they're through the front gates they start acting as if they own the place. Particularly the Jews. Most of the brown ones know a thing or two about humility. Empire and all that. Did them a world of good. They understand cricket, you see. But the Jews? When did you last see a Yid with a decent forward defensive on him? Eh? They're incapable. Money's the only thing they understand, you see. And they're dashed good at exams, too. That's the bugger of it.

My school was a living example to other establishments with a feeling for their history that once you let in people who . . . rather, once you allow the place to be dominated by chaps who aren't . . . from solid old-fashioned families, a school loses its social standing. Good eggs begin to steer clear, and before you know it, foreigners are flocking to you like flies around . . . um, honey.

*

The school was originally founded hundreds of years ago by one of the tradesmen's guilds in the City of London to educate the sons of poor workers. Since then, the school had relocated several times, finally settling on a site in the green belt just outside North West London. The boys came in every morning on a network of coaches which ranged from Watford in the west, through Harrow, Stanmore and Edgware across to Totteridge and High Barnet in the east.

When they chose the site, the governors must have felt jolly pleased with themselves, confident once and for all that they had excluded anyone who might even vaguely resemble the son of a poor worker from central London, and had found a catchment area consisting almost exclusively of the best, most prosperous suburbs. They failed to account, however, for the changing make-up of North West London, and by the time Thatcher was beginning to look as if even senile dementia wouldn't get her out of Downing Street, the governors had found themselves presiding over a cash-for-A-levels exam greenhouse for *nouveau-riche*, second-generation immigrants.

The governors had first attempted to stave off the impending disaster as early as the fifties, when they instituted a Jewish quota. The quota boys were excused from the religious half of morning assembly, and it is said that after the hymns and prayers, the headmaster would stand and intone the words 'LET IN THE JEWS!', whereupon the doors at the back of the assembly hall would open up to admit a line of boys in single file, who would take seats at the back of the hall for the school announcements.

It was extremely competitive to get a place in the Jewish quota, and as a result, the Jews did even better than they would have done had it not been for the additional selection procedure, giving rise to an embarrassingly segregated results table – Christians at the bottom, Jews at the top. It was difficult to retain the pretence that the extraordinary musicians, sportsmen, intellectuals and actors sailing their way into Cambridge were lucky to be allowed into the school, and the quota system had to be dropped. The segregated exam results, however, proved harder to dispose of.

*

This is why, at my school, someone like Piers Ward was an extraordinary phenomenon. He was the genuine article: a pukka toff, Anglican and everything. He even had the accent. E.T. would have been less conspicuous.

Piers was noisy, brash, rude, posh, and best of all, inert and stupid. This made him an excellent hockey goalkeeper. The only reason I knew him personally was because we played together in the school hockey First XI.

Thanks to the school's illustrious pre-Jew history, we had a sports fixture list that pitted us against all the most famous boarding schools in the area. As we arrived amid the dreaming spires of some Oxbridge replica or other, a whole row of Pierses would come into view, resplendent in identical brogues, cords and floppy hair.

While we got off the bus, they peered in horror at the bizarre collection of brown-skinned and big-nosed aliens stepping onto their hallowed ground. All of a sudden it wasn't Piers who was the freak, but us.

These boys were used to having the odd African Prince now and then, who would play on the wing in the school rugby team and be known as 'wog', but to see a whole bus-load of . . . of . . . *immigrants* always came as quite a shock.

One by one, we would have our hands reluctantly shaken by a Piers who would then take us off to a dormitory to get changed.

Not a changing-room, but a dormitory.

Where they slept.

This was their life.

They actually lived in this place.

The thought made us shiver, and we always changed in horrified silence.

Meanwhile, Piers Ward was slapped on the back, punched, rugby tackled and variously assaulted with all manner of sexually paranoid male greetings. A big crowd formed around him, gabbling about this sailing weekend or that shoot. None of us had ever imagined that Piers had friends. This extraordinary sight, of Piers talking to a group of people who gave every impression of liking him, gave further proof that everything which he found important was invisible to us. He simply lived in a different world.

This was when it first began to dawn on me that Britain wasn't dominated by Jews and Asians. 'Fuck!' I thought. 'I'm in a minority. This is terrible.'

Beating these rich, smug, racist, privileged wankers at hockey was an intensely satisfying experience. Or would have been. If we ever did. Unfortunately, their extra slick bobble-free water-shedding Astroturf mega-pitches were always too flat for us, and without the divots and molehills to hack through, we never managed to control the ball, and always got thrashed.

Having dribbled effortlessly through our knock-kneed defence, they would cast apologetic glances at Piers before thwacking yet another perfectly aimed shot into the roof of his net.

At the end of the game, we were shaken by the hand once again and told that we had 'put up a jolly good fight.'

My usual reply to this was, 'Fuck off, you rich cunt.'

On the bus home, Piers was always despondent. How he yearned to be at a school with decent people! How he hated his parents for not sending him away to boarding school!

Watching Piers' tear-filled eyes as we drew out of the school, past the twelve-foot razor-wired wall, through the spiked cast-iron gates, I began to wonder what family life could consist of for a real English person – not a Jew or an Asian – but a *real* English person like Piers. I couldn't imagine what his home could possibly be like if leaving that prison made him want to cry.

I began to form hideous and exaggerated images of what must indeed be an awful, chilling creature – the non-Jewish mother.

CHAPTER TWENTY

When Summer term began, the whole school changed its personality. People started dressing more casually, smiling, chatting in the sun, and things generally became a little bit more like the rest of the civilized world. Some of the nicer teachers started giving the odd class outside on the grass, and one could detect a marginal loosening in the sphincters of even the most up-tight disciplinarians. On one famous day in May 1982, a member of the physics department had even been known to open a window.

After all the hassles of rugby and hockey, the school switched its attention to wonderful, lazy cricket, the rules of which I have never fully understood but appear to differ only marginally from those of sunbathing.

After two terms of my A-levels, I felt that I had got a pretty good idea of which teachers had something to teach and which didn't, so I adopted a new policy of attending only those lessons from which I thought I would learn something. This left me vast tracts of free time in which I could concentrate on my tan. Since the gap between my stubble and my hairline constituted only a small stripe of skin most of which fell into the shade of my eyebrows, I had to concentrate on tanning my arms. Every now and then I would take off my watch and look at the ever-whitening band underneath it, which was the only way to measure my progress.

Thanks to an education system which was ideally suited to my small-mindedness, I hadn't had to take any biology or chemistry since I was fifteen, and as I lay in the sun, on a square of grass hidden behind the library block, I had visions of being joined in my happiness by millions of elated cancer cells swimming to the surface of my body to bask in the sun with me. I felt pleased to be spreading so much joy.

The first hiccup of the term came when I drank a glass of

water too quickly. The second, and more significant one, came in a conversation with Barry when he told me that he was in love with Mrs Mumford. This concept became rapidly less amusing when he informed me that she was also in love with him and was planning to leave her husband and children and move into a flat in Notting Hill with him. In a startling reversal of everything I had ever imagined, Barry told me that they had been having a long and passionate affair since one week after they first met.

'We've been having a long and passionate affair since one week after we first met,' was how he put it.

'But . . . but . . . you can't.'

'Why?'

'Because . . . because . . . what about me?'

'What about you?'

'I mean us. What about us?'

'What?'

'I mean, our friendship. I thought we were friends.'

'And? . . .'

'Um . . .'

'We *are* friends. So what?'

'Um . . . you just can't. What about me? It's not fair.'

'It's got nothing to do with you. I'll still see you, Mark. You won't even notice the difference. I've been with her for the last six months and you didn't notice anything. Why is it going to make any difference to our friendship now?'

I struggled to think of some objection.

'The cinema . . .'

'What?'

'The cinema. You won't be able to go with me to the cinema any more.'

'Of course I will, you prat. As long as no one else in the school finds out that we're living together, it won't make any difference to anyone except me and her.'

'But . . . Shit! . . . It's not fair.'

'What the fuck are you twittering on about?'

'Wittering. The word's wittering, you cunt.'

This was awful! How could he do this. It wasn't fair. I had to split them up.

Then I thought of something clever.

'What about her family? You're destroying her family.'

'I know,' he said. 'I think she should stay with them, but she is adamant that she wants to leave. Apparently her husband's a lazy shithead and it's about time he did some of the work with the children.'

'But – but – what a bitch! She can't do that. She should stay with her family.'

'Yes – I agree. For the kids' sake.'

'But . . . can't you persuade her to stay, then?'

'I've tried, but she says that she can't get enough of my body and has to have me all the time.'

Somehow when Barry said things like this it sounded more like modesty than showing off. It came from some trick of intonation which you can only acquire by spending several years being nice to people. I've often tried to copy it but it just makes me sound like a liar.

'One day I think we'll have a child together,' he said.

To this there was no reaction. I tried to make myself faint but it didn't work. When I opened my mouth no sounds came out.

I tried again. 'Bragghhlllnmmmnnnrrrror . . . bu . . . bugghrrhhriillipnnn.'

'I hope it's a girl,' he said.

I fainted.

CHAPTER TWENTY-ONE

Barry thought it was very noble of me to swallow my pride and help him and Mrs Mumford move into their new flat. It was the first time anyone had ever called me noble, and it wasn't really that accurate, given that I only went in the hope that I might be able to fuck things up.

My fake trip, which was intended to send Mrs Mumford's wardrobe far enough down the stairs to smash it, went a little wrong when I managed to overact my stumble badly enough to send me shooting down the stairs with the wardrobe, cushioning its fall, and leaving me wedged underneath it on a second-floor landing, unable to move, while the two people I was generously giving up my time for laughed their heads off at the top of the stairs.

'This is great,' I shouted. 'Really – thanks a lot, guys – I really appreciate this. I'm getting thinner *and* taller. You should sell the wardrobe crush method to health farms.'

They laughed more.

'GET ME OUT YOU FUCKERS!'

They stopped laughing and moved the wardrobe.

Mrs Mumford didn't seem to mind that I had called her a fucker. I was going to apologize and tell her that the 's' was and accident and I had only really meant Barry, but it didn't appear that she was about to give me a detention. The whole situation was distinctly weird. It felt like incest. Or like seeing your granny in the bath.

I decided to try an experiment.

'Margaret?'

'Yes?'

FUCK! SHE ANSWERED! JESUS FUCKING CHRIST!

'Nothing.'

*

A couple of days after this, I was in a French lesson with Mrs Mumford when something extraordinary happened. She was half way through explaining one of those tenses which is only used to describe an action which usually occurs regularly and was commenced but then interrupted by a moving object on the first Wednesday of a Leap Year, when she just stopped talking.

This was an unusual experience in itself, but when she continued staring at the blackboard, and allowed the silence to go on and on and on, we sensed something exciting in the air.

When she turned round to face us, she didn't look angry, but calm. She sat down. Her face was concentrating on something, thinking hard, but with a hint of a smile. When she finally spoke again, her voice was lower than usual, and more confident.

'I am aware,' she said, 'of certain rumours circulating in the sixth form about a sexual relationship between myself and Barry. These rumours are not only potentially damaging to myself, my career, and my family, they are also . . .' she paused for a long, long time, blinking slowly, '. . . true. I am, I must admit, having an affair – an extremely passionate affair – with one of my students. I realize that this could result in my getting the sack, and I have tried to terminate our relationship, but – well – when I see him . . .' there was another huge pause, '. . . and his beautiful face, I just can't turn him away.'

She was completely still. She closed her eyes for what could easily have been a whole minute, and when she opened them again, they were moist and shiny.

'When he touches me, I can't resist him.' She blinked about five times, her eyelids closing so slowly that each time it looked as if she was falling asleep.

'It feels so good – it makes me feel young.' She smiled to herself, her eyes focused far, far away. 'I feel alive. He's so gentle, so tender – my husband was always a brute – his clumsy fat fingers used to maul me – I never felt a spark, but when Barry touches me, my whole body feels on fire.' Her face was going red. Her eyes now glazed over altogether. 'I feel like I'm lost – I forget everything – we move together like . . . like . . .' She blinked slowly and crossed her legs hard, rubbing her thighs together. Her eyes then closed completely, and she sat silently in her chair, bolt upright, her chest moving slowly and deeply, up, down, up, down. Her legs were still crossed, and her pelvis was rocking subtly but regularly, making tiny circles around the seat of her chair.

We were transfixed. The silence was absolute. Every single one of us was staring at her nipples, which were twice the usual size. I had an erection.

Many blissful minutes passed.

Then, suddenly, her eyes snapped open. 'Listen – listen – I deserve a bit of happiness. I am fed up with . . . with all the shit. I have had enough of working twice as hard as all the other teachers in this place who are all, of course, lazy men. I have had enough of clearing up all the shitty mess my stupid husband leaves around our boring house. I am fed up with boring children complaining about boring, stupid problems – so fuck it. Fuck it all. I, for once, am staking a claim for something I deserve – I've earned it for God's sake, and I'm not going to take any more shit from anyone. Yes – I'm still going to mark your essays, but I'm not going to cover them in comments that you can't even be bothered to read – yes – I'm still going to look after my kids, but I'm not going to cook every fucking mouthful that ever crosses their fat, spoiled lips – and no – my husband can just go screw. So I have moved out, and I am living with Barry, who I love, and who is kind to me.'

She stopped talking, closed her eyes again, took a deep breath, and let the air out slowly through her nose. The redness slowly drained out of her cheeks. My erection began to fade.

Then she spoke again, this time in her normal voice. 'I'm sorry – I didn't mean to go into all that. I hope I haven't embarrassed you all – but I think you understand what I mean. What I wanted to say was just this – that at last, for the first time in my life, I have something that I want, and I don't feel drowned by other people constantly making demands of me. For the first time ever, I feel in control of my life – I feel able to take decisions about what I do and do not want. This is the most important thing that has ever happened to me. So – what I mean is – I *am* having an affair with Barry, and if these rumours spread to the staff, I'll get the sack, so I'm asking you a favour. I want you, my favourite class, to kill the rumours for me. Only a few people know at the moment, and I'm sure that between you, you know who they are. I want you to explain to them my situation – I want you to tell them what I have told you. This is the only time I have been so honest in my whole life. I would never have thought it possible that I could be so happy. *Please*, explain to people my situation – I need this job if I want to live without my husband. I hope you understand. I know I shouldn't trust you, but you are Barry's friends, so I'm taking a gamble. If you're anything like Barry, I know I'm safe. Thank you – thank you for helping me. I'll go now, so you have some time to think about it.'

Then she left.

Fuck!

CHAPTER TWENTY-TWO

Two hours later, one thousand three hundred boys knew every detail of Mrs Mumford's sex life, including the shape her nipples took when she was aroused, and within a week she got the sack.

The version you have just read is almost exactly the story which spread around the school and lost Mrs Mumford her job. Although this doesn't correspond *literally* with the exact events in the classroom, the fundamentals of what she said are all there. I just coloured it in a bit. Helped her express herself. People will always quibble about details, but if you do a survey of North London you will get exactly the same story that I have just told you. It is without a shadow of doubt the accepted truth. That much is undeniable.

Mrs Mumford getting kicked out of the school was hardly the end of the world, but when I heard that Barry had been expelled, I was gutted. I almost felt as if it was my fault.

The following weekend I went to see them at their Notting Hill flat, and Mrs Mumford . . . Margaret . . . was understandably bitter. I told her how terrible I thought it was that the story had been so rapidly passed around, and we commiserated together about how untrustworthy men are.

While she went on and on about what an idiot she was, I took a good look at her, trying my hardest to keep a straight face. Since losing her job, she had undergone a drastic image change. Gone were the severe skirts, fancy blouses, belts, necklaces, serious shoes and thick make-up, all replaced by one bizarre, baggy, lurid . . . *thing*. I'm not very good on fashion terms, but it appeared to be a cross between a poncho, a pair of dungarees, and a carpet. The make-up, the expensive accessories, and even the hairstyle had all vanished. I suspected that she wasn't even wearing any underwear. All she seemed to have on was the one *thing*. I suppose the intended effect was that she would instantly look twenty years younger, but it didn't really work, and she actually looked as if she had just got out of the shower.

She read my expression, and tried to explain: 'I've left all my clothes at my husband's house. I didn't want to bring anything with me. I was going to have a symbolic burning of the clothes I was wearing on my final day, but I couldn't find anywhere safe so I threw them in a skip on Portobello Road. I'm compiling a new wardrobe from the shops of Notting Hill.'

I couldn't think of a more disastrous plan, but told her that her optimism was 'admirable'. I had read somewhere that this is the kind of thing mid-life crisis victims want to hear.

'Doesn't she look beautiful now?' asked Barry.

'Yes, she looks . . . um . . . admirable.'

'Thank you.' Her expression pleaded for more flattery.

'Yes,' I said, 'you look . . .' – (um) – '. . . um . . .' – (could I force the words out?) – 'you look . . .' – (push – push) – 'twenty years younger.'

'Do you really think so?'

Oh no! Disastrous response! I was exhausted. I couldn't offer any more.

Thankfully, Barry interceded on my behalf. 'Of course you do – everyone keeps telling you so.'

It was time to change the subject. 'Are you going to look for another teaching job?' I asked.

'Fuck teaching,' she said. When she said 'fuck' it didn't sound right. Her intonation showed that she was trying just that little bit too hard to make it sound effortless. 'Barry and I –' (How can you put 'Barry and I' with 'fuck'? It's all wrong.) '– are going to spend the summer fruit-picking in all the most interesting parts of the country, then I'm going to blow my savings on a trip for the two of us to India. October's the best time to go – just after the monsoon. We can stay there through the winter – living in grotty hotels, eating cheap food –'

'Then what?'

'What do you mean, then what?'

'Then what – What will you do?'

'Oh for God's sake, don't be so square –' (she was beginning to piss me off) – ' "then what?" has made my life a misery.'

I pretended not to understand. 'Then what has made your life a misery?'

'No – "then what?" has made my life a misery.'

'What "then what?" has made your life a misery?'

'You know – "then what?" – the question "then what?" is what has made me do such boring things with my life.'

'I see – "then what?" has made your life a misery.'

'Exactly.'

'But what will you do when you get back from China?' I got it wrong deliberately. 'How will you make a living?'

'India, not China.'

'But how will you make a living? What about Barry's education?'

'Jesus!' she screamed, 'don't be so fucking middle-aged!'

At this point she lost my sympathy. Not content with stealing my best friend, this wrinkly old tart was now telling me that *I* was middle-aged. That was too much. It was just too fucking much. I took a deep breath and tried to calm myself down. 'Right,' I thought, 'listen here you prolapsed menopausal slag, I'm going to show you who's fucking middle-aged . . .'

I smiled politely.

'How old were you in the sixties?' I asked.

'Why do you ask?'

'You must have been in your twenties. Is that right?'

'. . . Yes . . .'

'And I suppose you had a really wild time.'

'. . . Well . . . sort of.'

'Were you really into the Beatles?'

'Yes – everyone was.'

'It must have been amazing seeing them live.'

'Live?'

'Live. You know – in concert.'

'Oh. Live. Well – I never actually made it to one of their concerts. What are you on about any – . . .?'

'Right. Were you too spaced out on drugs or something?'

'Not exactly.'

'Were you on the hippy trail to India, then? Or passed out in a police station in Marrakech?'

'No.'

'Or maybe you were having sex on acid in Hyde Park?'

'No.'

'Or were you, by any chance, revising hard for your modern languages exams at Cambridge University?'

'Um . . . well . . . I suppose something a little more along those lines.'

This was going well.

'What degree did you get?' I asked.

'A First.'

'From Cambridge?'

'From Cambridge.'

'In which year?'

'1965.'

'I see. There was still half the decade left, though. What about '67 – the summer of love and all that.'

'Summer '67. Um . . . that was . . . doing up a starter home in Finchley.'

'With your husband?'

'With my husband.'

'Who was also from Cambridge?'

'Who was also from Cambridge.'

'What degree did he get?'

'A First.'

'In what?'

'Economics.'

'Then what?'

'A job.'

'In the City?'

'In the City.'

'While you looked after the –'

'Yes.'

There was an embarrassed silence.

Then Barry piped up, 'I think it's good to catch up on what you've missed.'

There was another embarrassed silence.

This woman was a psychological disaster area. I had to save Barry from her. It was for his own good. I trawled my brain for a fitting lie.

'Besides,' I said, 'you can't go fruit-picking this summer, Barry. Because of our pact.'

'What pact?'

'The pact. You know – from that day –' I had to think of something good.

'What day?'

'The day. You know – at that place.' I wasn't doing very well.

'What place?'

'The place. You know – London.' He would give up soon.

'Where in London?'

'The middle. You know – the West End.'

'What?'

'You remember. We were walking around Leicester Square that day after the film, and we made a pact that this July we would spend a month Inter-railing together in Europe, then we went to a pub and you drank a lot and passed out.'

One of the nicest things about Barry was that he had only a passing familiarity with the concept of lying.

'Are you sure?'

'Of course I'm fucking sure. Can't you remember? I've already bought my ticket.'

'Oh no.'

'I can't believe you'd forget a thing like that. Jesus, Barry, you can be so selfish sometimes.'

'I'm sorry, Mark. I just forgot. I must have drunk too much.'

'So because you get drunk once, I have to spend the whole summer trudging round Europe on my own. You bastard, Barry.'

'Oh no. I'm really sorry. Mags – what am I going to do?'

She looked up. Her eyes were wet. 'Go. I'll buy you a ticket. Mark's right – I need a little time to sort myself out. A month on my own will do me good. I'll need to sort out a lawyer to deal with my husband. I have to work something out with my kids. And I still haven't told my parents what I've done. Oh God, my life's a mess. I'm out of control. I'm an idiot.'

She started to cry. She cried loudly, wetly and for a long time, so I left.

Poor Barry.

It had never occurred to me before to go Inter-railing, but now that it was all fixed, it seemed like a good idea. I had always thought it sounded rather futile, bombing around Europe's capitals in a state of poverty and catatonia, but now that I was going to be doing it myself it began to sound like fun.

I would have to get a job first, but if I worked through June, my July holiday would be paid for. It had turned out to be an excellent afternoon, with my whole summer fixing itself up for me almost without effort.

I felt a bit guilty about what I had done to Mrs Mumford, but . . . well –

CHAPTER TWENTY-THREE

The event which really captured the school's imagination that term was a mock election which had been set up by Mr Wright to mirror the one happening in the real world. Every boy was to get a vote, with each party led by a member of the lower sixth. In the run-up to polling day, a debate in the style of *Question Time* would be staged in the school hall, and the final vote was to take place just before the end of term, a few weeks ahead of the real election.

At first everyone was resistant to the idea, purely because Mr Wright was a nob, but after a slow start, election fever gradually spread through the school. The best party leaders organized representatives for each year group, and staged political rallies which took place on the playgrounds and playing fields.

By the day of *Question Time*, the election had narrowed down to a two-horse race, with support evenly balanced between the Eric The Half-a-Bee Party and the Des for Pres movement. The Pink Party was suffering from the classic third-party squeeze. Labour, Conservative and LibDem also had representatives, but no one quite knew who they were.

In the final minutes before the great debate, there were nasty clashes between Bee and Des supporters which resulted in one boy having to go to Matron.

On stage, the Eric The Half-a-Bee Party performed best, debating cogently for the rights of all half-animals (not just half-bees) to a life free from the spectre of discrimination. This expansion of range was an eleventh-hour policy announcement which drew roars of approval from supporters.

The Des for Pres movement, by contrast, had little to offer by way of policy, and was exposed as a mere personality cult. This cult, incidentally, was built around an upper-sixth former who was famous for having failed his English O-level four times, for having a stupid name, and for being generally very thick. Des, true to form, failed to notice that the Des for Pres movement was taking the piss out of him, and slowly came to relish his time as a focus of attention for the school. He was constantly pestered for autographs throughout the campaign, and was always given a standing ovation at any political event he attended. Once he had got over his bewilderment at the presidential campaign which had sprung up around him, he began to develop a magnificent line in little smiles and false-modest waves with which he acknowledged his followers. Despite the party's undeniable policy weakness, for me, Des' gradual acceptance of himself as a revolutionary hero provided an irresistible depth to the Des for Pres campaign. Personally, I was a dyed-in-the-wool Des for Pres man.

The Pink Party fell apart altogether in the course of the debate. One question from the floor led to an all-out row on stage between the two Pink speakers, causing a walk-out and the birth of the breakaway Rose Party faction.

The surprise hit was the T Party who came from nowhere to propose a winning policy package advocating increased use of all objects whose name began with the letter 'T', along with compulsory weekly means-tested tea parties across the board.

This debate was supposedly chaired by Mr Wright, but for the first half hour, he just sat on stage looking perplexed and dismayed. Then, suddenly, he jumped up and marched to the front of the stage, pushing the Eric The Half-a-Bee vice-president out of the way.

'STOP!' he shouted. 'Stop this! This is nonsense! What are you all talking about? What on earth are you all talking about? This is ludicrous! Absolutely ludicrous! I just don't understand. You're supposed to be the *crème de la crème*. I hand you a golden opportunity to engage in some intelligent political debate, and this is what you do with it! I came here, having worked jolly hard for you all, hoping that in return I would be rewarded by the opportunity to find out how young people feel about politics. And this is what I find! I'm stunned. Stunned and disappointed.'

There was a tense, shocked silence.

Then another voice rose from the platform.

'I, Simon Meyer, as President of the Eric The Half-a-Bee Party, would like to be the first person to endorse every point so cogently proposed by both halves of Mr Wright. We shall enshrine them in our constitution.'

Huge applause. Stamping, cheering, standing ovation.

Mr Wright left.

The following day, it was announced in assembly that any party without a direct counterpart in the General Election would be banned. No party would be allowed on the ballot paper without the permission of Mr Wright.

The Des for Pres movement responded with an immediate and deadly blow, transforming themselves into the Green Party. All the other made-up parties fizzled out, transforming the election into a more-or-less genuine survey of the school's political leanings.

Although this meant that no one attended any of the remaining debates, it did produce some interesting results when polling day came around. Mr Wright counted the votes, and produced a series of graphs breaking down the results according to each year-group.

The sixth-form results were a statistical anomaly, since a mixture of ballot-rigging and intimidation tactics resulted in an 85 per cent vote for the Green Party.

The first year voted 90 per cent Tory, 8 per cent LibDem and 2 per cent Labour, with a gradual slide of opinion through to the fifth form which came out at roughly 70 per cent Tory, 20 per cent LibDem and 10 per cent Labour.

Mr Wright was gutted. He sulked for two weeks, setting written work for his classes from the blackboard, and hardly speaking to anyone.

We all found it hilarious that he was so upset, and the only person who tried to cheer him up was Joel Schneider, who kept on offering him gifts of blue rosettes. Mr Wright wouldn't accept these presents, which I thought was very bad form. And the spirit with which he received Joel's free career advice ('Why don't you move to Russia, sir?') was equally sour.

CHAPTER TWENTY-FOUR

Meanwhile, in the midst of the school's rock-solid Thatcherism, despite the efforts of the more liberal teachers to stop the lower school working out competitive chemistry averages, however much we all fought with one another to claw our way to the top of whatever little pile we happened to be standing in, there was one thing which drew us all together regardless of social differences, of wealth, of chemistry marks, of beauty, and of sporting ability: one thing, and only one, brought us together: the Penis.

I don't mean the literal penis – the wobbly little piece of meat we all carried between our legs – I mean something far more powerful, infinitely more potent. I am referring to the *symbol* of the Penis – a talisman which all of us carried close to our hearts, and which was never far from our minds.

The Penis as a symbol bore very little resemblance to the actual object, and was only ever drawn in one of two ways.

Like this:

Or, for the artistic, like this:

These drawings, these symbols, were the mark of companionship which magnetized the minds of every member of the school, synchronizing our thoughts and turning us into one homogeneous family, if not almost into one person.

Like dogs pissing on trees, not one boy in the school could look at a clean, unmarked surface without thinking, 'that needs a Penis drawn on it'.

However, unlike those of dogs, our marks were indistinguishable and contained no identifiable authorial feature. The symbol served not to stake out territory or claim prowess, but as a purely communal mark of togetherness and harmony. *Everyone* could share in the joy of a wittily placed Penis.

Obviously a big one was funnier than a small one, but then anyone could draw a big one if he felt like it. Everything was possible. In the world of the Penis (if not in the world of the penis), we were all equal.

Anyone at all sceptical about the ability of men to work in harmony and sympathy should look on this as an irrefutable example of modern man at his very best. Maybe the first generation of New Men is only just arriving – we, the children of the seventies, the first generation to be raised by feminist mothers – we are arriving at last to overturn decades of slander against the male gene. Wait for us! We're completely different from everything you've ever seen before.

All over the school, etched into desks, Tippexed onto chairbacks, felt-tipped onto walls, inked on exercise books, graffitied throughout text books, fingered into dusty window-sills and car windows, drawn on hands, scratched with a foot into playground gravel, laid out in sausage and mash on school dinner plates; everywhere, the universal mission to spread the stamp of the Penis obsessed us all, pushing us on to ever greater feats of imagination.

(It is worth noting that the more aggressively heterosexual and rugby-obsessed a group of boys were, the more they tended to draw Penises all over each other's bodies and possessions.

However, even the Christians weren't above the odd quick scrawl in a hymn book.)

The greatest day in the history of the Penis came without a doubt in the final week of my lower sixth.

It was traditional at my school for the Summer term to end with a five-a-side football tournament which would take place on the fields in the furthest corner of the school, behind the car park. Technically speaking, this was on the other side of the Berlin Wall, and as a result the matches achieved spectacular attendance. It was the only time of year when there was a genuine excuse to cross the iron curtain. One couldn't possibly go just to look at the girls – that would be stupid – so we all went to the five-a-side football, just to look at the girls.

Of course, by the end of the lower sixth, my year had already seen all the girls, but it was worth going anyway, to watch the younger boys seeing the girls for the first time. With an extra something given to the afternoon by the element of sexual performance in the football, the day was a true bonanza of hormonal agitation – definitely not to be missed.

The tournament took up a week of lunch-times, with the grand final happening on the Monday of the last week of term. Traditionally, this final was also the last chance for the boys leaving the school to display their virility through some act of daring or skill, in front of an enormous audience. As a result the staff came out in force to try and stop whatever was going to happen from happening.

These parting shots, final dollops of daring from boys who had already sat their A-levels and were now effectively beyond the jurisdiction of the school, usually displayed nothing more than how spectacularly unvirile they were, and consisted only of a water fight with the odd bit of egg and flour-throwing if you were lucky.

However, the year above me was, for a change, genuinely rebellious, and they arrived at the five-a-side final pissed, in a fleet of cars which they drove onto the pitch, stopping the final altogether, and turning it into a stunt driving show which featured some impressive wheel-spins and hand-brake turns. Meanwhile, the staff police-force looked on aghast.

The following morning it was announced that the culprits had all been expelled, about which the boys concerned clearly did not give a fuck. However, it did give them an excuse to exact a spectacular revenge.

No one knows exactly how they did it, but it is easy enough to guess. They must have driven back to the school during the night, broken into one of the groundsman's sheds and stolen a rugby pitch line-painting machine, because when we arrived at school on the final day of term, the first thing we all saw from our coaches as we drew into the school grounds was a huge – a giant – a fifty-metre Penis sunning itself on the main cricket pitch, unfurled from the entrance to the headmaster's office.

I cannot think of those brave boys without a warm glow radiating my heart. They spread so much joy to us all that day. Such happiness everywhere – it was incredible. For the first time in my life, I felt that I could imagine what it must have been like being alive in Britain on VE-Day. It was the perfect end to the school year.

MY GRAND TOUR

CHAPTER TWENTY-FIVE

After school broke up, I went straight to my local temping agency to sign up for a job. They can't have believed what I said about fluent shorthand, because two days later they rang me up to offer me work as a filing clerk for £3.50 an hour.

I turned up at the offices of Lentrust Insurance Services in Harrow at nine o'clock the following morning. I was given an I.D. badge, which was a bit of card with the word 'visitor' written on it, and shown to my post.

On the second floor of the building was a huge open-plan office containing about fifty people, half of them sitting at computer screens, half of them answering telephones. Along one wall was a solid bank of cardboard folders, each one stuffed with papers, and labelled with a pair of numbers on the side. The first one, at the near end of the room said '80250-80259', and the last one, at the far end said '201190-201199'.

In the corner of the room was a waist-high pile of papers, each one relating to an insurance claim on a faulty piece of electrical hardware, each one with a number in the top left-hand corner between 80250 and 201199. My job was to put each piece of paper in the right folder. If the number was less than 80250 ('which it shouldn't be'), then I had to give it to Annie and it would go to the Hemel office.

('It can't be more than 201199 – we haven't got there yet.')

I had been told by friends that working as a filing clerk was boring, but this was truly an extraordinary experience. I thought that I had experienced boredom before, as a passive sensation of inertia or frustration. But this feeling was something entirely new. This boredom was something far more active – it was a vivid, almost gut-wrenching sensation, involving not only the brain, but every part of the body. It swept over me in giant, engulfing waves, a bit like what everyone always says about sex, only different.

This boredom was an astonishingly powerful emotion, and something I had never experienced ever before. If I had been filing things in alphabetical order, at least I would have been using my brain in some tiny, life-affirming way, but filing purely by number destroys the soul. Worst of all, it requires just enough mental effort to stop you day-dreaming, and not a brain cell more. If your job is stacking boxes or mowing lawns, with a little bit of imagination you can spend most of the day swimming in the Bahamas, making love to Darryl Hannah or playing a concerto at the Albert Hall; but if you are filing in numerical order then that's *it*, you spend *all day* filing in numerical order.

The first three hours are the worst, since they appear to last several months. After that, little systems emerge, tiny short cuts like putting the ninety-three thousands to the bottom of the pile because their files are behind the photocopier. Little things like that make your day a little happier. I also tended to linger on the one-hundred-and-sixty-thousand-and-overs, because that end of the room was where the telephone answering girls worked, and I could eavesdrop on them.

As far as I could tell, they spent all day talking about soap operas and sex, interrupted by the odd telephone call, shifting seamlessly between a cockney chatting voice and a pseudo-posh sing-song telephone voice:

'My mate Sal told me that her Tone took her up the shitter once and it did absolutely nothing for her hello Lentrust Insurance Services can I help you?'

'Jesus, I said to her, Jesus, I wouldn't *want* a bloke with a dick that size, I mean it's bound to do you some serious hello Lentrust Insurance Services can I help you?'

'Not when I'm *on*. At least not usually. Blocked dishwasher? You want 427-2375, madam. Fucks up the sheets, doesn't it?'

'Here, did you read that thing about the woman and the horse? Have you still got a copy of the guarantee? Apparently she had to go to hospital. She'll probably have a half-horse half-baby. Only one year for a hairdryer, I'm afraid. Bet the horse loved it, though.'

When one of the men from upstairs came through, they would all answer the phone at once, heads down, all in the posh voice. And I would go back to the less-than-one-hundred-and-sixty-thousand end to save the good numbers for later.

After a week I was still only a third of the way through the pile. I began to find myself spending my lunch hour in hardware stores, toying with lengths of rope.

When I noticed that there was an advertisement in the *Evening Standard* which ran every day, saying 'An enjoyable job outdoors talking to women,' I knew that my career as a filing clerk had come to an end.

CHAPTER TWENTY-SIX

Since Barry's expulsion from the school I had barely seen him. He must have been deeply involved in moving house and settling down with Mrs Mumford, while I was taken up with the end of term at school. Also, I felt uncomfortable about ringing him. Maybe it was a touch of guilt – I don't really know.

On top of this, I didn't have the phone number for his new flat. I always hated speaking to people's parents, but once I had started at Lentrust Insurance Services, I was so overcome with boredom that I managed to force myself to make the call. I spoke to Barry's father and we had an awkward conversation. He gave me Barry's new phone number, and I managed to say, 'You must have had a heart attack when you found out about this woman,' which was a particularly tactless comment given what was going to happen to him a few weeks later. Still, I don't suppose he could have noticed at the time.

When I spoke to Barry he didn't seem at all angry with me, and our friendship was instantly back to normal. This shouldn't have been a surprise, since Barry didn't have a clue that I had deliberately reduced Mrs Mumford to tears, and had lied through my arse to get him going on holiday with me, but still – I was pleased to have the confidence back to be able to talk to him without feeling bad.

During my long and successful career in filing, I spent most of my evenings at the Notting Hill flat. These evenings were always cosily pleasant, and I even got as far as developing a comforting Oedipus-type thing for Mrs Mumford. She really did have killer tits. And having given up on the hippie clothes, she looked reasonably presentable again.

I felt quite sorry for her actually, and I could see how positive it was for her that she was spending some time away from her family. Laughable, yes, but positive too. It was cool of her to make a stand, really. After all, the only thing worse than having a mid-life crisis is not having one – because if that happens, you've given up and you might as well be dead.

As I was having these thoughts, it occurred to me what a perceptive chap I was, and for the first time it dawned on me that my future career should be as a psychotherapist. Barry was in the kitchen cooking supper at the time, so I decided to have a go.

'Margaret?' I asked. Her first name now came naturally to me.

'Yes?' she replied.

'What kind of a relationship did you have with your mother?'

'Um . . . fine. Why do you ask?'

'Just wondering.'

'Oh.'

'Did she ever desert you as a child at any stage?'

'No.'

It was perfect. She was lying on the sofa, so I got up and subtly moved myself to behind her head like you're supposed to, so that we couldn't see each other's expressions.

'If you think back, are you absolutely sure?'

'Positive.'

'Was she a good mother? Did she breast-feed you?' I was really getting to the heart of it now.

'Yes, she was an OK mother, and I don't really remember if she breast-fed me – I was a bit young at the time.' Ahh – sarcasm as a defence mechanism. Interesting.

'Right. So you don't feel neglected in any way?'

'No, of course not.'

'Are you sure?'

'Actually – now I think of it, there was one time . . . yes . . . God, I must have been twelve. My father came home drunk and started touching me in funny ways. When my mother tried to protect me, he hit her. I remember clearly, now. The back of his fist smashed her on the nose – I remember blood spattering out onto my dress. She screamed, picked up a large saucepan and hit him over the head with it. He was knocked cold, and he toppled to the ground, falling on top of me. I couldn't move, but my mother dragged me from under him – it hurt my leg and I remember it tore my dress. A little tear just above the waist.'

Fuck! This was incredible!

'She pulled me out of the house – it was raining hard – and we just ran away – I didn't know where to – I was scared – we just ran. It was only when we were half way to the railway station that she remembered my sisters, so we turned round and went home.'

Jesus Christ! This was incredible! It explained everything. I couldn't wait to tell Barry. She was beginning to cry, now – I could see her whole body shaking.

'Ever since then,' she said – her voice was unsteady, 'I've had a suppressed agony – a fear of the adult world – of parenthood. I've always known that I could never be a good mother.'

This was brilliant! I felt incredible! What power! I leant forward to take a good look at her face.

It was at this point that I realized she was shaking with suppressed laughter, not tears. Once she saw that I had noticed, she burst into hysterics and rolled off the sofa onto the carpet.

'Oh, Mark – you're so gullible,' she said when she had finally calmed down. 'I never would have taken you for such a dunce.'

Me? Gullible? A dunce? Fuck that – she was just a liar. What a fucking liar!

She got up off the floor and sighed, wiping the corners of her eyes. 'It's sweet,' she said, 'you're so transparent. I love young men.'

Then she ruffled my hair like a kid and strolled to the toilet mumbling something about nearly wetting herself.

'I didn't believe you,' I shouted after her. 'I'm not stupid.'

Fucking bitch.

CHAPTER TWENTY-SEVEN

My interview for the enjoyable job outdoors talking to women was odd in two respects. Firstly that it took place in a group of ten, and secondly that it did not require the interviewees to speak at any stage.

In fact it resembled a lecture more than an interview. A squat, muscled man dressed in pin-striped trousers with braces, a white shirt and a blue tie paced the room, fiddling with a cigarette and telling us how to do the job which we had all, evidently, already got. It seemed odd that there was no selection procedure, but he made it clear that we were free to leave the job whenever we liked. 'And if you don't like it, piss off,' was the precise phrase he used.

I was beginning to see why the job was advertised every day. It didn't appear that my nine colleagues and I were in job-for-life territory.

'We're called Nestegg Growth Professionals,' he said. 'What we offer is personal and specific financial growth and savings plans for women, specially catering for a woman's needs, if you'll excuse the pun.' I didn't know what pun he meant. Something to do with women and catering, perhaps? Who knows . . .

'How many of you have done sales? Thought not. The way we operate is this – telephone sales. Statistics tells us that cold calling is not an effective method. It results in what is known as a low effectiveness percentage. So what we do is this – send you –' (he pointed at us) '– out there –' (he pointed out of the window) '– with these –' (he pointed at some leaflets) '– leaflets.'

'What you do is, you find a woman and give one of these leaflets which explains the services which we provide for women. Then you tear off the bottom of the leaflet – the detachable section – actually I suggest you do that before you give it to them – and you ask them their name and telephone number. You give in your detachable sections at the end of the day, and a few days later a member of our telesales staff phones them up, asks if they remember the leaflet, asks if they read it, then tries to sell them a pension plan. For every name and telephone number you give us, we pay you fifty pence. But, and this is a big but, for every hoax number you give us, we dock your wages. Too many hoaxes, and you won't get anything. So don't piss us around. We'll know what you're up to. Any questions? You all ready to start work?'

Three people left.

'Right. That's got rid of three. Let's see how long the rest of you last. GAVIN! This here's your supervisor. GAVIN! He's going to look after you on the street. GAVIN GET HERE! He knows all the best places to cover. GAVIN, YOU CUNT!' Gavin entered. He was exceptionally ugly. And huge. His face had a recent-looking scar which, attractively, went from his left nostril down through his lip to his mouth. His body was covered in slabs of fat-verging-on-muscle. 'Gavin will look after you. He takes care of any problems, threats, things like that. It's in his interests.'

Jesus! This was much better than filing!

Gavin took the seven of us to the cross-roads at Camden Town.

THE CAST:

Paula. An alcoholic middle-aged Irishwoman who always wore a tracksuit.

Wayne. A bricklayer between jobs who looked more like an Aussie surfer. He was distinctly ESN, but had considerable charm and was shortly to get Trish pregnant.

Trish. A chirpy cockney lass straight out of an English Tourist Board film for gullible American tourists. She was of indeterminate age, but appeared to be older than fifteen and younger than thirty. She always wore a baseball cap (usually backwards), and had the amazing ability to talk incessantly about any subject without ever being boring.

Oliver. Wore a tie, knew about wine, gave up the job after twenty minutes.

Nell. Recently graduated from Bristol University, Nell was finding it difficult to choose a career, and scanned the *Guardian* jobs pages at every spare moment. She almost always wore a green beret, and had a lopsided, bland face. She found Gavin difficult to relate to.

Pete. Quiet, broody, but a decent enough chap. Had the same stubble problem as me. Just out of prison for GBH.

Me. A rich Jew.

Gavin. The supervisor.

We were not the most homogeneous of groups. But this was *life*. This was the real world.

I had seen social realist drama before, and watched the odd soap opera, but up until now that world had been no less fantastical than your average Hollywood movie. And now suddenly I found myself in an episode of Eastenders! I was mixing with poor people. It was fantastic! I felt as if I had landed on the set of an MGM musical, and everything I said came out as a tune.

All I had to do was roughen my accent a little bit, and I was one of them. And no one laughed at me! No one knew where I was from, and they didn't ask. Everyone just assumed that I had it tough in life. What a dream! I wished the other boys at school could have seen me. I felt so cool.

The person I got on with best was Gavin. He was a pathological liar and a psychopath. He thought that Nell was the funniest thing he had ever seen. The mere sight of the *Guardian* sent him into fits of laughter.

Have I mentioned Gavin's teeth yet? They lived the wrong way round, with the top set nestling behind the bottom set, an arrangement which is distinctly unbeautiful. It also gave him the table-manners of a poodle. His diet wasn't that far off a poodle's either, since all he ever ate was McDonald's hamburgers, with the odd chip here and there if he was on a health push.

My relationship with Gavin was unusual in that I don't think he had ever had a relationship before. He was under the impression that his job was less to protect us, and more to try and piss us off so much that we resigned. There was a certain gulf between office policy and street ethics here, but I assumed that Gavin knew what he was doing, and went along with him. His particular speciality was with women. If he tried taking the piss out of Trish or Paula, they just turned to each other and started discussing how small his dick must be, so he focused most of his energies on Nell.

'Why do you cut your hair short, Nell?'

Silence.

'Is it something you learnt at university?'

Silence.

'I don't mind if you're a lesbian, you know, I think three-in-a-bed is a great idea.'

'Listen – I'm not a lesbian just because I cut my hair, and even if I was, it wouldn't matter. Lots of my friends *are* lesbians, but I'm not. But I could be if I wanted to. And lesbianism isn't about three-in-a-bed, it's about two in a bed. Two women. No men.'

'You seem pretty keen on the idea for someone who isn't a lesbian.'

Silence.

'I bet you haven't got a boyfriend, though.'

Silence.

'Have you got a boyfriend?'

Silence.

'Maybe your boyfriend's got long hair. Maybe he's a poof.'

Silence.

'Is he a poof?'

'SHUT UP! I haven't got a . . . I mean it's none of your business if I . . . Just shut up, OK.'

'Sorry, you're right. I'm being nosy.'

Silence.

'Aren't you going to accept my apology?'

Silence.

'Come on – be a sport.'

Silence.

'What's that you're reading? The *Environment Guardian*! Now there's a fucking joke. Eh – Mark – she's reading the *Environment* fucking *Guardian*! If you believe in the environment why do you waste all that paper every day? Why do you waste all that paper?'

And so on.

Personally, I was bored of people like Nell, so I always took Gavin's side, and laughed whenever I thought I could detect a joke. He was used to being either ignored or scorned, so I rapidly became an ally. He started giving me extra time off, and would sit me down in a café, treat me to a cup of tannin, and entertain me with stories from his past.

Except that they weren't stories from his past. As far as I could tell, they all came directly from his overactive, sick imagination. But he was a gifted, experienced bullshitter, and I had a lot to learn from him.

As we got to know each other better, his past became more colourful. The following is a list of the subject matter which we covered together:

- Life in the army, including details of Gavin's dishonourable discharge for drug offences.
- Life as a mercenary in South America, including how to deal with bombs, what it feels like to kill someone, and the joy of camaraderie among desperadoes.
- Whether or not I, Mark, had the moral strength to be able to shoot someone point blank.
- A brief tour of the globe, covering the liberally sprayed locations of Gavin's progeny.
- Black women in bed.
- His relationship with his ten-year-old son in London, whom he had met several times.
- Buddhism, pronounced Boodism. (Almost the same as the black-women-in-bed conversation.)
- The time someone tried to attack Gavin on the tube with a

knife and Gavin threw him across the carriage and stamped
on his head until blood came out of his ear.

Each day started with breakfast at the Wimpy in King's Cross,
then we would all get onto the tube and head off for a location
of Gavin's choosing: Uxbridge shopping centre, Brent Cross,
Camden, Wembley, Kingston, Shepherd's Bush market, Brixton
– all the most glamorous parts of London were ours.

There was plenty of time on the underground for conversation, and apart from Gavin, everyone seemed to like each other.
Somehow even Nell fitted in. And people actually liked me!
This was what came as a real surprise. At school a newcomer
had to perform an act of violence, or publicly humiliate a perennial victim in some way in order to gain social approval, but
here people just assumed that I was OK.

I began to think that maybe hard people weren't that hard
after all.

Most people gave up the job within a few days, so by the
time three weeks was up, I was a veteran. Only Trish and I
remained from the original team. The reason why Trish was
still doing the job was that she made a fortune. Most of us
struggled for every phone number, often resorting to begging
('Of course you don't want a pension plan – I just need your
name and phone number – I get fifty pence for each one, and all
that happens is you get one phone call and tell them to piss
off'). But Trish seemed to get a phone number off every single
woman she approached ('Hello, there, luv. How are you? What
are you up to today? You doing the shopping? Here you are
darling, you take one of these, put it safe in your bag and give it
a look over when you get home. What did you say your name
was? Right. Smashing – thanks a lot for your help, love. Right –
that's all I need you for – now, if you can just give me your
number ... OK, thanks – someone'll be in touch with you
about the leaflet, then. OK – thanks a lot – see ya later – ta ta.')

I was just beginning to entertain the fantasy that Trish fancied me when she told me that she thought Wayne might have
got her pregnant. 'Contraception never was my strong point,'

she said. 'I used to use the cap but that got on my tits. Now I just improvise.'

'Is that effective?' I asked.

She laughed. 'EFFECTIVE! I wouldn't be up the duff if it was effective, would I? He was supposed to pull it out at the last minute, but you know what Wayne's like.'

'I don't know him *that* well.'

'You know what I mean. Up top. One sarnie short of a picnic. Slow, like.'

'Oh, right.'

'He's sweet, though.'

I decided to try a line I had picked up from the telephone ladies. 'I bet he goes like the clappers,' I said.

Trish laughed for about ten minutes. 'Here – you can't say that! What are you, a poof or something?'

Evidently I hadn't quite understood things properly yet, but my month was up, my money was earned, and I was meeting Barry at Victoria Station that Sunday to head off and discover the world. The Inter-rail ticket had cost only £160 and gave us the right to take any train in Europe at any time for the next four weeks. Unfortunately we didn't have much money left after buying the ticket, so we wouldn't be able to eat very much and would have to sleep on trains most of the time, but still – I was excited. And with luck, by the time we got back Barry would have forgotten about middle-aged women.

Trish and I swore to keep in touch and never spoke to each other again. Gavin shook my hand and told me to have a nice life. I said I would try.

CHAPTER TWENTY-EIGHT

Meet Barry at Victoria Station at 10 a.m. Get on the train to Dover. Everything seems to be going smoothly. After one hour I am bored of trains, and decide that I am going to hate Interrailing. After one hour and ten minutes, I settle into a rhythm, and decide that I like trains. The holiday will be fun. Barry is beginning to piss me off a bit, though.

Afternoon ferry – boring. Full of school kids who have never been allowed to play arcade games before. Barry feels sick, which cheers me up a little.

Arrive in Calais at 11 p.m. If we get the next train to Paris, we will arrive in the middle of the night and will never find a hotel and will have to sleep rough and will probably get killed. This is our first major problem.

We settle for a B&B in Calais, which costs three days' budget each. The concierge smells of French faeces (more cheesy than the English variety), as does our room. We have to share a double bed, which gives me an all-night erection.

MONDAY 8TH JULY

Severely achy penis. Barry asks for an egg and bacon breakfast. The hot chocolate is delicious. 9:30 train to Paris.

Paris smells wonderful – of Gauloises. I tell Barry and he agrees, but I can tell that he thinks Gauloise is the name of a politician. I can see him wondering how someone so pungent keeps getting elected.

We go straight to the youth hostel, where we queue for a bed. At 3 p.m. we get to the front of the queue and are told that there are no more beds. We can't afford to stay anywhere else in Paris, so in order to avoid sleeping rough we go straight to the nearest railway station and look for a suitable night train. After much queuing, we discover that there is a night train to

Bordeaux which takes long enough for us to get a decent night's sleep. The train leaves at 7 p.m. By the time we have sorted all this out, it is 5 p.m. We therefore have two hours to see Paris. Unfortunately we haven't eaten yet today so most of this time is spent in the nearest restaurant, which happens to be the Q Quick Burger Bar. Still, we have time for a little stroll around the city, and Paris seems to be a nice place.

No spare seats on the train. Barry sits on the floor outside the buffet car and I spend the night sitting on the toilet.

TUESDAY 9TH JULY

Morning — arrive horribly early in Bordeaux. Both exhausted. Head straight for the city park for a snooze.

Wake up at 2 p.m. and run all the way to the youth hostel to discover that the last bed has just been taken. Not enough money for any of the hotels, so we decide to take the night train to Marseille. It doesn't leave till 8 p.m., so we have several hours to explore Bordeaux. Verdict: very pleasant — must go back some day. Good, cheap restaurants.

We find a supermarket with a bottle of wine for only 20 francs and buy it for the train.

Plenty of space on the train. Compartment to ourselves. I stretch out. Get drunk. Sleep like a log. Wake up. Vomit. Sleep like a log again.

WEDNESDAY 10TH JULY

Hangover. Green teeth.

Pull into Nice station. Must have passed through Marseille several hours ago. Take a nap on the platform.

Bus to youth hostel. Get beds. Shower. Bus to beach. Sleep. Eat. Bus to youth hostel. Sleep.

THURSDAY 11TH JULY

The entire female population of the hostel follows Barry and me to the beach. Women of several hundred nationalities fawn over him all day using every possible variation of bad English. I feel like the invisible man.

Barry spends all day describing his passion for Margaret Mumford to jealous women. Their nipples go hard when he mentions sex.

I complain to Barry that I hate beaches and remind him that we came to Europe for the culture. We decide to get the night train to the Loire Valley.

It takes us an hour to check out of the youth hostel because Barry insists that he can't leave without his 'MY AUNTIE WENT TO TRINIDAD AND TOBAGO AND ALL I GOT WAS THIS LOUSY T-SHIRT' T-shirt. I suggest that it has been nicked from his bed, but Barry feels it to be more likely that the T-shirt is playing a game and has walked away to hide in a corner. He refuses to leave without it because Trinidad and Tobago isn't called that any more so he can't get a replacement and his aunt will be upset. Clearly he has a strange aunt.

Eventually he agrees to leave without the T-shirt, but by the time we get to the station we have missed the last train going north. Since we no longer have a bed in Nice, we have to get on the only night train out of the city, which is heading for Bordeaux.

FRIDAY 12TH JULY

Arrive Bordeaux. V. tired. Sleep in the city park all day. For supper, I eat one mouthful of a goat's cheese sandwich, which tastes significantly worse than a human turd. Night train to the Loire Valley.

SATURDAY 13TH JULY

Arrive in Blois. The youth hostel is way out of town, so we decide to hitch there. Unsuccessfully. End up walking, which takes hours.

Barry is still going on about Mrs Mumford. I call her an old bag and he sulks for the next two hours.

By the time we get out to the youth hostel, which is in a field on the edge of a farm, we can't be bothered to go back into town again. There are ten other people in the same situation, so Barry spends the afternoon chatting to them (about Mrs Mumford) while I sulk.

An active day. Up early. Breakfast. Bus into town. Hire bikes.
Oh.

Shit.

It's Sunday.

No bikes.

One shop in the whole town is open. It's a hardware store.
Quincaillerie. I knew that word would come in useful one day.
We spend an hour or so in the *quincaillerie.* Then two hours in
a café having lunch. Back to the hardware store. Quick browse.
Then bus back home to the youth hostel.

Just as we're pulling out of town, five hundred people in
fancy dress march past in the opposite direction playing musical
instruments and waving bits of military hardware around.
Barry's looking out of the other window so he misses it, which
cheers me up immeasurably.

We spend the afternoon in the same field talking to the same
ten people. One of them, called Bella, is a second-year student
at Bristol University. It turns out that Bella knows Nell, and she
is a lesbian after all.

An active day. Up early. Breakfast. Bus into town. Hire bikes.
Cycle to the Chateau de Chenonceau with Bella and her friend
Briony.

Chenonceau's nice. Briony isn't. Luckily she spends all day
trying to have sex with Barry, so I am left alone with Bella for
most of the afternoon. As an experiment I try flirting with her,
which, to my surprise, not only proves enjoyable but also seems
to evoke a response differing in several respects from revulsion.
This is distinctly exciting. We have a romantic dinner *à quatre*
in Blois, then head back to the youth hostel. I talk to Bella until
midnight, rapidly falling in love with her. Eventually, we kiss.
She is very good at it. My heart skips a beat, dances a tango,
then runs naked through Trafalgar Square. At last! I have tasted
love!

When I am absolutely certain that she likes me, I ask the

obvious question: 'Why me? You don't think I'm ugly?' This is my first chance to get a proper answer. It should give some clue as to how the remainder of my sex life will shape up. I am desperately, *desperately*, DESPERATELY fishing, trawling, harpooning for a compliment.

'I like ugly men,' she replies.

This is not the answer I was hoping for. Still, at least it's honest. I wanted her to say that I was beautiful, but I suppose I wouldn't actually have believed her. At least it gives some glimmer of hope for the future. Maybe there will be other girls who like ugly men. Maybe women think like that. Bizarre!

Bella can tell that her comment has upset me, so she gives me the biggest, wettest kiss yet. Yup – I am definitely in love.

We say goodnight, and I race back to the dormitory to tell Barry what has happened. But he's not there. I lie on my bed and wait for him. I can feel my body tingle with happiness all over.

Two hours later, the tingle has faded, and Barry still isn't back. The curfew has long passed, so he probably won't be able to get in. This is annoying – I want to tell him my story. I go to the window to see if he is locked out, and there he is, pinned to the ground under a cherry tree, naked, with Briony riding him like a pogo stick.

Upstaged again.

Bastard.

TUESDAY 16TH JULY

When I wake up, Barry is in the bed next to mine. He must have climbed in somehow. My tingle is back again, and I don't feel angry with him any more. I shake him, and tell him my cunning plan. Barry is impressed with me, and thinks we should give it a shot. The idea is this: I have breakfast with Bella, ask her where she is going next, then, whatever the answer, I say, 'What a coincidence, that's where we're going. Shall we go together?'

Pretty clever, eh?

Ten minutes later:

'Hi Bella.'

'Oh, hi.' She doesn't look up.

'Um – . . .'

'Fuck, I was pissed yesterday.' She still doesn't look up. I can feel bad news in the air.

'Um . . . are . . . are you two . . . er . . . off somewhere today?'

'Yeah.'

'Right. So are we. Um . . . where abouts are you . . . um . . .'

'Home. Our ticket's run out. Pass the jam.'

Desperation. The end. Possible suicide.

'Are you deaf? Pass the jam.'

I pass the jam.

They take the next bus. She doesn't ask for my address.

This is the third day Barry and I have spent in the field in front of Blois youth hostel. This time we are alone. We don't talk much. We decide to leave France.

WEDNESDAY 17TH JULY

Morning train to Paris. Two hours in Paris. (I feel as if I am getting to know the city well.) Afternoon and night train to Barcelona.

We both sulk.

Between Toulouse and Carcassonne, Barry asks me if I think Margaret is too old for him.

Just after Narbonne, I tell him yes.

Between Perpignan and the border, he tells me I must be a wanker, then.

THURSDAY 18TH JULY

Arrive Barcelona.

Visit Barcelona – nice.

Night train to Madrid.

FRIDAY 19TH JULY

Arrive Madrid.

Visit the Prado – bit boring.

Back to youth hostel in time for curfew. Smelliest dormitory yet – difficult to breathe. I dream all night about being force-fed goat's cheese.

SATURDAY 20TH JULY

Visit the rest of Madrid. Nice place – good weather. Can't find any of the Gaudi buildings, though.

Night train to San Sebastian.

SUNDAY 21ST JULY

Our compartment on the train to San Sebastian is shared with a German couple, who, like all hippies from that country, are trying unnaturally hard to be laid back. They want us all to sing Beatles songs together, but Barry and I only know the words to 'Yesterday'. Eva and Adolf, or whatever their names are, insist that this is cool, that they dig 'Yesterday', so we close the compartment door and start singing. Once we get going, it dawns on me that I don't exactly know *all* the words, but the great thing about old-fashioned songs is that you can just sing the first verse twenty times and it sounds exactly like the real thing.

I don't normally like singalongs, but this is fun. Then I remember that the Beatles did a famous cover version of the cub scout song, 'We All Live in a Yellow Submarine'. This one's even better because you only need to know one line and you can pelt it out for half an hour without getting bored.

Just when we're beginning to sound good, some arsehole from the next carriage complains that it is 2 a.m. and he is trying to get some sleep. He is a real grouchy old fuck, which leads us into an interesting conversation about how true it is that people who have never travelled are amazingly small-minded.

'These people who just work work work – they have a lot to

learn from us,' says Eva. We all agree with her and decide to teach the old bastard next door a lesson about love and tolerance by singing as loudly as we can all night.

By the time we arrive in San Sebastian, we are understandably tired, so we spend the morning napping on the beach. Then the four of us go in search of a room. On the way, we meet up with two Danish girls who are both wearing pink shoes, purple track-suit trousers, pink track-suit tops, purple hair-bands, and carrying purple and pink rucksacks. They come with us to the youth hostel.

The youth hostel is full, so the six of us ask around the cheap hotels, all of which have no vacancies, and none of which are cheap anyway.

We decide to sleep on the beach, but just as we are settling in for the night, a friendly local approaches us and tells us in graphic detail about the current fashion in San Sebastian for dropping boulders on the head of sleeping tourists, then stealing their money while they are unconscious.

Despite the fact that this is clearly a lie, we all believe him. Especially the Danish girls, who go into a pink and purple panic. This makes me angry and jealous, because I also want to panic but they have got there first. The Germans try and panic mellowly, but find it difficult. Then Barry panics, which sparks off the Germans, who get going on a proper panic. Now I am panicking too.

Somewhere in the background, I get the feeling that I can hear the friendly local laughing, but I can't be sure because I am too busy with my panic.

When we calm down to boiling point, we decide to head off together to the edges of the city and look for a secluded spot to bed down.

Eventually we settle for a landing at the top of an outdoor staircase serving a luxury apartment block. It is perfect – quiet, just the right width for six sleeping bags, and with a stunning view out over the bay. If it had been a hotel room, it would have cost a fortune. Apart from the Danish girls, we are all happy – this is a hundred times better than any youth hostel.

Within five minutes, four of us are on the ground, lined up in our bags. Three quarters of an hour later, the Danish girls have unpacked their rucksacks, got out their pyjamas, gone round the corner in shifts, got changed, come back, packed their clothes into their rucksacks, gone round the corner in shifts, removed their make-up, cleaned their teeth, unrolled their sleeping mats, unrolled their sleeping bags, taken their vitamin pills, repacked the rucksack with the toiletries, pills and pastes at the proper rucksack depth, taken off their shoes, combed and tied back their hair, put on clean pairs of night socks, and got into their bags.

Then they start dealing with their contact lenses.

The four of us watch the whole show, incredulous.

In the middle of the night I am woken up by a furious, whispered argument between the Danish girls. After much debate, one of them gets out of her bag, unpacks her rucksack, takes out her purple track-suit trousers and her pink track-suit top, puts them on over her pyjamas, puts on her pink trainers, and disappears round the corner. Shortly after this I hear a loud vowelly swear-word from below, then the distraught Dane reappears with wet trainers.

It is clear from her face that this is the worst night of her life. I find it hard not to laugh. It becomes even harder to control myself when I hear her explain in a quavering voice what happened. Great command of Danish is not required to catch the gist of her explanation, which is something along the lines of, 'I'm so depressed. I want to die. I've urinated on my pink trainers. No one told me that travelling was going to be like this. It's so humiliating. You step outside Denmark and suddenly you find yourself weeing in the open air. Without a toilet. And why didn't mummy ever tell me that you mustn't point your bum uphill?'

My sleeping bag shakes so much that I have to pretend to be having a nightmare about being force-fed goat's cheese.

MONDAY 22ND JULY

By the time I wake up, the Danish girls have gone. The first thing I do is look for the urine mark on the stairs. It is still there, so I show it to Barry and tell him the story behind it. He is so impressed with the tale that he tells Eva, who in turn tells Adolf, and we all have a good laugh together.

It occurs to me that her pee might spell out the word 'Danish' in the way that pigs from that country have been trained to do with their bacon fat, but this doesn't appear to be the case.

We head off together for a day of sunbathing.

The word crowded simply cannot convey the state of the beach. Two words, very crowded, do a distinctly better job. Now I come to think of it, extremely crowded conjures things up perfectly.

I had expected to find empty beaches and rolling surf, but we rapidly discover that while all the foreigners go to Southern Spain, all the Spaniards go to Northern Spain to escape the foreigners.

Eventually, Barry and I find a pebble to sit on, which we share.

That evening we go back to the same staircase to sleep.

TUESDAY 23RD JULY
Another day on the beach-cum-commuter-train-cum-flea-pit. I am getting on quite well with Barry, now that he has stopped going on about Mrs Mumford all the time.

It dawns on us suddenly that we have got less than two weeks left and have hardly seen anything yet. Our main priority is Amsterdam, so we decide to get out of Spain and take the first night train going North.

WEDNESDAY 24TH JULY
At 4 a.m. the train terminates and a guard kicks us off the train. It turns out that we are in Bordeaux. Luckily we know the place well by now and stumble to the city park, which we get to at about dawn. We climb in, go to our favourite spot and fall fast asleep.

Perfect timing – we wake up with an hour to spare before the night train to Paris. Bordeaux feels like a second home now, and we take supper in our favourite restaurant. We can afford a good meal because we haven't paid for accommodation since Madrid.

THURSDAY 25TH JULY

Arrive Paris. Breakfast. Quick stroll. I feel like a local here, too. Off to Amsterdam. Train fucks up. Arrive Amsterdam 2 a.m. Scary.

We don't want to take on the city at this time of night reading a map and wearing our Karrimor 65-litre mug-and-rape-us-please,   we're-gullible-and-ignorant-and-carry-lots-of-cash-sacks, so we decide to play safe and bed down in the railway station with the junkies, dealers, whores, pimps, gangsters and lunatics.

FRIDAY 26TH JULY

Dawn. We flee the railway station.

Get to the youth hostel and take beds in the dormitory, which we will be sharing with ten other people, mostly junkies, dealers, whores, gangsters and lunatics.

The pimps must stay at the YMCA.

The first thing we do is to go to the nearest café and order a 'special tea', with a big wink at the waiter. It's nice enough tea, but doesn't seem to have any effect, so we order another one. 'And make sure it's very special,' I say to the waiter with an extra-big conspiratorial wink.

Barry says he can feel the second one taking effect, but I get the feeling that the waiter (who is treating me like a bit of an idiot) has been ripping us off. So I beckon him over. 'Excuse me,' I say, 'it says "moon cakes" on the menu here, can you tell me if these cakes are special?'

'Pardon?'

'Are the moon cakes special?' I wink again, just so he can't miss the point.

'If you are asking me if the moon cake contains hashish, which is a legal drug in this city, then the answer is yes.'

Jesus! He's a bit of a cowboy, this one.

I blush and look round to see if anyone heard. What a crazy guy! He didn't even lower his voice. 'I'd like one of those then please,' I whisper.

I eat the moon cake, but still no effect. Terrible rip-off. If I hadn't been breaking the law myself, I would have reported that waiter to the police.

We pay the bill – no tip – and leave the café. Just outside the door, the buildings go all wobbly, my legs turn to rubber and I enter a coma. Barry carries me to the city park, where I have a weird dream about being force-fed goats.

It takes me the whole morning to sleep off the worst of it, but I wake up mid-afternoon feeling pleasantly stoned, and we head for the famous sex museum.

Despite everything that I had been told, I suspected that I was an unshockable person and thought that I would enjoy the sex museum. When I actually see all the pictures, though, I am appalled. I can truly say that I have never seen anything so repulsive in my life. The photographs, of group sex, fetishism, and women with animals, actually make me feel sick. They are truly repulsive. I am not even the least bit turned on.

Weird evening wandering around the city, stoned.

SATURDAY 27TH JULY

Get up, get stoned, wander round a bit. Get more stoned. Pass out. Wake up. Go shopping. Buy a souvenir penis. Get more stoned. Go shopping. Buy seventeen souvenir vaginas. Eat. Visit the sex museum again. Eat. Go to bed.

SUNDAY 28TH JULY

Feel a bit rough. So I get stoned.

I feel like getting in touch with my heritage so I go and visit Anne Frank's house. It is very moving. But I puke on her floor and I have to leave in a hurry before anyone spots me. Feel very rough. I sit down and have a special tea. Feel a bit better. Go back to the sex museum. Have a nice supper with Barry.

We spend the evening eating moon cakes and wandering around the red-light district watching fat women finger themselves in shop windows (v. enlightening).

Get to bed around 3 a.m.

Have an odd dream where I am the only person in the auditorium of a theatre. On stage there are fifty Kim Basinger look-alikes, all of whom somehow also resemble my mother. They are all wearing nothing except a pair of pink trainers, and are having sex with slabs of Danish bacon. I am also wearing nothing except pink trainers and am trying to hide my erection behind a miniature French dictionary, which is too small for my penis, and I cannot decide whether to expose my balls or my helmet. Whichever Kim Basinger I look at stops having sex with the bacon and offers me a piece of goat's cheese.

MONDAY 29TH JULY
—

TUESDAY 30TH JULY

Don't quite understand it. Went to bed on Sunday, woke up on Tuesday. Odd.

After a leisurely but confused breakfast, we are hit by the fact that we have less than a week left and are still only a quarter of the way through our original plan.

So after one last look at the sex museum, we get on the next train to Brussels.

Arrive Brussels early evening, take a look around (bit bland), have an argument over Barry always walking too fast, and take the night train to Berlin.

WEDNESDAY 31ST JULY

Arrive Berlin. Leave bags at the station. Take a look (bit grey). Big row over Barry slurping tea. Night train to Prague.

THURSDAY 1ST AUGUST

Arrive Prague. Quite tired. Quick stroll (not much in the

shops), nap in the park, major dispute over nicked biro, night train to Vienna.

FRIDAY 2ND AUGUST

Arrive Vienna. Pleasant. Barry accuses me of nose-picking. I counter with his annoying sniff, leading to a lengthy body-habits argument. Over lunch we realize that we've only got one full day left on our ticket. Big panic. Next train homewards.

Arrive Munich at midnight. Quick peek outside – doesn't look like we're missing much. Train to Paris.

SATURDAY 3RD AUGUST

Arrive Paris (the old friend) at lunch-time. Half an hour to buy a baguette and take one last look, then next train to Calais. The cost of the baguette is split evenly, but Barry takes it upon himself to eat at least two thirds of it (if not more) while I am in the train toilet, leading to our biggest row yet. Almost a punch-up.

Night ferry.

SUNDAY 4TH AUGUST

Home.

Sweet home.

I don't want to see Barry again for at least a year.

CHAPTER TWENTY-NINE

By the time I got back to Harrow, I needed to spend a week in solitary confinement in order to regain a taste for humanity. I gave my parents a full and proper description of the holiday in three sentences, then hid in my bedroom. I didn't read or watch television or go out, but spent my time eating and sitting in the corner drooling, trying to remember the difference between Vienna and Madrid (or do I mean Bordeaux) – or wasn't that Prague? No, Paris! Barcelona?

I had learnt a lot from my trip.

In my daze, I thought frequently about how much I hated Barry. I was overjoyed not to have to put up with any of his tiny mannerisms, habits, phrases or smells. Then, one morning, I realized that he was my best friend, that we had just experienced an amazing month together, and that he now knew me better than anyone else in the world outside my family. I suddenly felt closer to him than ever before.

My hibernation ended, I recovered my faculty of speech, and I phoned him. He told me that he had arrived back at Notting Hill to find the flat occupied by a pair of TV weather forecasters, who said that they had moved in to the flat a week before. He'd then gone to his parents' house, where he had found a letter from Mrs Mumford waiting for him, explaining that she had gone back to her husband and children.

Barry said that he had spent all week crying.

Although in one way this completed a perfect summer for me, I did feel a little upset for Barry. I had known that this would happen – that a few weeks without sexual ecstasy on tap would bring the delights of a life of drudgery rushing back to Mrs Mumford, but I hadn't considered it all week. I had been thinking exclusively of Barry the travelling companion who I wanted to throttle, and had forgotten about the existence of Barry the friend whose life was on schedule for collapse.

I felt that I should have been with him as it all happened, but if I had seen him crying, and above all *sniffing* (two quick short bursts, right nostril flaring, left nostril contracting, one high-pitched gurgle from the sinuses), not to mention that repulsive almondy smell of his deodorant, I wouldn't have been in a position to offer much comfort.

While he told me what had happened, I suddenly felt a stab of guilt, and promised that I would go straight round to his house. I had to ask for directions, because it was the first time I had ever visited his family home.

Barry opened the door, and though he wasn't actually crying, his eyes were red and puffy. My first impulse was to give him a kiss, but I resisted and put a manly hand on his shoulder.

'The bitch,' I said.

He turned away from me and walked wordlessly up the stairs, so I followed him. We arrived in a cramped, over-decorated bedroom with the odd token attempt at a teenage poster on the wall: Bob Marley lying on pink satin sheets and Kylie Minogue smoking a joint (or something along those lines, anyway). Barry immediately started crying, full throttle.

I did what I could to comfort him. 'Fucking women. They're all the same. They all shit on you in the end.'

This didn't seem to cheer him up very much.

'You'll find another one. There's plenty more fi –' I stopped myself there. Never let it be said that I'm insensitive.

'I can't believe that she'd . . . that she'd . . . that she'd . . .'

'Do that to you?'

'Do that to me. We were so . . . we were so . . . we were so . . .'

'In love?'

'In love. Do you think she was . . . do you think she was . . . do you think she was . . .'

'A little old for you?'

'A little old for me.'

'Do I think she was a little old for you?'

'Yes. Do you think she was a little old for . . . for . . . for . . .'

'You.'

'Me. Do you?'

'Well . . . I mean it's difficult to say at this stage. I suppose if you're sexually compatible, there's nothing to stop you having a very fulfilling relationship. I mean if you found her attractive, there's no reason not to . . . um . . . most people don't find women that old at all sexy, but if you . . . not that's she wasn't fantastic, I mean she was an exception for her age . . . I mean very well preserved and all that . . . so once you're over the attraction hurdle you can . . . um . . . How old's your mother exactly?'

'What?'

'Just – how old's your mum?'

'What do you mean?'

'Nothing. Nothing at all. I just wondered.'

'My mum's sort of forty-five or something like that. But look, I haven't got a thingy complex if that's what you mean.'

'Are you sure?'

'Of course I'm fucking sure. I haven't wanted to shag my mum for years.'

'You never know, though. That's the whole point. It's subconscious. I thought I'd grown out of wanting to shag my mum, but only the other week I had a dream where she looked like Kim Basinger, and bingo – it was hard-on city.'

'Your mum doesn't look anything like Kim Basinger,' he snivelled.

'I know. I don't know how she did it. It was incredible. But I dreamed it. So you don't need to be Freud to know that my subconscious wants me to have sex with my mother.'

'What did your mum do in this dream that turned you on so much?'

'Oh – er . . . I can't . . . um, remember the details, really.'

'Shit! That's so embarrassing. Did your mum know that you were turned on?'

'No – she couldn't see. I was hiding my dick behind a pocket dictionary. Look – it's not important. The point is that my subconscious put a nice face and big tits onto my mother in order to trick me into fancying her.'

'You can't have been that turned on if you could hide your whole dick behind a pocket dictionary.'

'Will you shut up about my fucking dream! I wish I hadn't told you now. What I'm trying to say is this. I've been reading all about it – I think I'm going to be a psychologist one day. We *all* want to have sex with our mothers. It's a fact. It's been proven. But we're so afraid of wanting to have sex with our mothers that we pretend to ourselves that we don't find them sexy – only, it all goes wrong in dreams, when our subconscious tells us what we really want to do, and has us rogering them senseless on the kitchen floor.'

'I see. Right. Actually, now you mention it, I did have one weird dream a few weeks ago.' Barry was beginning to cheer up.

'What?'

'In it, I'm a little kid, and I'm in my bedroom, and my mum comes in and starts teaching me French verbs. Then I tell her that I need a pee, and she carries me to the toilet and holds me in the air to make me tall enough to get it into the bowl, but I can't produce a proper wee. All that comes out is these little white dollops. I don't know what they are, and I get scared, but my mum is kind and holds me there and just keeps saying that it doesn't matter and I can try again. But all that comes out is white dollops.'

'Jesus!'

'I didn't think twice at the time, but now I . . .'

'You didn't think twice at the time! What are you, an idiot?'

'No – you know how it is. You just, you know, wake up, think you're a pervert for a few seconds, then forget the whole thing ever happened.'

'Fuck!'

'What do you reckon? It's a bit freaky isn't it?'

'You know how surprised I am?' I said.

'How surprised?'

'This surprised.' I indicated with my finger and thumb.

'One centimetre?'

'Be fair.' I showed him again.

'Two centimetres.'

'Yup – two centimetres surprised, i.e. not very much.'

'You think I'm better off without her?'

'Yeah – of course you are. You're young – you should be playing the field. Not sitting in a flat with a twisted wife/mother figure, storing up a lifetime of mother-shagging psychological trauma for yourself. Jesus, for a while there you were well into Bates Motel territory.'

'You could be right. I did love her, though.'

'Who, Margaret or your mother?'

'Margaret, you tosser.'

'Just checking.'

'Have you seen the letter she wrote me?'

'Yeah – she rang me up in Amsterdam and asked me to check her punctuation.'

'Really?'

'Of course she didn't, you prick. It's called sarcasm. S – A – . . .'

'All right, all right. Calm down. Here, read this.'

He passed me the letter:

Dear Barry,

This is the hardest letter I have ever had to write. Don't think that I don't love you. You mustn't ever think that I don't care for you with all my heart. I love you as much as my own children. [Uh oh!] *But I have to leave you – I have to save us from ourselves.* [Vomit] *What we have is unique, unrepeatable, and we will always have it in our hearts.* [Bucket number two, please.] *But we cannot carry on like this. I am not a young woman any more. Although there is a fiery spark between us, there are other, more permanent bonds that I have with my family, bonds which cannot be easily broken.*

Loving you was the best thing that ever happened to me, but that's all it was – a thing that happened to me [Hello? Which planet are we on?]. *There are other things, more solid things, which I have built myself, with my own two hands and with the hands of my family. These things cannot be knocked down by a quick thunderbolt of passion, however big it may seem at the time.* [Good point.]

I may hate my husband, but I also love him, just as I love you, but also hate you. [A fine distinction.] *And my children are very special to me – I can't just cast them aside like pieces of waste paper.* [True, true.] *Some people are women of passion, brave women, irresponsible women; others are women of duty, caring women, with responsibilities and duties, and I am one of those. You showed me a new side of my character – one that can laugh and scream and be spontaneous and have orgasms, but a little time on my own to think about things has shown me that this is not who I am. This is not me – this is a different me. A me who is lying and pretending to be someone who she isn't – at least not in her heart.*

If only I could be a woman of passion – but I'm not. I am a woman of duty. I salute you for what you have taught me, and I wish I could have been a more receptive student for your lessons of love.

I have begged and pleaded with the school, explaining that the fault was all mine, and they have agreed to take you back as a student for the upper sixth. For myself, I will be seeking employment elsewhere.

You will always be with me in my heart.

Ever yours in love and in death,
Margaret

I gave the letter back to Barry.

'Isn't it the saddest thing you've ever read in your life?' he asked.

'Yes – um . . . It's very . . . um . . .'

'Moving?'

'Moving. Yes.'

CHAPTER THIRTY

The most extraordinary thing about my visit to Barry's house that day was not that it took him less than ten minutes to get over his love affair with Margaret Mumford, nor the news that his lover was a sentimental illiterate. The *really* amazing event of the day was the discovery that Barry had a sister. An *older* sister. Can you think of anything more exotic? It had never occurred to me – it had never crossed my mind – it just didn't seem possible that such a person could exist. He had never mentioned her, and I had never dared to assume that such a fantastic, wonderful, *accessible* female could be.

I know what you're thinking. You want to know why someone who is supposedly in the middle of a major quasi-homosexual best-friend-fancying identity crisis is so excited at the thought of a sister.

Well – let me straighten things out a bit here. Literally. This is not the story of one man's coming to terms with his sexuality against all the odds in a homophobic environment. And if you are hoping for a sickeningly PC 'out and proud' ending, then you can forget it now. I'm sorry to spoil the fun of your sordid speculations, but the time has come to break the news – I am not, and never will be, a successful homosexual.

So why all the fuss? Why the hell is this story of any interest? Who gives a shit about yet another middle-class private-school clever dick who can't even muster the imagination to be margin-ally queer? Who gives a fuck about *you*?

Well I'm . . . I'm . . . I mean I thought I was gay. For a while. I really did. Cross my heart, hope to die.

I'm . . . er . . . Jewish. That's a bit unusual.

And my toes – they're bendy, and much longer than average.

Look – I'll come clean. I'm not going to play the coy adolescent any more.

What I'm trying to get at is this:

Take your average guy, who has been so conditioned by everything he has ever seen that he has never considered the possibility that he might be anything other than heterosexual. He has learnt from films and advertisements and soap operas and books and magazines, that when you look at a woman, you pay attention to her breasts and buttocks, then, that evening, when you are masturbating, you reflect on the varieties of breasts and buttocks that you have seen that day, with erotic consequences. This guy has spent his entire post-pubescent life obediently following these rules, and has found that it works satisfactorily for him. Although he has never actually been through the mechanics of intercourse, he has found that the images available to him provide perfectly adequate wanking fantasies, and therefore he has never considered the possibility that he might be in any way unusual (other than being Jewish and having bendy toes, of course).

Then, one day, a boy turns up at school who gives our friend a hard-on every time he thinks about him.

What happens then?

There.

That's a bit interesting.

Isn't it?

When I first heard that Barry had a sister, I was happier than a magazine in a magazine rack. OK, so I still stared at Barry a bit too much, and my admiration for his physique was maybe a hint over-enthusiastic, but I didn't want to do anything about it. Not *really*. Just a bit. But not a real bit, just a fantasy bit. It was his sister I was interested in, now.

So. I am descending the stairs at Barry's house, trembling at the thought that I am about to meet a Barry with breasts and no penis.

She is called Louise.

First impression: bit plain.

Second impression: actually quite horny – looks very like Barry.

'So you're Mark,' she says. 'You don't look that bad. Barry tells me that you nick biros, pick your nose, and smell of almonds.'

A good start.

'It's him that smells of almonds,' I say.

This is a very odd thing for me to be saying. I haven't even said hello yet. It somehow feels inauspicious to be opening our relationship with the words, 'It's him that smells of almonds.' I wonder how many successful marriages have been forged with this phrase?

'He's right,' says Barry. 'I smell of almonds. Mark's the one with asparagus pants.'

I only just stop myself from saying, 'my pants do not smell of asparagus,' on the grounds that this would almost certainly lay a curse on my chances of ever being found attractive by Louise. My opening line is a bad enough omen as it is.

Since I cannot think of anything to say other than the naming of a vegetable more apt for the odour of my groin, I decide to make an excuse and rush home. This is a wise choice. Now that I have chosen to be in love with Louise rather than Barry, I must spare my time with her for moments when I am more composed.

As I walk home, I decide that Louise is just right: not too sexy, not too ugly – I reckon I might stand a chance. She's got similar hair to Barry, but it's a bit darker – mousy rather than blonde. Her features are basically the same as Barry's, but just, well, it kind of looks as if they've slid down a bit. Her eyes, though, are identical to his – they really are. That's the incredible thing. Also, she's a bit – fat's not the right word – plump, I suppose. Just, kind of, cuddly looking.

It occurs to me that maybe, if I didn't know Barry, if I didn't know what she was trying to look like, I wouldn't find her attractive. But as it is, I've decided: she's the one for me.

FINISHING SCHOOL

CHAPTER THIRTY-ONE

First day back at school.

It was fun to be surrounded by so many people all pretending that they were not having fun pretending to have no fun in front of so many people.

However much people moaned, it was clear that everyone was secretly bored of their holidays and pleased to be back in a strict, pleasureless regime. The sheer joy of communal moaning, coupled with the exquisite thrill of giving false directions to minuscule, tearful boys with creases down the arms of their blazers made for what was always one of the most enjoyable days in the school calendar.

I felt a little bitter that I *still* couldn't use the word 'college' to describe my place of education, a privilege that seemed long overdue, but other than that I was pleased to be back.

Almost the first thing I saw as I walked down the drive from the coach park was Mr Davies, head of the Design and Technology (i.e. metalwork) department, standing in front of a cracked window, holding a tennis ball in his hand, red with anger, lecturing a group of spotty thirteen-year-olds with his favourite who-do-you-think-you-are-you-shouldn't-be-doing-this-you're-supposed-to-be-the-*crème-de-la-crème* speech. This brought back all the school's identity crises to me in a depressing surge.

Two of the boys were Asian, and the other one was white. It was clear from where I stood that who-do-you-think-you-are stuff was aimed at the Asians, while the *crème-de-la-crème* nonsense was mainly for the white boy. When Mr Davies started taking their names down for a detention, things got more complicated.

'Phathwhat?'

'Pathmanathan. Hari Pathmanathan.'

'Pathwhat?'

'Hari Pathmanathan. The Hari is short for Hariharan.'

'Spell it out.'

'P-A-T-H-M-A-N-A-T-H-A-N.'

'P-A what?'

'P-A-T-H-M-A-N-A-T-H-A-N.'

'M-A-N what?'

'H-A-R-I-H-A-R-A-N P-A-T-H-M-A-N-A-T-H-A-N.'

'Right. You're in trouble. I'm going to get your real name off your form master. What form are you?'

'2–19, sir. That is my real name, sir. You can check.'

'Just shut it, Phathmin . . . Shut it, boy.'

'You. What's your name?'

'Shah. Angus Shah.'

'THAT'S IT! I'm not in the mood for any more jokes. You've both got two detentions. All three of you, I mean. Two detentions each.

'You – Shah – are you also 2–19?'

'Yes, sir.'

'And if your first name isn't Angus, you've got three detentions.'

'Right – now you. Name and form, boy.'

'Ben Herschfeld, 2–19.'

Mr Davies tried to write it down, but had obvious difficulties.

'That's with an "E", sir. There's also a "C" between the "S" and the "H", and a "D" not a "T" at the end.'

'Shut up, Hurstfield, or you'll be in more trouble.'

'Herschfeld, sir.'

'Right. I'll be talking to your form master. You're all in . . . um . . . big trouble.'

Poor Mr Davies. He must find the first day back from his cream-coloured, thatch-roofed, cucumber-sandwiched, vicar-infested summer very depressing. I brushed past him as close as I could, waving my giant hooked nose in his face.

The big news on the first day back was that Brian Coote, the fattest, least popular boy in the school, now had purple hair.

The story behind it was that one day during the holidays, he had decided that his lack of a love life could be put down not to his unpopularity, ugliness or obesity, but to the colour of his hair. With the help of a knowledgeable friend, he chose a black, indelible dye, which he washed in. After he had dried and brushed his hair, pleased with the deep black colour it had gone, he rang his friend and asked him if he needed to use it every time he washed his hair.

'Yes,' replied the friend, on an impulse seizing the opportunity to make Brian look shamefully and irreversibly ridiculous for several months. After all, the chance to force long-term daily humiliation by a thousand adolescents on one of one's friends doesn't come by every day, and it would have been a shame to waste it.

One wash later, fat, ugly, unpopular, had become fat, ugly, unpopular, dark purple hair, subject of universal mirth.

For weeks to come, people would block his path in the corridors, finger his hair and laugh in his face.

Brian, I imagine, did not have a fun term. Everyone knew that his mother had died only a few months earlier, but since no one had liked him beforehand, the death of his mother didn't seem a good enough reason to change anything. Besides, I think we all felt that it would have been embarrassing to start being nice to him all of a sudden, because it would have been obvious why we were doing it, and that would have been like reminding him about his mother's death. It was far better to just carry on in the same way as before, then it would be easier for everyone to forget what had happened.

I was particularly impressed with the friend who perpetrated the trick, because it couldn't have been his intention from the start. In fact, when he received the telephone call, he wouldn't have known that he was going to be asked that question. He could only have had one or two seconds to think of the joke, assess the consequences, decide that the joke was more important than the friendship, and say, 'yes'. Admirable opportunism, indeed.

This enterprising approach to cruelty was particularly popular at my school. You always had your eyes open for inventive ways to make your friends' lives worse in some unusual or amusing way. Though it didn't really have to be inventive, or indeed unusual, since making someone miserable was in itself inherently funny.

One perennial favourite was the combination-lock trick. There was a phase following an edict by the headmaster about rigid-sided bags protecting schoolbooks when the richest, youngest or most timid boys (a perfect selection of victims) all bought briefcases, many of which had combination locks. In their enthusiasm to rush out at break-time, many rich, young or timid boys forgot to conceal the number of the combination, so if you went to the bag racks, several bags would open first try, then you could just reach in, change the combination, close the case, shuffle the numbers around and leave. Although you rarely got to see your specific victim, you often saw red-eyed boys struggling with locked cases, a sight which never failed to warm the heart.

This hit'n'hope approach to cruelty never particularly appealed to me. I always preferred the personal touch, and had an excellent relationship with a fat, deformed, pompous twerp called Philip Thackeray.

Philip Thackeray always wore flashy watches and expensive clothes which looked ridiculous on his misshapen body. It was clear that he was from a sexy, pushy, ambitious family, into which he had inexplicably been born looking like a troll. This made him a leader in the competitive field of school body-paranoia, and an ideal candidate for psychological torture.

He had the kind of thin, stubborn hair which wouldn't go into any kind of parting, so had to be brushed forward. Philip Thackeray's forward-brushed hairstyle was under permanent threat from a particularly obstinate cow's-lick which he plastered down with water every morning. So, whenever I bumped into him at school, all I had to do was flick his cow's-lick once, and that was it – a tuft of hair would stick up from the side of his head, making him look like a skewed Tintin for the rest of the day.

Every morning, I looked forward to this moment. 'Hello Philip' – flick the hair – Philip goes mad and tries to kill me.

The pleasure of distressing someone to the point of delirium with a mere flick of the wrist was a rare and delightful one. By the start of the upper sixth, I was beginning to grow out of this kind of stuff, though. Also, once he discovered hair gel, it didn't work any more.

CHAPTER THIRTY-TWO

During lunch break of the first day, I went for a walk with Barry to Pike's Water, a small lake, roughly twenty minutes' walk from the back playing fields, through the forest behind the school. It was a beautiful, secluded spot – strictly out of bounds, but now that we were in the upper sixth, that really didn't matter. Once we were there, we sat down on a tree stump, and Barry said that he had some important news.

There was a long silence, then he told me that in the last week of the summer holiday, his father had died of a heart attack.

I couldn't believe it. Only a month before, I'd . . . I'd seen his car, parked outside the house. I racked my memory, but other than at the parents' evening, I couldn't recall ever having met him. I couldn't even really remember what he looked like.

The way Barry told me was extraordinary. He just seemed completely matter of fact about it.

'Aren't you upset?' I asked.

'Yes,' he replied.

Then that was it. I couldn't think of anything else to say. It didn't seem as if Barry was about to say anything either, and for over a minute we just sat there in silence. He wasn't crying or anything, so I couldn't exactly give him a hug. I didn't know what the fuck to do. It was the most embarrassing conversation of my life. After a while, I couldn't take it any more, so I changed the subject, and this seemed to cheer him up.

After our holiday, and then this piece of news, I felt as if I had a secret bond with Barry. I now knew him better than I had ever known anyone outside my family. In fact, other than my brother, I think he was the only person in the world that I actually really understood.

During the first term of the upper sixth we spent almost all our time together, going for walks in the countryside around the school, lounging in the sixth-form common-room and, most amazingly, talking about subjects other than sex. I told him that I would like to get to know his sister better, and he told me that he was planning on taking a break from relationships, then that was it – we talked about other things. The subject only came up once, when he mentioned something about having doubts over his sexuality, which I found hilarious. The thought that Barry, of all people, was worried, just made me piss myself laughing. Poor boy – he really was so dim, sometimes.

My relationships with my other school-friends were the same as ever – quite fun, but still on an I'd-ruin-your-life-if-I-thought-people-would-find-it-funny basis. With Barry, though, I felt that I was getting somewhere unusual. I hate the word intimacy – it sounds so childish – but there isn't a better one. We didn't have to cry together or take saunas or dredge up childhood memories, we just – just felt – relaxed . . . right – it felt right. And there was less sexual tension than before.

I began to notice that when no one was looking we walked a little closer together than usual – side by side, but with our shoulders brushing in a way that wasn't normal. We never talked about it, and I only became aware of it after it had been happening for a while. I couldn't tell whether it was me or him, but one of us must have been aware of it, because when we got back to public places, we stopped doing it.

It's difficult to express these things without sounding like a bit of a tosser, but with Barry, I felt more relaxed than I had ever been with anyone else, more at ease, more ('whole' is a bullshit word, but you know what I mean).

It was strange – I didn't quite know where we were any more. It now seemed obvious that Barry and I were never going to – you know – do anything. But I hadn't realized that Barry knew I wanted to do anything *before* – and now it became clear that Barry understood that I suddenly *didn't* want to – you know.

Is that clear?

The really weird thing was that now that I had firmly decided to make absolutely sure that I was 100 per cent straight, all of a sudden Barry started being physically affectionate to me. But not in an I-want-you-back way, just in a nice way.

This is all crap and I shouldn't have got onto the subject, but the point is – almost as soon as the thought of Barry stopped giving me hard-ons, we started, sort of – falling in love. And I don't mean he started giving me hard-ons again, or even that he gave the impression that he wanted to give me hard-ons. Which is why I couldn't figure out how, or why, or in what way we were in love. It was odd – it was physical, but not sexual. Which is odd. Because if it was physical, then it was obviously a *bit* sexual, but it didn't seem sex-sexual, just friendly sexual.

Anyway – we didn't talk about it, so none of this shit really matters.

Fuck me. I'm beginning to sound like Mrs Mumford.

Jesus.

CHAPTER THIRTY-THREE

Mr Burn (a charming, funny, kind man who bore an unfortunate physical resemblance to an ape) left the staff one week into the term, following a nervous breakdown, so my English A level was split in two, and taken over by a pair of teachers who, supposedly, were still sane.

There had been an alarming spate of breakdowns among the staff of my school in recent years. Well – not exactly alarming – more funny, really. Still, it was a shame that it kept happening to the nice ones. The grumps, idiots and fascists all appeared immune, however hard we worked on them.

Half of my English A level was given to Mr Dunford, a boring, fat old bastard, nicknamed Bob (Boring Old Bastard). He was one of those teachers who took life so seriously that the minute you set eyes on him, you felt yourself regressing ten years. Thus, in the upper sixth, his crushingly earnest lessons always teetered on the edge of the surreal, since we all felt in the mysterious grip of an eight-year-old's sense of humour.

For example, when Mr Dunford read an excerpt from *Middlemarch* involving a minor character called Mr Kek, the entire class was reduced to a state of dribbling hysteria, purely because 'kek' happened to be that term's current terminology for poo. I don't think we even would have noticed the connection if it had been any other teacher, but somehow, hearing Mr Dunford put on his I-was-born-in-the-wrong-century-at-heart-I'm-an-eminent-Victorian voice, in order to read about Mr Kek the butcher, was the funniest thing we had heard for weeks.

I'm not telling you this story because I hope you will find it amusing that my teacher accidentally said 'Mr Poo'. Oh no. My point is just that it's funny that *we* found it funny. Fifteen intelligent boys on the verge of adulthood, studying an eight-hundred-page novel for a demanding exam, all reduced to anally fixated giggles by the fact that Mr Dunford took life seriously. It was a curious phenomenon.

The problem of excess amusement was not one which ever cropped up with my other new English teacher, Mr Lowe. He had less charisma than a spoon.

His favourite colour was slime green, in which he bedecked himself every morning. The colour would lighten gradually throughout the day under the gentle but steady cascade of dandruff from his head. He was quite tall, but had a stoop which made him look short, and would have appeared scrawny if he hadn't worn clothes which made him look fat. His most distinctive disability was that of his eyes, one of which was nearly blind while the other was almost normal. This put his glasses on a permanent slope, with the heavy lens resting on his cheek and the light lens hovering around his eyebrow.

He had an agonizingly quiet voice, which always spoke at a volume just above audible and below a whisper, and at a speed somewhere between soporific and funereal. He was one of those people who could only have been a teacher. If he hadn't been a teacher, he would have had to be a tramp.

His lessons gave one a mixed sensation of boredom, frustration and the immediate need to leap from a high window. You could sense that even the dopiest boys wanted to give him a slap around the face and a good talking to: 'WAKE UP! SPEAK UP! DRESS PROPERLY! WASH! GET A HAIRCUT!'

The only thing to look forward to would be his celebrated temper tantrums. I had only ever seen two of these, both when he was my teacher in the second form. The first time, it took me completely by surprise – one minute I had been happily dozing off in the corner, the next, Alex Denzer was standing on a chair in the middle of a room, with Mr Lowe screaming, 'THERE! HOW DO YOU FEEL NOW? IS THAT BETTER? DO YOU FEEL LIKE NELSON? DO YOU FEEL LIKE NELSON NOW? UP THERE YOU FEEL IMPORTANT, DON'T YOU? AND THE PIGEONS ARE SHITTING ON YOU, AREN'T THEY? DO YOU FEEL LIKE

NELSON NOW? DO YOU? NELSON . . . DENZER . . .
DO YOU?'

Dandruff was flying everywhere.

Then, unfortunately, the bell went.

The following day Mr Lowe brought a home-baked cake to school, which he gave to Denzer by way of apology.

For two months after this, he had remained calm, then one day a boy hid in a box during a drama lesson and Mr Lowe threw a stage door at him.

Not that I really give a shit, though.

To be honest, I don't find these people very funny any more. In fact I find the whole thing distinctly unfunny. It used to be pleasantly surreal, but now it has gone beyond a fucking joke that these weirdoes insist on treating me like a twelve-year-old and have the power to tell me what to do all day. It's just not funny any more. In fact, it really, genuinely pisses me off.

I have had enough of being treated like a child.

Enough.

So, I am taking a stand. I am refusing to tell you the story about how Mrs Lowe once had to call the fire-brigade to free her husband's toe from a bathtap. I am too old for that now. It no longer amuses me.

Actually I think it's hilarious that Mr Lowe is dopey enough to get his toe stuck in a tap, but I find it distinctly less hilarious than I would have a year ago. So there.

Toe in a bathtap! What a dickhead!

CHAPTER THIRTY-FOUR

In my new persona as a mature upper-sixth former, most of the time that I spent with Barry was at his house. And most of the time that I spent at Barry's house, I also spent with his sister.

For the first time, *EVER*, in my whole life, things with a female seemed to be going to plan. It was fantastic.

Ahh, Louise – darling Louise.

She liked me. She actually fucking liked me.

It didn't even occur to me to wonder very much about whether or not I liked her. I was just permanently spinning with the fact that there was loads of eye contact going on, and even the odd accidental touch that wasn't instantly flinched from. This kind of thing had never happened to me before. It made my heart race, and pumped me full of adrenaline.

I suppose I ought to tell you a bit more about her. Well – she's . . . um . . . mmmm . . . yes – nice, really. Just, a nice person. Very like Barry, in fact.

I can't think of that much to say about her, really. I mean, if I think about her objectively, she's a bit strange. And if things hadn't been so exciting, I think I might actually have found her really quite annoying. I'm not saying she *was* annoying – far from it – we always had a great time together – I just mean that she didn't exactly have a great sense of humour. And she tended to get annoyed about very small things. But I'm not whining here, because I really did fancy her, and there was always this sense that things were going to happen.

She was two years older than Barry, and was still living at home for some reason which I never really figured out. She tended to have the odd job here and there, but never really stuck at anything, and never actually got anywhere. She was what you might call a bit of a loser. Nice girl – very nice girl – just a touch screwy in the head.

The great thing was that without me even having to try too

much, things between us started to gain a seriously horny momentum. Normally, I'm petrified by the thought of making a pass. But with Louise, somehow things seemed to just happen on their own. Without having to agonize over this knee-touch, that lingering glance and the other slightly-longer-than-usual-goodbye-kiss-that-wasn't-so-long-that-it-couldn't-also-at-a-push-have-been-a-normal-goodbye-kiss, without even noticing that I was missing out on all the embarrassing bits, we found ourselves touching, and holding hands and having slightly-longer-than-usual-goodbye-kisses.

I think maybe it was because Barry was always there that things were so easy. The three of us always had an excellent time together.

We didn't go to amazing places, or do particularly creative things, we didn't make each other laugh all the time, and we certainly didn't have fascinating political arguments. I don't know what it was that was so good – it didn't seem to matter what we did, or even if we did nothing – we just had fun. Not learn-about-yourself, change-your-personality fun, just enjoyable fun. And because Louise was Barry's sister, it was as if I knew her well from the start. I never had to make an effort to project my personality or any of that crap. It was all just so smooth.

And before long, Barry began contriving situations which left Louise and me alone together. By the way they exchanged glances, I even got the impression that this wasn't against her will. And once, after a particularly subtle 'must dash – I'll be gone for at least an hour' from Barry, she kissed me. On the lips. Not a wet, slobbery tongue-ing, but a slow, dry, gentle, lingering kiss that was the most sexual moment I had ever lived through.

I couldn't believe that she was doing it to *me*. My first thought was that she was taking the piss. But she wasn't. It nearly knocked me out.

And a week or so after that, Louise asked me if I thought we should make love. A week! Can you believe it? It was like being in a film. I only just managed to stop myself from leaping in the air and running a lap of honour around the living room.

I told her that I thought we had reached the stage of our relationship when making love seemed like the right thing to do.

'Let's go up to my bedroom,' she said.

From the moment she said the word 'bedroom', I had a concrete erection. I almost created a whole new chapter in the history of premature ejaculation by spunking in my trousers half way up the staircase, but just managed to keep it in.

As we undressed, the concrete faded into vulcanized rubber, and by the time we were naked, sprawled across the bed, ready to penetrate, I had a wrinkly deflated balloon between my legs. I had never seen it so small. Maybe once, trying to have a pee during a snowball fight at the age of five I had seen it at this size, but other than that, it was definitely a record.

'It's all right, you're bound to be afraid first time,' she said.

'How do you know it's my first time?' I replied. I had meant to put the emphasis on the 'know', which would have made me sound enigmatic and mysterious, but it accidentally came out with the stress on the 'how', turning me into an embarrassed schoolboy. Which, essentially, I was.

'Barry told me,' she said.

'Jesus. Thanks Barry.'

My penis shrank more, beating the five-year-old-with-hypothermia record.

'That's one of the reasons I like you so much,' she said.

What! I couldn't fucking believe it! What the hell was going on in her head?

'I'm sorry,' I said, 'I don't understand.'

'I like you how you are. You're not old and cynical. You're fun. You're transparent.'

'What! What the fuck do you mean transparent?'

'All right – don't get angry. It's a compliment. Look. All my life, I have gone out with older men. When I was . . . when I was fourteen, I lost my virginity with a thirty-one-year-old. Since then, the men have got a bit younger, but they have always, *always*, been older than me. And I'm fed up with boring, world-weary, cynical, rich men who pay for everything and tell me what to do. I'm just bored of it.'

'Sounds all right to me.'

'Look – I had a bit of a . . . well, the last guy I went out with was a bastard, a *real* bastard, and it all got so . . . well, we got in one of those self-destructive relationships where we were just punishing each other all the time . . .'

'. . . know them well . . .'

'. . . and, when it all ended, I just shut down. That was it. Everything just stopped for me. I fell apart. And with Dad dying at about the same time, things were just, you know . . .'

Fucking hell! Was this her idea of foreplay?

'So for the last month, I've been at home trying to put my life together – to figure things out. I've always been in such a hurry . . . Look – for a year, I had hardly even seen my brother. My *brother*, for God's sake. I'd just been spending my time working, and pissing around with these awful men who just . . . Anyway – this month, the best thing has been just getting to know Barry again. It's been amazing. I'd forgotten what a great person he was. He's so kind and gentle and easy to talk to, and . . . God . . .'

Now if I was in bed with someone who had incest fantasies about Barry, then we were *really* on dodgy ground.

'Barry's been talking about you such a lot, and saying such nice things about you. He really respects you so much, you know. And everything he said made me feel a lot of warmth for you. I just knew that anyone who Barry liked such a lot, had to be an amazing person. It was as if I fell in love with you before I even met you. I could tell that you were going to be exactly what I need at this point in my life. And when you first came round, and you were all coy – it was just so sweet, I really . . . you know . . . I just like you how you are.'

'Great. I'm really flattered that you find me attractive because I'm coy and transparent. Thanks.'

'No, no, no, no – you've got completely the wrong idea – I want you because . . . because . . .'

'I'm Barry's friend?'

'No – because . . . um . . .'

'I'm inexperienced and you can boss me around?'

'No – because . . . just – I like you. I really do.'

Then she gave me this incredible kiss and I melted and we made love.

Hallelujah!

Yyyyyyyyyeeeeeeee haaaaaaaahhhhhhhhhhh!

GGGGGGGOOOOOOOOOAAAAAALLLLLLLLLLLL! BRAZIL – ZZZZZZICO!

Thank you, God.

People say that the first time you have sex it is a let-down. This, quite categorically, is a lie.

The first time you have sex it is without doubt superb amazing incredible mind-blowing perfect best-ever brilliant. It is only with the benefit of hindsight, having discovered how much better it can get (that it can last more than three minutes, that pausing is allowed, etc.) that people say their first sexual experience was a disappointment.

The minute I finished having sex with Louise (which was not very many minutes after I started having sex with Louise), I knew that I had discovered something truly fantastic. And if it never got any better or lasted any longer, I would have had no complaints. Further improvements would be just a bonus.

I did want to ask one tiny little post-coital question, though.

'Louise . . .? You know what you were saying earlier about how you've been through all this stuff and it's very complicated and you've got all your reasons why you like me, and I'm too young to understand and – anyway, it's all the same to me, but I did want to know – am I . . . I mean is it . . . am I – am I handsome enough?'

She laughed and gave me a big kiss. 'I like ugly men,' she said.

Damn.

Not the answer I had hoped for.

But this time I didn't mind.

CHAPTER THIRTY-FIVE

So, for the second half of the first term of the upper sixth, I put an extra little swagger into my walk – a subtle I'm-not-a-virgin-any-more spring in my step, which I think people began to notice. I detected just that little bit more respect from strangers.

Despite the fact that the average age for my year at school was eighteen, the vast majority of us were still virgins. At an ordinary school, we would all have had children by now, but the place inculcated us with some magical potion – essence of abysmal social life – which must have been sprinkled over our meals, stopping us from doing anything imaginative with our spare time.

It was not as if this potion took away the desire for sex. Every boy in the school was an obsessive masturbator, and it was virtually impossible to spend a whole day without engaging in some kind of debate about quantity ('quarter of a pint, no sweat'), frequency ('five times a day, minimum') or potency ('stains on the ceiling, man, stains on the ceiling').

It was such a popular topic of conversation that I often thought the school hymn book, jammed into every junior school blazer pocket, ought to have been replaced with copies of *Portnoy's Complaint*. In fact, it seemed logical that if, instead of singing a hymn at morning assembly, the chaplain had stood up, read a few pages from *Portnoy's Complaint*, and then led us all in a communal wank, we would have faced the day with greatly improved powers of concentration.

('Please rise. Place the holy book on your seats. Put your hands together. On your penis. And jerk off. WATSON! ARE YOU PRAYING? Stop at once or I'll make you stand up in front of the whole school and do it! If you really can't hold back, I suggest you buy a copy of *The Tablet* and use it in the school lavatories.')

*

Other than my new walk, the major news of the term was that a member of the music school staff had been assaulting boys on a private boat for the last ten years.

Everyone knew that for a long time Mr Newton had been taking his favourite pupils for sailing holidays, but no one had ever asked why. Nor had anyone noticed that his favourite pupils varied enormously in studiousness, but somehow always had blond hair, blue eyes, regular features and a ruddy pre-pubescent glow to their cheeks. In a school crammed with Jews and Asians, these boys were not easy to find. And how did a mere teacher manage to afford his own sailing boat? Well – it's not so hard, really, if you don't have a family to support.

Although it doesn't require great insight to put together these facts and come up with dodgy conclusions, no one had ever made the connection.

At least not until one particularly angelic fourth-former turned up in the headmaster's office carrying a tape.

He had been playing the tape to his friends since the start of the year. He claimed to have recorded it in secret on the boat while he was playing a hypnotism game with Mr Newton. The boy was unclear about exactly whether or not he had been successfully hypnotized, and his answers were impossible to make out from the tape, but Mr Newton's questions were clear enough, in an absolutely recognizable voice. And I quote:

'Do you like girls? Do you like sexy videos? Do you like magazines? Are you capable of producing semen yet? Do you like playing with yourself? How often do you do it?'

The little angel had played the tape to all his friends and all his friends' friends and most of his friends' friends' friends, before someone suggested that he play it to the headmaster. Which he did.

Mr Newton vanished from the staff. His departure was never announced, and his name never appeared in the 'Teachers Leaving' section of the school magazine. He was eradicated from history.

(Needless to say, the boy who had hoped to win friends by

playing the tape was ruthlessly tormented as a homosexual for the rest of his school career, and left before the sixth form.)

The whole affair was an absolute joy – the kind of thing that makes attending school worthwhile.

After such excitement, the rest of the term seemed bland. The only other notable event was the discovery by Michael Fox (the boy with a square head) from a careers handbook that Aberdeen University ran a Theology with Brewing course.

CHAPTER THIRTY-SIX

My relationship with Louise developed in a strange way. In moving from friends to lovers (I adore that word – it sounds so mature), nothing seemed to be at all different, other than the odd shag. I didn't think this was normal, but whenever I tried to go soppy or have hour-long telephone conversations she always cut me off before I had got going. I don't believe all that shit about conditioning, but I do think it would have been a bit more normal if she had been the over-keen one. I just felt that I was in an odd position to be the one desperate for a lingering glance or a smile or a touch. It really ought to have been her.

Don't get me wrong – everything was great – the sex was amazing, and we got on really well; but I couldn't help worrying about the fact that she was only ever physical with me in bed. Outside the bedroom she just treated me like an ordinary friend, and hardly ever touched me. In fact, she had touched me much more in the past, when we were at a kind of flirting stage, and now she actually seemed to be less friendly to me than before.

I mean, that's fine by me, and I was lucky to have her, but I just felt that it put me at a disadvantage. I'm not trying to turn it into a tennis match, and I certainly wouldn't want a relationship where I was obliged to stare dreamily into my girlfriend's eyes all night – I just thought she was a bit *too* cool about the whole thing. I was straining every muscle in my body to try and be as cool as I could, but whatever I did, she somehow out-cooled me. It was almost as if . . . as if she didn't really give a toss about me.

I had heard people whingeing on about how they were 'used' by some man in a relationship, and I always thought they must be thick arseholes with a victim complex, but I couldn't help thinking that . . . that maybe . . . that Louise was . . . well, it just seemed that Louise wasn't into the whole thing. That for her, it was a bit of a joke.

Look – I'm not complaining, here – it really is all the same to me, and even if she had hired me as a sex slave and never spoken a word to me, it still would have been fine – I wanted to learn about sex, and that was what I was doing. I had no complaints. But I just – wasn't very happy most of the time.

Which was not what I would have expected in the circumstances.

I started watching soap operas to try and see what a guy is supposed to do in this situation, but it was no help because it only ever seemed to happen to the women, and I certainly didn't feel like breaking down in tears on the family sofa and having an emotional togetherness session with my mother in which she comforts me and accidentally lets slip that I am adopted/illegitimate/suffering from a fatal disease.

In fact, I have to admit that the situation was seriously weird. I was getting my physical affection from a guy who had thrown me into a year's worth of paranoia about my sexuality, my sex from his sister, who never touched me with my clothes on, and was meanwhile sustaining an apparently normal friendship with both of them.

Weird.

No handy tips from soap operas on this one. Even *Prisoner In Cell Block H* was no help. I couldn't avoid feeling that Barry and Louise were talking about things behind my back, or that they knew something I didn't. Something in the back of my head told me that I was having a trick played on me. Or maybe it was just my ugliness paranoia, which was beginning to steal top spot from sexuality on my hit parade of neuroses.

There's nothing that bores me more than fucked-up people who spend all their time having traumas and nagging other people to listen to all the problems which they've created for themselves purely so they can have the pleasure of telling other people how unhappy they are. And I am proud to say that no one has ever come crying to me with their woes. But with events taking the turn that they had, I found myself in a strange position. Because I didn't want to cry on anyone's shoulder or any bullshit like that, I just wanted to talk things through with someone – to get them straight in my head. However much I thought about it on my own it never sounded right. I just needed to say it all to someone – explain it from the beginning.

The only people I could have tried were Barry and Louise, and obviously I couldn't do that, so I didn't know what to do. I could feel it all festering in my head and turning sour. I was finding it harder and harder to stay cool with Louise, and was becoming increasingly clingy, which I could tell was beginning to get on her nerves.

So when Dan came home from university for Christmas, I talked it through with him. I asked him if he had five minutes, and I told him the whole story.

Somehow this took three hours – God knows what I said – and at the end he didn't give me any advice at all, he just smiled. Which made me feel a lot better. Then he told me that I had grown up a lot, so I hit him and we had a fight which I lost by having my head sat on. I gave him a good Chinese Burn, though.

After that I felt a lot better.

But this is not the point. My hormonal problems are not of interest. I was simply trying to conjure up my state of mind approaching the incredible party which was to be thrown by Barry's mum that Christmas Eve.

When all the life insurance money had finally come through, Barry's mother found herself much richer than she had ever been before. Barry said that she had gone through a strange phase of grief during which she went out every day to dance on her husband's grave. As we neared the end of term, she was just beginning to come out of it, and decided that she would give 5 per cent of the money to charity, spend 5 per cent on a huge Christmas party, and use the rest to live off.

She said that she didn't care if the house got trashed, because she was going to redo everything in order to 'eradicate every trace of the boring shitcake I wasted half my life on'. When Barry told me about the party, I asked him if I could bring my brother along.

'Brother! I didn't know you had a brother,' he said.

'What do you mean?'

'What do you think I mean? Since I have known you, you have never told me that you had a brother. I can't believe it!'

'What's so unusual about having a brother? Most people have brothers.'

'No – I just can't believe you haven't told me.'

'Why should I have told you?'

'What?'

'Well – you know – he's at university – he hardly ever comes home.'

'He's still your brother.'

'Yes, but if I've barely seen him for two years, why should I have told you about him?'

'You just should. He's your brother. I'm your friend. It would have been nice to know that he exists, that's all.'

'OK, OK. Sorry already.'

'Sorry already?'

'Sorry already. It's an expression.'

'I've never heard it.'

'No, you wouldn't have done.'

'What does it mean?'

'It just means sorry.'

'Sorry already means sorry?'

'Yes. It's a Jewish expression.'

'Oh.'

'Oh, already.'

'Oh, already. What's he called?'

'Who?'

'Your brother.'

'Dan.'

'Dan. What university is he at?'

'Cambridge. Doing History. In his final year. Five foot eight, less hairy than me, more intelligent, marginally less ugly, no taste in clothes. Any more questions?'

'No. No. Bring him to the party, though. You must.'

'You won't like him,' I said.

I just knew.

CHAPTER THIRTY-SEVEN

The school careers library was a tiny, unsupervised room where sixth-formers went to smoke and look for the Theology with Brewing reference. Adjoining it was an even smaller room, where each boy was handed his UCCA Form and given careers advice about what to do with his life. This advice was merely a formality, however, since seven years of brainwashing had made us all want to do exactly the same thing.

The whole careers department was a wonderful idea, but a poster on the wall saying 'GO TO OXBRIDGE OR DIE' would have served the purpose just as well, and saved a lot of money. Remarkably, almost one third of the pupils *did* end up going to Oxbridge. The other two-thirds were thought of as statistical freaks, even though they actually made up the majority of the school. They were, so to speak, the shit that inevitably collects on the soles of a good pair of brogues. In all careers matters, the Oxbridge boys came first.

My personal careers talk was given by Mr Hodge, a History teacher who had never taught me, other than for an extremely brief 'Personal Relationships' course in the fourth year. (This was the school's attempt at sex education. It consisted of a slide show from which no one learnt a single thing, partly because we'd seen it all on video in far more graphic detail, but mainly because Mr Hodge bottled out and flicked straight past all the cock and vag pics, only stopping when he got to the two-month and three-month foetus diagrams, which he flustered over for the entire lesson.)

I had assumed that Mr Hodge's eye-wrinkling, cheek-squeezing and agonized pausing were confined to Personal Relationships lessons, but coming across him again in the sixth form, I was surprised to discover that they were even worse in casual conversation. In fact, he had some of the strangest facial mannerisms of anyone I had ever spoken to, halting communication in the middle of sentences to place his glasses on the table and massage his features into bizarre contortions with both hands, while he pondered which word to use next.

Despite the fact that he had the body-language of a mentally subnormal child, Mr Hodge was considered to be one of the most intelligent members of staff, and was said to have good contacts with several colleges at Cambridge. These 'little chats' with the school's Oxbridge applicants were the highlight of his year, giving him the opportunity to pontificate at great length on the infinitesimal differences between the colleges, obsessing over smaller and smaller details, contorting his face into ever more ludicrous shapes as he talked about the gardens at Trinity Hall, the punts at Trinity, the food at Clare, the playing fields at Jesus, the ducks at Emmanuel, the buggery at Peterhouse (joke) . . . on and on, leaning further and further back in his chair, with his eyes glazing over and a distant smile passing over his lips.

When I asked him whether there was an English department at Birmingham, he sat up with a jerk, blinked about fifty times, squeezed his ears, and scurried out of the room to look in a reference book.

Approaching the Christmas holidays, everyone was jockeying for position, trying to gain whatever official titles they could in order to have something to write on their UCCA Form which would make them sound interesting to universities. Boys came to blows over who was secretary of the School Astronomical Society (which met once a year to look out of a Maths Department window) or chairman of the Music Appreciation Society (which never met, but would have put on a record and had a chat about it if they had) or official transport co-ordinator of the School Rambling Club (which went for a walk once, many years ago).

I would like to say I was aloof from the UCCA Form panic, but actually I was as involved as everyone else, desperately trying to concoct lies which would make me sound like an enthusiast for something. I didn't expect that my profound enthusiasm for watching television and wandering around with Barry and Louise would make a particularly startling impression. ('*Stop the interviews! I want THIS one. He knows a lot about sitcoms, and is familiar with three different routes to St Anne's Shopping Centre coming from the Kentucky Fried Chicken opposite what used to be the Granada.*')

Barry, on the other hand, decided that he wasn't an academic person. He didn't bother with university applications and instead took a place on a counselling course in Central London, with a view to getting involved later in charity work of some kind. In the eyes of the school, this was the career equivalent of leprosy.

CHAPTER THIRTY-EIGHT

While my social life moved further and further away from school, the rugby boys who had dominated ever since the first year now seemed to be slipping behind, and were still going to the same old parties. The only difference was that the girls now hated them, so they had actually regressed to the stag nights of pre-girl, fifth-form days. They didn't see it as a regression, though, because they also now hated the girls, and were pleased to be back to the good old uninhibited, all-boys-together setting where they felt best.

This group had expanded in the lower sixth to include people like Neil Kothari and Dave Samuels, but by now these fringes had dropped away (Dave and Neil seemed to spend most of their time wobbling records backwards and forwards in the garages of Wembley and Chalk Farm), and the hard-core rugby clique was back to its purest, most sexually repressed core. The sofa buggery game, which had faded in popularity towards the end of the lower sixth, was now making a major come-back as a morning break activity, and the School Animal, who had been somewhat side-lined for the last year, now retook his position at the top of the social heap (which was, incidentally, at the bottom of the sofa heap).

The stag parties, which of course I never went to, were supposedly very wild, very drunken, and left lots of room for spirited play between chaps. At one of them, the School Animal had reputedly got so turned on that he went upstairs and climbed into bed with Matthew Gold's divorcee mum. When he started feeling her arse, she woke up, slapped his face, shouted at him for ten minutes, and kicked him out of her room. He decided that she was playing hard to get, and tried again half an hour later.

Meanwhile, I was making the depressing discovery that having a sex life was even more complicated than having no sex life. My gggggooooaaaalll-Brazil-Zzzico phase seemed to have lasted about three days before I was swamped by a whole new range of paranoias which I had heard of before but never really taken seriously. I had certainly never imagined that they would afflict me.

In fact, the most frightening thing that has ever happened to me in my whole life occurred one evening when I was in bed with Louise. We had been lovers, *amants*, fuck-bunnies, for around a month, and sexually things were beginning to get rather hectic. She was . . . well, a very demanding person, and I was finding it all a bit knackering. The colder she was towards me as a friend, the more she seemed to want to eat me alive in bed. It was as if she had decided that she didn't like me as a person any more, but that this was what turned her on more than anything else.

Once she actually bit me, and when I screamed that it hurt, she slapped me in the face. After that, I was too frightened to complain. That's the bizarre thing: I was actually frightened of her.

Anyway, as I was saying, the most frightening thing that has ever happened to me in my whole life took place in her bedroom one evening: we were having sex, when . . .

I don't know how to say this.

I'm no prude, and my vocabulary is more than fruity enough to deal with complicated moments, but I just don't know how to put across what happened . . .

Well – she was doing a bit of the old pipe of peace, when suddenly I noticed that she was moving down, and trying to . . . that she was starting to lick my . . .

Deep breath. Hot sweet tea. Out with it.

Let's just say, she put her tongue where the sun don't shine.

As you can imagine, this was a rather intimate moment, and I somewhat altered the atmosphere by shrieking, leaping out of bed, and running to the far corner of the room.

This did not make her very happy.

'What the fuck do you think you're doing?'

I was trembling with fear. 'I . . . I . . . was about to ask you the same question.'

'Very funny, Mark, you little runt. I was making love. What are *you* doing?'

'Um . . . running away.'

'Yes. And why, Mark, are you running away?'

'Um . . .'

'WELL?'

'Because I'm scared.'

'And why are you scared, you little coward?'

'Um . . .'

'WELL?'

'Um . . . because . . .'

'YES?'

'. . . because you licked my bum.'

'You are pathetic. Do you realize that? You are a typical, suburban, boring, unadventurous, childish little squirt. I don't know how you can live with yourself.'

'I don't know how you can lick my bum.'

'You know you enjoy it.'

'What!? Of course I don't enjoy it – it frightens the shit out of me.'

'Of course you enjoy it. You're just too repressed to admit it. There's nothing you want more in the whole world than for my gorgeous fucking brother to take you up the arse.'

'WHAT!?'

'Play your cards right, and you might just strike gold, too. You're far too fucked up to actually give it a go, though.'

This was more than I could take. I swore at her, and at my clothes, until I was fully dressed, then I walked out.

You would think that an argument like that would be enough to end a relationship, but we seemed to have one of these every single week, and still managed to carry on like any other couple.

The strange thing was that none of our rows ever seemed to have any repercussions. The day after a marathon screaming match, Louise would behave as if it simply hadn't happened. And since she gave every impression of having forgotten that we had almost killed each other the previous evening, I never thought it was tactful to bring it up. So I just lived with it: some days we'd argue, some days we wouldn't, and if I wanted to go out with her, that was how it had to be.

She always bossed me around, but I found it very difficult to make a stand, because the minute I made the slightest objection to anything that she suggested, she would bark at me, tell me I was selfish, then go ice-cold for the rest of the night. And because she got so angry when I tried something small, like changing our plan for the evening, I knew that things would be awful if I ever told her that I was upset about anything more important. So I never said a word about what was going on in my head. During arguments, heavy-duty insults of all kinds flew between us, but when it came to the things that I was really worried about, I couldn't mention them. I never said that I thought she was cold towards me, and I didn't even consider telling her that I thought she didn't love, or even like me.

I should have tried to get out of the relationship, because it really wasn't doing a lot for my self-esteem, but it never occurred to me to try and chuck her. It wouldn't have seemed possible. She was the one who made the decisions, and I think I was just waiting for her to get rid of me. She consistently gave the impression that this was about to happen, which always secretly felt like a huge relief, but she never actually went as far as to end it.

It was a bit like sitting through *The Fly* all over again. I could move to the back, but I couldn't let myself leave until it had finished.

CHAPTER THIRTY-NINE

The party that Barry's mum threw on Christmas Eve was incredible. Without doubt the best I had ever been to. Every single room in the house was used, with each one turned into a different decade of the century: the garden was the 1910s, with hundreds of water pistols lying around so that you could act out World War One. The twenties was in one of the upstairs bedrooms, with Barry's granny (on his mother's side) DJing on a wind-up gramophone, playing all her teenage 78s and teaching everyone how to do the Charleston. The thirties was in the toilet, and the forties was in the living room with a live swing band (five old men) dressed in army uniforms.

The kitchen was supposedly the fifties, with a few chrome stools giving the room the vaguest resemblance to an American diner. Hamburgers were on offer and James Dean movies played on a hired TV set. The sixties was in Louise's bedroom, with compulsory bowl haircut wigs given out and everyone doing the twist to Beatles records (which didn't feel right but was a good laugh anyway).

The best room was the seventies, which was in Barry's bedroom. All the furniture had been taken out, and the room was ankle-deep in flowers. It was lit by one red light bulb. The only other thing in the room was a barrel of massage oil.

No one had been able to think of anything for the eighties, but half way through the evening, Barry drew a picture of Margaret Thatcher which he pinned on the garden fence for people to throw darts at. This got a bit confused with World War One, though, and the picture was ruined when everyone started squirting it with water.

Most of the money had been spent on drink, which flowed in enormous quantities for the whole night. The amazing thing about the party was that there seemed to be equal numbers of guests from every generation. And while Barry's granny's friends started off in the twenties, Mrs James' friends in the sixties, with Barry's generation evenly split between the seventies and World War One, by the time midnight had passed everyone moved freely throughout the house, and danced with whoever was there. Wherever you went, you saw hilarious things, whether it was a stoned eighty-year-old getting a massage from her grandson, a fat bank manager doing the Charleston, or ten women between the ages of fifteen and seventy munching on hamburgers and earnestly discussing James Dean's sex appeal.

After a slight lull in activity at around two o'clock, World War One suddenly took off, with a grand battle developing between the greyhairs and the juves. We were seriously outnumbered, but made up for it when we found buckets in the kitchen, which we used to take Barry's gran hostage.

Things got complicated when Barry decided to change sides on the grounds that he was a double agent. This led to everyone else deciding that they were at the very least triple, if not quadruple or quintuple agents, resulting in a huge, soaking wet free-for-all.

It finally came to a halt when the trumpeter from the dance band played the last post from an upstairs window, declared a cease-fire, and proclaimed the Jazz Age officially open. He told us to go into the hall of mirrors to witness the signing of the Versailles Treaty.

We all assumed that he meant the living room, so we went in and Barry's mum dished out a cup of Ovaltine to each of us from a huge soup tureen which she had brought through from the kitchen. We all sat on the floor, and the dance band took their places on the stand.

They took off their army jackets, and this time, instead of playing the Glenn Miller stuff they had been doing earlier, they came out with the most incredible bluesy, moody, moving, uplifting music that I had ever heard in my life. I couldn't believe that such old men could produce such amazing sounds. Every single person in the room was transfixed.

When they were improvising, I had this amazing sense that

the musician was talking straight to me. And because it was all being made up on the spot, it felt like it had all been created solely for that party, and could never have sounded as it did, other than at that moment in that place with those people. And since it wasn't composed and wasn't recorded, it was all unrepeatable – the second each note came out, it floated away and was gone. You had to be completely in the moment to catch it. I had never got so lost in a piece of music. It was as if the musicians were describing the party back to us – telling us what we had done, what fun it had been.

There was an atmosphere of total stillness and attention in the room, and a kind of shared warmth that went with the sensation that we were all feeling the same thing. It was perfect. Without anyone having to say anything, or make a speech, we all felt completely together. It was a weird sensation.

I'm not normally the kind of arsehole who goes around loving humanity, but that evening I really did have to make an exception. Even Louise seemed to be in a good mood, and we had a superb time together, though that *was* the evening when I decided that she was actually quite ugly.

Barry spent most of the party with my brother.

CHAPTER FORTY

Dan had intended to go back to Cambridge for the New Year, but he ended up staying in Harrow for a whole fortnight after the party. He hadn't spent such a long time at home since before university.

Even if his sartorial progress seemed to have stalled (a Bhutanese yak-wool jumper with knitted moose-heads was the biggest hit in Dan's Winter '87 wardrobe), he seemed exceptionally happy, and we got on better than ever. The age gap between us was at last beginning to feel insignificant.

However, other than a brief re-visit to 'Sally: Statue of a Skipping Girl' (for which we unfortunately forgot to take the turd in a bag), we didn't manage to see each other very often. I was spending most of my time in physical and emotional mutual abuse sessions with Louise, and Dan seemed to be out with friends around the clock.

He wouldn't tell me who they were, so I presumed them to be some kind of weirdo set from his university. That would have accounted for the heinous jumper. Still, he seemed to be having an incredibly wild time with them – most evenings he didn't even come back home. Dan insisted that he was just spending the night at friends' houses when he missed the last train, but I could tell by the way he was acting that there was something saucy going on.

I didn't force him to admit it, though, because he'd never been very confident about that kind of thing, my brother. I was just happy to see it happening, because lovely though he is, Dan can hardly be called a ladies' man.

Most of my remaining Christmas holiday was evenly split between worrying about Louise, worrying about my A levels, and masturbating. There was something particularly comforting about a good, old-fashioned sixty-second wank – it reminded me of my blissfully simple life as a virgin schoolboy.

I did find it a bit worrying that I was *still* tossing myself off despite having regular sex with Louise, though. I wondered if I would ever be able to kick the habit. The thing is, in some ways I actually preferred the masturbation to the sex. I didn't prefer the sensation – don't get me wrong, I'm no perv – it was just that the flexible timing of it made sure that a wank almost always hit the spot, where sex was sometimes a bit of a hassle.

It seemed strange – within two months I had gone from 'the meaning of life; our reason for being on the planet; the motivating force behind most action and thought; the central desire upon which my entire future is dependent,' to 'a bit of a hassle'.

It wasn't that sex didn't live up to expectations, it was just . . . oh, I don't fucking understand. Ask someone else. It's too depressing.

Towards the end of the holiday, while I moped around the house, and my brother stalked the city distributing his seed, I was struck by an amazing thought. It occurred to me that if *even* my brother, of grey polyester trousers with pockets on the thigh fame, he with Bhutanese yak-wool moose heads on his chest – if *he* was getting his oats, then university surely had to be the best place in the world.

That day, for the first time, my A-level motivation kicked into gear. If I could just get decent exam results, and avoid being garrotted-for-kicks by Louise, then I was bound to end up swamped by horny, laugh-a-minute, sane girls.

I went back to school with a red-hot, throbbing purple fountain pen, desperate to get cracking on some serious work.

CHAPTER FORTY-ONE

Lent term (which really ought to have been called Passover term) was dominated by university interviews. My first one was at York, where I had a friendly chat about a few novels with a nice man in horrible clothes who gave me a B-B-C offer. My second one was at Bristol, where I had a less friendly chat with a less nice man who wore more horrible clothes and gave me an A-B-B offer. Neither my fourth or fifth choice universities gave me an offer or an interview, since they thought I would almost certainly end up somewhere else. This only left Cambridge, my first choice, who eventually summoned me for a mid-February interview.

Having read in the alternative prospectus (compiled by the students) that Trinity was the richest college and gave lots of book grants and travel grants to their students, I had applied there. In principle, my interview was pretty much what I expected (a hostile grilling from an unpleasant man in hideous clothes), but the severity of it surprised me. I was to have two interviews, one at 10:30 with Dr Chambers and one at 11:00 with Dr Morne. I arrived ten minutes early for Dr Chambers, and heard voices coming from inside the room. I agonized for five minutes over whether or not to knock just to let him know that I had arrived, by which time I was only five minutes early, so I knocked. He didn't answer, so I assumed that he knew I was there and was just finishing off the previous interview.

By 10:35, I had already been standing there for a quarter of an hour, and still no one had asked me to come in. I was in a state of high tension. What do I do? What the fuck do I do? Maybe he didn't hear the first knock, in which case I must knock again, but I'm done for anyway because he will think I am five minutes late; or maybe he did hear the knock and is just running late, in which case I mustn't knock again because he'll think I'm rude for interrupting his interview twice and implying that he's deaf. Or maybe he did hear, and it's all a test to see whether or not I'm assertive. After thirty seconds in which my muscles behaved as if I was in the Arctic and my sweat glands as if I was in a sauna, I finally knocked on the door. It came out much louder than I had expected.

Almost immediately the door opened. His clothes were extraordinarily bad. 'Bit late,' he mumbled, and showed me over to a large sofa. I followed him, bright red, still trembling, covered in sweat, trying to decide whether or not to explain what had just happened. I decided against it just as he put a photocopied sheet in my hands.

'Read this over a couple of times – I'll be back in a mo.' Then he left the study, and from an adjoining room carried on the telephone conversation which had obviously been what I had heard from outside. Shit! I should have knocked more loudly first time round. Shit! I looked down at the sheet of paper which was vibrating rapidly in my hands and tried to focus on it. By placing it flat on the arm of the sofa I could just about stop it from moving around, and I then dragged my eyes into focus on the words. Dr Chambers was talking so loudly on the phone that I could barely concentrate, though, and when I heard him beginning to draw the conversation to a close, I panicked. Shit! Have I used up all my time? I haven't even read it once yet! Shit! Shit! How much time have I used? I couldn't have read it this fast, even if I *had* been concentrating. Or maybe it's a test of reading speed. Shit. Read quickly.

Fuck. That was too quick – I can't remember one word. Concentrate. Read slowly. Relax. Read.

I read:

Self-consciousness which is at first only the Notion of Spirit, enters on this path with the characteristic of holding itself to be, as a particular spirit, essential being; and its aim, therefore, is to give itself as a particular individual an actual existence and to enjoy itself as an individual in it.

In holding itself to be, *qua being-for-self*, essential being, it is the negativity of the 'other'. In its consciousness, therefore, it appears as the Positive in contrast to something which certainly is, but which has for it the significance of something without intrinsic being; consciousness appears split into this given actuality and the *End* which it realizes by superseding that actuality, an End which, in fact, it makes an actuality in place of that which was given. Its primary End, however, is its *immediate* abstract *being-for-self*; in other words, seeing itself as . . .

'So – tell me a little about the passage you have just read.'

'Ah –'. I opened and closed my mouth several times. This must have given me a particularly intelligent air. 'Ah – I would say it's about self-consciousness, and about how to feel . . . er . . . individual compared to other people.'

'But surely, self-consciousness which, on the whole, knows itself to be reality has its object not in its own self, but as an object which initially is merely for self-consciousness.'

'Um . . . Could you say that again?'

'Surely self-consciousness which, on the whole, knows itself to be reality has its object not in its own self, but as an object which is merely for self-consciousness.'

'Yes. I agree.'

'But how can you agree if you are of the opinion that individuality is primarily expressed as a relationship to an other, an external. Surely self-consciousness which primarily observes self is completely at odds with a "society" –' (he made the inverted commas in the air with his fingers) '-oriented position.'

'I see. Right. What I meant was that self-consciousness is mainly a private thing. More than a public thing.'

'So you're an arch Thatcherite?'

'Am I?'

'Surely you can see that to exclude all reference to society in the generality of the self-consciousness debate is to abandon all hope of creating an alternative to market ideology. Can't you see how dangerous the "private self" position is in a post-industrial world? I'm shocked to find your generation so oblivious to notions of spirit in this debate – an attitude which is without doubt in step with the erosion of the most basic foundations of . . .'

My brain seized up. This didn't matter too much for the remainder of my interview with Dr Chambers, who did all the talking anyway, but it was rather embarrassing when, half an hour later, I found myself upstairs in Dr Morne's study, unable to think of an answer to the question of why I wanted to come to Cambridge.

When I finally staggered out into Trinity New Court, it took me several minutes to remember who and where I was. I felt as if I had undergone the mental equivalent of a car crash.

Standing there reminded me of my school hockey matches. There was something aggressively English about the place that put me on edge. Yup, I was *definitely* in a minority. I wandered past the church, or chapel, or whatever you call it, and I heard voices singing inside. They were singing loudly, but not taking-the-piss-loudly, this was proper enthusiasm-loudly. They were using the right words and everything.

I poked my nose around the door, and saw that it wasn't a service – just the choir rehearsing. The conductor, who looked like he was just a student, saw me, and told me to sit down and have a listen. And he didn't say it weedily – he said it in a commanding, people-usually-do-what-I-say voice, so I did what he said. Now I looked at them, all of the choir looked reasonably well-fed. Some of them were quite good-looking as well. And when they sang, it was incredible. They were superb musicians – I had to admit it was a beautiful sound. I couldn't believe they were all so competent and keen.

And they weren't lonely old people who are about to die – these were young, healthy-looking types.

It was lucky that I was already sitting down, because I might have collapsed. *Fuck!* I thought. *FUCKING HELL! I can't believe it! This is incredible! I live in a Christian country! The whole bloody nation, outside North London, is swarming with fucking Christians! Jesus Christ, what kind of a country is this? How come I haven't noticed before? Fuck – maybe people do watch Songs of Praise.*

This, my miniature spiritual revelation in Trinity College Chapel, or Church, or whatever you call it, frightened the shit out of me. I raced for the train station as fast as I could. I had to get back home.

It was only a couple of hours later, sitting on the Circle Line, pulling out of Farringdon Station (aaahhh – lovely, familiar names), that I realized what an absolute howling wanker Dr Chambers was. There was no way I could have understood what he was talking about. It must have been some elaborate wind-up that I didn't understand. If I had been one of the Pierses, I probably would have told him to piss off, and we'd have been chortling over glasses of sherry within minutes, discussing subjects for my first year dissertation.

CHAPTER FORTY-TWO

While everyone else struggled with interviews and university offers, Barry was having his best term since arriving at the school. He had a guaranteed place on his counselling course and could take his A levels without the pressure of having to get any particular result. This seemed to have a strange effect on his work rate, though, and rather than working less, he seemed to be working harder than ever before. He said that he wasn't stressed, but just felt that for the first time he understood what his subjects were about, and was beginning to enjoy schoolwork. His teachers gradually began to notice the difference, and he became recognized for the first time as a hard-working and intelligent student.

Half way through the term, his house-master even summoned him for a special talk and asked him whether he couldn't be persuaded to put in a late UCCA application. He promised to ensure good references and A-level predictions. 'It will be such a waste if you don't even try,' pleaded the house-master.

Barry told me that he toyed with, 'Waste of what, you small-minded, university-obsessed git? Bend over, give me an UCCA Form to roll up and I'll shove it where it belongs.' Instead, he settled for, 'Sorry – I'm not really an academic person.'

I still spent a lot of time with Barry during the lunch hours, but outside school I saw him less and less. Since things had started getting strange with Louise, Barry and I seemed to have drifted apart. Both of us now worked most evenings, and at the weekends he kept on going away to work and visit friends.

I didn't really know what he was up to, but he seemed very busy all of a sudden, and didn't have much time for me. Or maybe it was me that didn't have time for him. I don't know what it was, but we just seemed to miss each other. And when we did get together, things weren't the same as before. I was often worried or unhappy about Louise, and Barry seemed pre-occupied by something of his own.

In the past we had always told each other everything, but now we both knew that we were keeping secrets from each other, and this affected everything between us. There was nothing particularly wrong – we never argued or anything like that – it was just that we didn't spark each other off any more – it wasn't exciting, it was just comfortable. But in a slightly uncomfortable way.

I wanted to tell him about Louise. In fact, I wanted to *ask* him about Louise, but I never could. He didn't give a single clue about what he thought of her as a person, and I couldn't bring myself to ask. I desperately wanted someone to say to me, 'Yes, she's difficult, but she's worth it,' or something which would reassure me about what was going on. I needed someone to tell me that I was sane, and that Louise was the irrational one, but I could never speak to Barry about it, because I was too afraid that he might take Louise's side.

Keeping all this to myself must have created some of the distance between us, but I couldn't help feeling that most of the coldness was coming from him. I could sense that he was hiding something from me. He suddenly seemed utterly disengaged from our friendship, and from everything else at school other than his work. Mentally, he was just somewhere else.

This pissed me off. It was as if he had lost interest in me as a friend. He only ever perked up during an endless series of conversations about my childhood which he kept on drawing me into, and even then he almost seemed more interested in Dan than in me, which was ridiculous.

The whole thing made me worry that maybe Barry and Louise had both turned against me. I began to feel excluded, and resented that Barry had taken her side.

My rejection from Cambridge hardly came as a surprise. Since the thought of ever setting eyes on Dr Chambers again made me feel nauseous, I wasn't too depressed about not being given a place to study with him. Involuntary vomiting during seminars probably wouldn't make for an ideal student.

('*Mark – do you feel that guilt is the foundation-stone upon which all tragic drama is built?*'

'*Hhhhhhhhhuuuuuurrrrrrrrrggggggggghhhllllll hhuurrgggg hhh hhuurrgggghhh HHHHHHHHHUUUUUUUURRR-RRRRRRGGGGGGGGGGGHHHHHHHLLL!*'

'*Interesting. Did you remember the mop this week?*')

My form-master told me that the school was 'most surprised' by my rejection from Trinity. He also said that the head of English had contacts with certain other Cambridge colleges, and would be doing his best to 'put in a good word for me with the powers that be'. Not long after this, I was summoned for an interview by Selwyn College, who reversed the rejection and offered me a place conditional on three As at A level. I felt that I ought to be grateful to the school, but in all honesty I didn't really give a shit. It was good news for me, but bad news for the poor sod whose place I had taken by having strings pulled. I felt bad at having profited from the very bullshit I most hated about the school.

I took the offer, though. I'm not a ponce.

CHAPTER FORTY-THREE

Getting three As, however, was going to be a problem. I had always been good at English, and French was a piece of piss as long as you read the texts in translation (my A-level book was *Le Grand Meaulnes*, which is without doubt the crappiest, most juvenile book ever written). But maths – maths was horrible.

The problem was not so much that the course was difficult, more that my teacher, Mr Gaskin, was an incompetent moron not capable of communicating even the most basic mathematical concepts. If the classes hadn't been streamed, this would have presented no obstacle, since the school had plenty of coherent, articulate boys who could have done the entire A level in two weeks and spent the rest of the year explaining it to the rest of us. Unfortunately all these boys were in the top set together (and half way through a degree course by the time the A levels came round), while my class, the second set, consisted of ordinary mortals who couldn't understand what all the newly shaped squiggles meant.

Luckily, though, there had been an error, and Paul Berhmann (a South African Jew with a boil on his nose) had accidentally been placed in the second set, so when the bell went after a fruitless hour of Mr Gaskin's verbal dysentery, all the boys who wanted to pass the A level would gather round Paul, who explained everything in five minutes.

By Easter, Paul's group of students had grown to include almost the whole class. Mr Gaskin grew a bit suspicious that no one wanted to leave the room at the end of the lesson, but he never hung around to find out what was happening because he was always desperate to get to the staff room for a fag.

Mr Gaskin was a nice man, though, and we all liked him despite his flaws. He did have one particularly annoying habit, however, which was that he took every available opportunity to grope his students. While the shoulder-brushing, the arm-patting and the standing-so-close-that-his-rancid-breath-shot-straight-up-your-nose-and-made-your-eyes-water was never really a major problem, it was his habit of squeezing onto the edge of your chair and putting his arm round you when you asked him a question that really turned stomachs.

Now I'm quite willing to admit that when Barry first turned up at school, I acted like a bit of a whoopsie myself, but I have to say, when an old man with permanent sweat-patches and green breath starts fondling me, I want to puke.

The strange thing was that school opinion did not brand Mr Gaskin as one of the queer teachers. According to student wisdom, only the quiet, skinny types in the English department who were vaguely limp-wristed, did no sport and made the odd snide comment about the games masters were 'fucking benders'. The married men who touched and eyed up little boys but did their bit for the school's sporting life were always assumed to be straight.

Personally, if I happened to be a gay teacher, I know for sure that the first place I would head for is the pert, heaving buttocks of a lower-school rugby practice. In fact, even in my very straightest moments I have to admit to a flicker of arousal when I see pretty boys hurting each other. But no. Apparently gay people sit around in staff rooms, reading novels. Yes, novels. And that's a fact.

When the Easter break came, I still had a lot of work that I needed to do on my maths. Barry told me that he wanted to have a period of intense revision during the holidays, and he suggested that we hire a place in the country and go away for a week, together with his sister (who felt like a holiday despite the fact that she'd been doing sod all for the last six months). We planned to study each morning, and go for long walks during the afternoon.

Amazingly, that very evening my brother phoned from Cambridge, saying that he had a lot of work that he needed to do for his finals, but felt like getting away from it all for a while.

'Shit,' I said. 'That's incredible! That's an incredible coincidence. Only this afternoon, Barry suggested to me that I go away with him and Louise over Easter.'

'What a coincidence,' he said.

'Listen. I've had an amazing idea! How about the four of us all go away together? It'll be a lot cheaper if there's four. What do you reckon?'

'Gosh. What an amazing idea,' he said. This sounded almost sarcastic, but I ignored it.

'I know you don't know them and everything, but you'll like them – I promise. Louise is my girlfriend – you've met her, and Barry's at school with me – he's her brother.'

'Let me see – Barry . . . Barry . . . um, I *think* I met him at that party. Tall, dishy, blond hair.'

'I suppose so. That's him,' I said.

'Great – that's all sorted, then. Look – I've spoken to a letting agency, and there's a place we can have in Cumbria from the third to the tenth of April which sleeps four and will only cost forty-five pounds each. You can drive up from London in Louise's car, pick me up in Cambridge and we can all head up there together.'

'Fuck! You're very well organized. How come you . . .? Shit . . . I mean . . . Brilliant! That's um . . . perfect . . . I suppose that sounds fine. I'll check with Barry and Louise that they're happy for you to come along and everything, then I'll ring you back and you can put down a deposit.'

'I'm sure they won't mind. We're all set, then.'

'Brilliant.'

'Excellent. I'm really looking forward to meeting Brian and Lisa again,' he said.

'Barry and Louise,' I said, 'Barry and Louise.'

'That's it. That's it. I hope we all get on.'

'Me too. You never know, really, do you?'

'No,' he said. His voice was all wobbly.

'Dan? Are you all right?'

'Fine. Fine. Absolutely fine.'

'Your voice sounds funny.'

'I'm fine . . . I . . . just . . . er . . . I'm just . . . er . . . pleased that you've come up with such a good idea, that's all . . .'

'Oh, it wasn't me really. You've done all the work. It's just a nice coincidence, really.'

'Yes. What a nice coincidence!' Now his voice was very wobbly.

'Are you sure you're all right?'

'Frog in the throat. I have to go.' Then he put the phone down.

Poor Dan, I thought. He's not usually like that. He must be under terrible stress.

CHAPTER FORTY-FOUR

Everything about the holiday seemed perfect. Even the drive up the motorway was fun – for the whole journey, the car bubbled with an inexplicable sense of hysteria. Dan was brilliant – even though Barry and Louise were strangers to him, he instantly seemed completely at ease with them, and we all just laughed all the way. Barry was in a particularly strange mood, and whenever we saw anything even vaguely unusual out of the window, he made some comment, or sometimes just a silly noise, which sent Dan and Louise into stitches, shortly followed by me. A few times, I asked whether they'd been drinking, which just seemed to make them laugh more than ever.

We stopped at a supermarket in Kendal and bought enough food and drink to last us for a few days. By the time we had found the cottage it was late, so we dumped our bags in the living room and started on supper straight away. Barry and I washed and peeled, Dan and Louise cooked. There was still the same bizarre atmosphere. For some reason, everything was funny. We all just kept on laughing at strange things. I didn't know who or what had started it off, but it infected us all.

When the food was ready, we all moved from the kitchen to the open fire in the living room and ate off our knees. By the time the meal was over, the atmosphere was even stranger than before, but not in such a nice way any more. We weren't laughing so much now, and I realized that there was something odd in the eye-contact going on. It was as if . . . I don't know . . . it was as if Dan was at the centre of everything rather than me.

I was just beginning to feel uncomfortable, and was about to say something about it, when Dan spoke.

'Mark,' he said, 'do you notice anything strange here?'

'Yes. I do, actually,' I said.

There was a long pause. Then Dan spoke again.

'There's something we want to tell you.'

'What do you mean, *we*?' My blood started pumping faster. I could feel that something terrible was coming.

Dan put his head in his hands. 'Shit, I wanted to do this nicely. I think I've given it away already.'

'What? Given what away?' I was speaking loudly, now.

I looked across at Barry, sitting on a sofa next to Louise. He was looking frighteningly serious. She was trying to look serious, but had a smirk around the edges of her mouth.

'Given what away?' I said. 'Will someone tell me what you're talking about.'

'Look,' said Dan. 'This holiday wasn't just a coincidence. We planned it as a way of getting you on your own so that we could break some important news to you.'

I was sweating now.

'What? What news? And what's all this *we* stuff?'

There was another silence. No one could actually say it.

Then Louise leaped up, exasperated. 'For fuck's sake, Mark. Can't you even guess? Jesus Christ – do you have to make them say it? Just *think*, for once in your life. Look at the pair of them. Do they look like they hardly know each other?'

'No – they don't.' My heart was thumping unpleasantly hard. 'What's been going on?'

'Mark,' said Dan. 'We got you to come here, because we thought it might be the easiest way to tell you that Barry and I are . . . well, we're in love.'

I froze. Time stopped.

'Oh, my God! *You* two.'

'I'm sorry,' said Barry. 'I should have told you earlier.'

'Earlier? Fucking hell – how long has it been . . .?'

The three of them looked at me.

'Dan – you're not . . . And Barry . . . Fuck. *Both* of you. I don't believe it.' I looked at Louise for confirmation that something extraordinary had just happened, but she was just smiling, and staring at me as if to say, 'you're a fucking moron.'

'You're a fucking moron,' said Louise. 'How can you not have noticed?'

'Noticed what? I mean I've noticed now, but how could I notice . . .? I mean what was . . .? how have . . .? Are you – have you been – are you . . .?'

'Benders?' said Dan.

'*Are* you?' I said.

They looked at each other, then they both reached out and held hands. It made me feel strange in my stomach.

'So have you two . . . have you two been . . .?'

'Afraid so,' said Barry. 'Ever since Christmas.'

'What!? At that party? Fuck! I don't believe it!'

'It all started in the sixties, before Barry was even born,' said Dan.

'That was just a kiss, though. We first had sex in the trenches of World War One,' said Barry.

'Jesus! Jesus Christ! Dan – you're my brother! How come I didn't even know? I mean, how long have you been . . .? You know . . .'

'You can say it, it won't hurt.'

'Gay. How long have you been gay?'

'Ever since I was born, darling.'

'But when did you . . .?'

'I came out just over a year ago in Cambridge. Barry's my first proper lover, though.'

'Jesus! I can't believe it! And Barry . . . you're . . . Barry . . . what the . . .? I mean what are you? What's going on? Are you a . . .? Are you a –?'

'A what?'

'Bisexual – are you bisexual?'

'I don't know. I think this is what I'm really into.' He touched Dan's leg. 'At school, there's a lot of pressure to conform – I think that's why I was a bit over-enthusiastic. I'm not really into the woman thing at all.'

'It's just a phase he went through,' said Dan.

'Ha fucking ha. Very witty,' I said. 'I wish you weren't so fucking smug about the whole thing. You're both beginning to piss me off.'

My brother looked at me sharply. I looked back. The three of them were sitting in a line, opposite me: Louise and Barry on the sofa, Dan perched on the arm-rest with his hand curled around the back of Barry's neck. I suddenly felt as if I was in a fucking job interview, or something. As if they were all in some club together, and I was begging to be allowed in. In an instant, my confusion evaporated, and I just felt angry.

I looked hard at Barry.

'It's disgusting,' I said. 'Both of you – you're disgusting.'

There was a long, tense silence.

'I think you should take that back,' said Dan. 'It's very insulting.'

I was breathing heavily. I couldn't stop myself from blinking too fast.

'What do you mean take it back? You know I'm telling the truth.'

'What?' said Dan. I could see him beginning to get angry.

'It's disgusting. It's unnatural. You've nicked my best friend, turned him into a fucking bender, and now you're just sitting there laughing smugly about how clever and different you are.'

Barry stood up.

'You're jealous,' he said. Although he had said it calmly, I could tell that he was angry.

'No – I'm just repulsed. You're repulsive.'

'Please, Mark. Don't behave like this,' he said.

'It's disgusting,' I said.

The three of them looked at me as if I was a giant gate-crashing turd.

'You are pathetic,' said Barry.

'*I'm* pathetic. That's a joke.'

'I know why you're behaving like this,' he said.

I grunted.

'Do you remember the first time we met?' he said.

'No.'

'It was in the changing rooms, after rugby during my first week at the school. We didn't say anything, but that was when we became friends.'

'What the fuck are you talking about?'

'I was getting changed, and you were watching me with your eyes on stalks, your tongue hanging out, and your groin humping a schoolbag.'

I didn't know what to say.

'Do you remember?' he said.

'Fuck off.'

'You know I'm not making it up. Why do you think I picked you as a friend? I knew from the start that we were ... similar.'

'What are you talking about? *I* picked *you* as a friend. Anyway – what do you mean similar – are you saying I'm gay?'

'No – I'm just saying that we shared a degree of confusion. That's why we were attracted to each other.'

'Attracted?'

'YES!'

'You were attracted to me?' I asked.

'Not as much as you were to me – but I thought you were OK. Have to admit – I prefer your brother.'

'I can't fucking believe this! Everything's happening at once. It's too much.'

'Mark,' said Dan, 'nothing's happening at once. It's all been unfolding with exceptional slowness over the last two years, but you've just been too thick to notice anything until it's jammed down your throat. What the hell did you think I was doing spending all that time in Harrow? Admiring the architecture?'

'I can't believe it! This is all too much. I can't believe that my brother *and* my best friend are both gay. It's unbelievable!'

'It's not that surprising, really,' said Barry, 'you're the classic fag hag.'

'I am not. I am *not* a fag hag.'

There was a pause, while they all looked at me.

'What's a fag hag?' I asked.

'A fag hag, strictly speaking, is a woman,' said Dan, 'but it is basically any straight person who spends their time hanging around gays in order to escape problems with their own sexuality.'

'Fuck off! Will you all fuck off! You're the ones who are bent, so how the fuck has this turned into a character assassination of me? There's nothing wrong with *me*.'

'There's nothing wrong with us, either, you little shit,' said Barry.

'Of course there is – you're shagging my fucking brother.'

Barry grabbed my shoulders and shook me, shouting into my face, 'Oh, GROW UP! Will you just fucking GROW UP!'

Then he pushed me away, and stormed out.

I slumped onto the sofa. After a while I noticed that I was shaking, and my face was wet.

Dan tried to give me a hug, but I didn't let him.

CHAPTER FORTY- FIVE

We left the cottage the following morning. After we had dropped Dan off in Cambridge, no one said a word all the way back to London.

For two days, I sat at home doing nothing, trying to pretend that the whole thing hadn't happened. Impressively, thanks to the Valium-by-the-fistful effect of daytime TV, I succeeded.

Half way through the third day, though, my vision started blurring and I began to have weird sexual hallucinations involving Scooby Doo and Anne Diamond. Just in time, I managed to switch off the set before the OD fully kicked in. If I hadn't had a remote control, I never would have made it, and God knows what would have happened.

My vision soon returned, shortly followed by the memory that I had alienated myself from my best friend, my brother, and my girlfriend. I tried to recall whether or not there was anyone left on the planet who actually liked me, but I couldn't think of any candidates other than Anne Diamond and Scooby Doo. I almost switched on again, but luckily the remote had slipped between two cushions, so I didn't manage it.

After a couple of Mars bars and a pot of coffee, I felt restored to health, and decided to phone Dan in Cambridge to see if things could be sorted out. I knew that the only way to be forgiven was to do a bit of a magnanimity act, so I started the call with an irresistibly grovelling apology, telling him all the obvious stuff about how I had been shocked and angry, and had said a lot of things that I didn't mean.

'I know,' he said. 'I think we just told you in the wrong way. I didn't realize how jealous you'd be.'

I almost argued back, but decided to let it go. If it made him happier to believe that I was jealous, so what. Besides, I'd never done humility before, and I was getting quite a kick out of the fact that it actually seemed to be working.

'I really am sorry,' I said.

'It's not me you have to apologize to – I can take it. Barry's very upset, though.'

'Why?'

'Well – other than Louise, you're the first person he's ever told.'

'And you.'

'He didn't have to *tell* me.'

'How did you know, then?'

'How do you think?'

'I don't know, do I? That's why I'm asking.'

'I just knew. It was obvious.'

'What, straight away?'

'Yes.'

'Are you telling me that you walked into that party, looked at Barry, my best friend for over a year, and knew straight away that he was gay.'

'Exactly.'

'Bollocks.'

'It's true.'

'Bollocks.'

'Honestly. It was obvious. I reckon it took me about a minute to be completely sure. But once I had spoken to him, that was it.'

'What was it?'

'I knew.'

'You're lying.'

'I'm not lying, for God's sake.'

'Really?'

'Really and truly.'

'That's amazing. Have you people got a secret code or something.'

'We people? Have we people got a secret code? If you want to call it that, yes. It's called intuition – a concept utterly alien to heterosexual men.'

'That's rubbish – I've got intuition. I just choose to use it on women.'

'Don't make me laugh. Straight men have such a hard time trying to understand themselves, they don't even think about attempting anyone else.'

'You're wrong, actually. I've got plenty of intuition.'

'Yeah, right. You and Louise – the mind-reading couple.'

'Maybe we are. What do you know about it?'

'More than you'd think.'

'What – more intuition?'

'No – gossip. Even more reliable.'

'What's she told you? What have you heard?'

'Look – you're meant to be apologizing, not getting me to reveal which dismal secrets of your doomed relationship I know about. You started off wanting to know if Barry was upset.'

'Oh, yeah.'

'Aren't you going to ask?'

'I'm asking, for God's sake. Don't be so anal.'

'He's upset.'

'Shit. Is he angry?'

'Yes, very.'

'Really?'

'Of course, really. It's no joke. You managed to squeeze all the worst things you could possibly have said into the two minutes before he walked out.'

'Really?'

'Will you stop saying that? I'm not lying.'

'Sorry.'

'You insulted him very badly.'

'Yes.'

'And you have to apologize.'

'Yes. You're right.'

I phoned Barry straight away, but it was Louise who answered, which she took as a handy opportunity to tell me that I had behaved unforgivably, I was evil, and I was chucked.

After that, no one would take my calls, not even Barry's

mum – they all slammed the phone down as soon as they heard my voice.

I rang Dan back to tell him what had happened, and he said that I had to wait until Barry would talk to me, *then* I had to apologize. It seemed like sensible advice.

All in all, I was having a great week. Perfect preparation for my A levels.

What worried me most was that I couldn't help feeling more upset about Barry than Louise. I tried to force myself to feel things the other way round, but it didn't really work.

CHAPTER FORTY-SIX

The first day back at school after the Easter break was awful. When I got to the coach stop in the morning, I saw Barry for the first time since our argument. I tried to apologize, but he wouldn't talk to me. He wouldn't even stand near me. As soon as I approached him, he just turned around and walked away.

He made sure that I got on the coach before him, and when I sat at the back, he sat at the front. We were back where we had started almost two years ago.

I was quite willing to let him sulk for a few days to make it clear that he was pissed off with me, but when the same behaviour went on for three weeks, I began to get annoyed. I couldn't understand why he was being so childish. Even in the school corridors, if he spotted me, he turned around and walked away. It was laughable.

He developed complicated systems for avoiding me at every point in the school day. On the coach home, for example, if he arrived before me, he would surround himself with a group of seats that were already taken, so that it would be impossible for me to sit near him and start a conversation.

I just couldn't understand it. He almost seemed afraid of me.

The worst insult of all was that whenever I glimpsed Barry around the school, he never seemed to be alone. He had started hanging out with that scrawny geek from the year below, Robert Levin. (You remember – the guy who tossed off Jeremy Jacobs in a jacuzzi.)

It was during this Barry-thinks-I've-got-rabies phase that I first noticed my absence of other friends. It became apparent that I hadn't actually made the effort to talk to anyone other than Barry for the last year, so when Barry stopped talking to me I was suddenly at rather a loss for things to do. Everyone seemed to have forgotten who I was. I almost felt as if I ought to have been wearing a name badge. Or maybe a sandwich board saying, 'The end is nigh, but does anyone need a new friend to keep them company in the meanwhile?'

In fact, admitting friendlessness is not something I am into, and I can't think of anything more embarrassing than actually going out of your way to try and make new pals, so, since I had only a few weeks left at school, I decided to do a Clint Eastwood. I took to wandering around the school chewing a biro (bit worried about matchstick splinters) and giving off don't-even-think-of-talking-to-me vibes.

I was a little depressed to find that this worked ludicrously well. No one talked to me. No one at all. And probably not because they thought I was desperately cool, either.

In the upper sixth, your final term is only half length, because they set you loose for study leave (i.e. last-minute panic revision) after half term. You then only come back to school to sit your exams. The great thing about this system is that half a term is so short that you can't really do anything with it, so all the teachers make sure that you finish the syllabus before the Easter holiday, leaving the Summer term free for strolls, looking out of windows, and chatting about how stressed you are.

This quirk of timetabling conspired with my Eastwood-style social life to give me the impression that I wasn't actually in school. My body was there, but no one was talking to me, no one was trying to teach me anything, and it seemed very rare for anyone to actually focus their eyes on me. Fundamentally, I just wasn't there.

I don't mean to go all surreal here, but – what can I say . . .? The whole thing felt very weird. Then, one day I woke up as a butterfly and ate a rainbow for breakfast as I flew to school on a giant pea named Hope.

Joke. Don't worry.

Honestly, though – I almost gave up on TV and started reading foreign books. *That's* how strange I felt. And while I'm plastering on the weirdness, I might as well tell you the one really shocking effect of the whole thing. This is what really freaked me out. While all the other kids in the place started seeming sort of unreal, I began, in a bizarre way, to feel as if the teachers were like human beings. At least, more like human beings than the students.

Once, I was wandering around, aimlessly avoiding some lesson that wouldn't really have been a lesson anyway, when through the window of a classroom, I saw an argument between a fifth-former and Mr Dunford. I could see that the boy's neighbour was counting seconds on his watch. In other words, they were having make-Mr Dunford-angry-enough-to-move-his-belly-off-the-table races.

Watching this familiar sight, strange thoughts started floating around in my head. I looked at Mr Dunford and thought, he's not *that* fat. Maybe he likes his food: is that a crime? What's the point in hating him? When he's not being wound up, he's actually an OK guy. Boring, maybe, but not evil. Not a bastard. Just some bloke who's not that interesting, and who ended up as a teacher.

I don't know what it was that started putting thoughts like that into my head, but it was very depressing. I felt like I was having some kind of premature menopause, or something. Honestly. Losing the desire to take the piss out of teachers made me feel like there was a leak in my testosterone tank. I felt as if a vital aspect of my hunter-gatherer instinct was eroding. The whiff of teacher-blood no longer awoke my killer instinct, but made me feel like shaking my head, and tutting about obnoxious boys.

Me. Tutting. Can you believe it?

Baldness is next, I thought. And before I know it, my belt will be propping up my nipples.

CHAPTER FORTY-SEVEN

In a school environment, it is useful to have some way of expressing physical dominance over a weaker person without having to resort to a fight. The most common way of doing this was with a wedgie. A wedgie, in case you don't already know, is a mild form of torture which is carried out by reaching your hand into the back of someone's trousers, getting hold of their pants, then pulling upwards as hard as you can. It sounds harder to perform than it is. When someone isn't expecting an attack, it's remarkably easy to get a firm grip on their underwear. Try it sometime – it really is fun.

The worst wedgie I ever saw was in the fourth form, when I walked into the rugby changing rooms, and saw a boy, aged about thirteen, dressed in full school uniform, hanging from a peg by his Y-fronts. I am telling you this because that boy's plight best conveys how I felt during my last term at school. I was in limbo, dangling, angry but resigned, waiting for rescue, knowing that whatever I did, I wasn't going to look cool.

Then, after almost four weeks of waiting for Barry to come and unhook me, I suddenly realized why we weren't communicating.

He was afraid of me. I thought about all the time we had spent together, and all the things I knew about him. I remembered how we'd even shared a bed together in France, and I realized that he *couldn't* be gay. It wasn't possible. We used to be the same – he had been right about that – we had both had doubts, and maybe we had even been a bit obsessed with each other – but that was only natural in an all-male environment. Everyone goes through a phase like that. You just have to wait until you come through it, as a normal person.

I realized that Barry wasn't being mature. He was, as usual, being stupid. He was a year behind me, and he was confusing a phase with the real thing. And *that* was why he was avoiding me – because we knew each other too well, and I would have blown the gaff. I could see through him.

I'm not being homophobic, or anything – I realize that some people are gay, maybe even my brother, but not *Barry*. It wasn't possible.

I remembered all the stupid things he had done, and everything made sense. He had always been the kind of person who took things too far – he had always taken himself too seriously. He always wanted to be *different*. And he was avoiding me because I reminded him that he wasn't different. He was like me. He was normal.

If I could just talk to him, if I could force him to listen while I explained to him what he was doing, I knew that I would be able to get him back.

CHAPTER FORTY-EIGHT

In the last two weeks before half term, I started keeping an eye on him. At lunch-times I watched from a distance to see where he went, looking for an opportunity to catch him on his own, in a place where he couldn't run away.

With only a couple of days to go before school broke up, I saw an opportunity. It wasn't perfect, but it would do. I caught sight of Barry and Robert Levin taking the path out to Pike's Water together. Barry may not have been alone, but at least he was heading somewhere private, where we would be able to talk.

I followed at a discreet distance, crouching behind bushes so that they wouldn't see me if they turned around. I couldn't get out of my head the feeling that this was, in some way, my last chance.

They walked all the way to Pike's Water without noticing me. When they got there, I hid behind a tree and watched them. They sat down on the far side of the pond, and talked. I watched for several minutes, my heart beating faster and faster.

I had to go and speak to him. If I could only explain . . .

Then, suddenly, watching Barry look so comfortable with someone new, a horrible, painful emotion swept over me. It wasn't rational – I didn't know where it had come from or what it meant, but for the first time in my life, I hated myself.

I sat down, leaning against a trunk. My face was dotted with sweat. Now I was facing away from Barry, staring through the trees, looking back towards the school. Slowly, the wave of emotion dissolved into one, clear thought. I needed Barry back. But Barry didn't need me.

I stood up, blinked, hesitated for a moment, then walked across the footbridge to where Barry and Levin were sitting. When Barry caught sight of me, he stood up and tried to walk away, but Levin grabbed his sleeve and pulled him back down.

'Hi,' I said.

Neither of them answered.

'Barry?'

He didn't look up.

My body was shaking. I didn't know what to do. I almost needed to sit down.

'Barry?'

He still ignored me. I tried to think of what I would have said a few months ago, if I had been trying to stop him sulking.

'Bazza?'

No response.

'Bottom?'

A flicker of a smile.

I touched him on the shoulder, but he still wouldn't look at me.

'I'm sorry,' I said.

He looked up. It was the first time he had caught my eye since our argument.

'Barry – please. What do you want me to do, for fuck's sake?' Then I felt this thing – not a tear, but a kind of wetness in my eyes. I tried to blink it away, but that just made it worse.

When I saw the effect it had on Barry, though, I realized that I had done something right. He was stunned. He stared at me as if . . . as if he was impressed, or something.

For a while, he just watched; then he stepped forward, and put his arms around me. Just like that.

Funnily enough, that was the first time we had ever hugged.

When I opened my eyes, I saw Levin standing opposite me, looking hilariously pissed off.

'Barry,' he said. 'What do you think you're doing?'

'Fuck off home, Levin. This has got fuck all to do with you, you little cunt,' I said.

As soon as I had spoken, I regretted it. Barry took a step back, and I saw him look at Levin, nervously.

'See?' said Levin. 'You see what he's like?'

Barry sat down on a tree stump, and ran his fingers slowly through his hair. He thought for a minute, then let out a little snort of a laugh.

'What?' I said.

'Dunno. At least you're consistent, I suppose.'

'What are you on about?'

'He means,' said Levin, 'that you're a selfish, self-obsessed, mean-spirited, homophobic egomaniac. I'm paraphrasing, here, but that's the basic drift of it.'

'Will you just fuck off!'

'Don't get angry with *me* – they're his ideas. Personally, I think you're exactly the kind of guy I would want by my side when my father died, my mother had a nervous breakdown, I got chucked out of school and I tried to come out as gay. I think you'd be really supportive.'

'Robert,' said Barry. 'Please.'

There was an awkward silence. I didn't even know about his mother's nervous breakdown. I would have asked, but I was too angry.

'What have you been saying about me, Barry? I don't believe this,' I said.

He didn't say anything.

'You're meant to be my friend, you arsehole.'

Then we just stared at each other, not speaking. The conversation had somehow gone in a bizarre direction. I wanted to say something about his mum, but I couldn't think of a way to phrase it that wouldn't sound stupid. You're meant to send your love, I knew that, but I'd only met her a few times – I obviously didn't love her, so I didn't know what to say – I didn't know how to say it. And I didn't want to back down, either. It wasn't my turn to apologize. Barry had ditched me and pissed off with someone else – for the second time – and the tosser was waiting for *me* to apologize. I definitely wasn't going to back down.

When the silence became too embarrassing, though, I just had to speak.

'Are you cheating on my brother, then?' I said.

Barry laughed through his nose again. He was in serious danger of losing his sex appeal if he carried on like that.

'Nice one, Mark,' he said.

It sounded almost affectionate, which was weird.

'We're just friends,' said Levin. 'Try looking it up in the fucking dictionary.'

'Barry – I really can't talk to you with this tosser standing here.'

'That's OK, then, because I don't think there's a lot more to say.'

'What? Is that it then? Now that you've slagged me off, you feel satisfied, do you?'

'I haven't slagged you off, Mark.'

'I suppose this little prick made up all that stuff, then, did he?'

'No.'

'Then you've slagged me off, haven't you? I get cross with you – once – by accident, and you just use it as an excuse to run away like a little fucking girl, choose a new prick of a best friend to hold hands with in the playground, and you giggle away together, bitching about me behind my back. You're . . . you're just –'

'I haven't been bitching about you, Mark.'

'No, of course you haven't – in fact it sounds like you've been really fucking complimentary.'

'I don't enjoy criticizing you, Mark. I really don't. But I am allowed to tell my friend how I feel. You never took me seriously. You always let me down. You – . . .'

'Jesus, Barry – you're so full of hippie shit these days.'

'If that's what you want to call it,' he said.

There was another long, embarrassing silence.

'Wanker,' I said.

'Tosser,' he said.

'Arsehole,' I said.

'Prick,' he said.

'Poof,' I said.

'Cunt,' he said.

'Twat,' I said.

'Shitface,' he said.

'Baboon,' I said.

'Platypus,' he said.

'Filet O'Fish,' I said.

'Cuddly toy,' he said.

'Washing machine,' I said.

'Electric ice-cube dispenser,' he said.

'Twig,' I said.

'Abraham Lincoln's last fart in a bottle,' he said.

'The complete prose of Cilla Black in four volumes,' I said.

He smiled.

'You do realize that I think you're an arsehole,' he said.

'Oh yes,' I said. 'I think you've made that abundantly clear.'

'Good,' he said.

'And I hope you appreciate that you are the biggest jerk I have ever met,' I said.

'Absolutely,' he said.

'Good,' I said.

He looked at me, smiling and not smiling at the same time. Then he took Levin by the arm, and they walked away, through the trees.

I sort of thought that we had made up – that it had been a pretend argument rather than a real one. But the strange thing is, Barry never really spoke to me again.

I suppose I ought to come over all mature here, and wring my hands over how badly I let Barry down, and how I'm a crap person – oh woe is me, blah, blah, blah – but I really can't be bothered with all that, because Barry was just as crap towards me as I was towards him. I might have started the whole thing off, but I certainly tried my hardest to fix things up again, and he just didn't let it happen. So I stand by the belief that he behaved like a little girl.

I'm better off without him.

And I still think I could have cured him. If Levin hadn't turned up and ruined everything, Barry would have accepted my apology, then I could have set about getting him back again. I wanted to help him.

And I do still get on with my brother, which proves that I'm not homophobic.

CAST IRON
COOKING FOR
VEGETARIANS

{ *Also by Joanna Pruess:* }

The Supermarket Epicure: *The Cookbook for Gourmet Food at Supermarket Prices*

D'Artagnan's Glorious Game Cookbook

Eat Tea/Tea Cuisine: *A New Approach to Flavoring Contemporary and Traditional Dishes*

Supermarket Confidential: *The Secrets of One-Stop Shopping for Delicious Meals*

Soup for Every Body: *Low Carb, High Protein, Vegetarian and More*

Fiamma: *The Essence of Contemporary Italian Cooking (with Michael White)*

Seduced by Bacon: *Recipes and Lore about America's Favorite Indulgence*

Mod Mex: *Cooking Vibrant Fiesta Flavors at Home (with Scott Linquist)*

Cast Iron Cookbook: *Delicious and Simple Comfort Food*

CAST IRON
COOKING FOR
VEGETARIANS

JOANNA PRUESS

PHOTOGRAPHY BY BATTMAN

Skyhorse Publishing

Skyhorse Publishing books may be purchased in bulk at special discounts for
sales promotion, corporate gifts, fund-raising, or educational purposes. Special
editions can also be created to specifications. For details, contact the Special Sales
Department, Skyhorse Publishing, 307 West 36th Street, 11th Floor, New York,
NY 10018 or info@skyhorsepublishing.com

www.skyhorsepublishing.com

Library of Congress Cataloging-in-Publication Data is available on file.

ISBN 978-1-62914-324-8

All photography by Battman, except for istockphoto images on pages 115, 189, and
190 and shutterstock on page 214.

Printed in China

To Nicole, Ben, and Justin: You are, as always, my source of pride and inspiration.

And for my late mother, Harriet Rubens, who worked very hard to remember those recipes from so long ago.

"One is considered fortunate nowadays if by chance one of these iron utensils is handed down to them from the second to the third generation."

—*Aunt Ellen*

CONTENTS

LUNCHEON & OTHER NIBBLES

1

VEGETABLES & OTHER SIDES

23

MAIN COURSES 45

DESSERTS 67

SAUCES & STOCKS 91

APPENDIX 102

Acknowledgments

My profound thanks go to:

First, Ann Treistman, my wonderful editor at Skyhorse Publishing, for another timely idea that evoked many happy memories, and for shepherding this project through with passion and wisdom;

Alan Batt (Battman) for your evocative photographs, easy disposition, and for going far beyond the call of duty to make the food look so real and tempting;

LeAnna Weller Smith, designer, for perfectly capturing the spirit of yesterday and today in this book and your generous, creative spirit;

David G. Smith—a.k.a. the Pan Man—for expert guidance in all matters relating to cast-iron cookware, including the history and care, and for loaning me archival materials;

Joel Schif—a prominent disciple of antique cast-iron cookware, and generous source of printed materials and information;

and to Jane Crosen for your copyediting and amusing, informative insights.

Thanks to the following for your pots and palates, testing and other useful thoughts:

Haejin Baek, Michael Berk, Sarah and Glenn Collins, Moira Crabtree, James Derek, Joe DiMaggio, Jr., Bobbie D'Angelo, Teresa Farney, Dianne Flamini, Lucio Galano and Louis Valantasis, Clara, Tony and the entire Grande family, Pam and John Harding, Elyse and John Harney, Bob Lape, Deb Lape Lackowski, Lisa Ligas, Stephen and Sally Kahan, Carole and Winston Kulok, Sally and Gene Kofke, Geri and Kit

Laybourne, Michael Pesce, Jane and Jack Quigley, Wendy Raymont, Janet Roth, Dick Saphir, Kathy and Tim Scheld, Anne Semmes, Roberta and Sandy Teller, Debbie Lewis, and Judi Arnold of Dufour Pastry.

Thanks to Rick Waln who has helped me in so many different ways.

Finally, to the relatives, acquaintances, and friends over the years who left us recipes and happy food memories. . . .

Introduction

Life certainly seems more challenging today, even compared with just a few years ago. Whether those earlier times were ever really kinder and gentler, or just rose-colored dreams, is debatable. For whatever the reasons, these days many of us crave the comfort of the familiar in one form or another. That yearning is most obvious in our food choices: simplicity is the new sophistication and fussy fare seems dated.

Mac and cheese—just like Mom's or dressed up—appears on restaurant menus. Even in fancier restaurants, some homey dishes like Brussels sprouts are served in the same cast-iron ramekins and casseroles in which they are cooked, sometimes smugly sharing the table with Limoges porcelain.

Old-fashioned fare and cookware not only satisfy our hunger, on a primal level they reassure us by their link to the past . . . and seem so right for today.

Old Is Newsworthy

Long before my great-grandmother simmered chicken and dumplings in her Dutch oven, cast-iron cookware was appreciated. The Chinese began melting and forming the metal into vessels in the sixth century BCE. By the Middle Ages, tools and cookware that were cast in iron were so valuable they were listed as hereditary property in European estates; and in the fifteenth century, three-legged, dark gray iron cauldrons were common in hearths and fireplaces.

The pots arrived in the New World with the earliest European settlers. By the mid-nineteenth century, as Americans pushed beyond the Mississippi River across the plains to the Old West, thousands of pioneers hitched their oxen or mules to covered wagons. Often, a thick-walled pot with a tight-fitting lid—the Dutch oven—was on the back of each chuck wagon. It was essential for cooking meals.

For the forty-niners who went to California during the Gold Rush, "cooking was in black iron spiders (monumental cast iron frying pans on legs, originally designed for open hearth cooking and now pressed into service over the campfire) and Dutch ovens. Meals were dished up with the sky as roof and the earth as dining table, around a fire of sage, twigs, or buffalo chips," writes Ann Chandonnet in *Gold Rush Grub: From Turpentine Stew to Hoochinoo*, (University of Alaska Press, 2006).

David G. Smith, a pre-eminent cast-iron cookware historian (a.k.a. the Pan Man), veteran collector, and co-founder of the Wagner and Griswold Society (www.wag-society.org), says that the first piece of cast-iron cookware made in the American Colonies was a small kettle cast in 1642, in Lynn, Massachusetts.

Today, celebrated chefs and cooks like Emeril Lagasse, Tom Colicchio, and Martha Stewart are among many who have joined the cast-iron bandwagon as enthusiastic advocates.

Why Cast-Iron Now?

Teresa Farney, a friend and food editor of the Colorado Springs *Gazette*, asks: "Do you really need to dish out hundreds of dollars for designer-label, high-end cookware when there's good old cast-iron around? Durable, functional, and relatively inexpensive, cast-iron has so much going for it, it's a wonder more cooks don't use it. Maybe it's because cast-iron seems so old-fashioned compared to all the modern-looking $300-plus industrial cookware sets."

"Among its strengths is that the heavy metal retains heat well, which helps food cook quickly and evenly," Farney adds. The reason many people say that they buy a large black skillet in the first place is because they remember their mom or grandmother using it to make the best fried chicken and wonderfully crusty loaves of breads. As a result of that weight—the cookware's only major drawback—the pans take longer to heat up than, say, stainless steel or aluminum. A quick rule of thumb is to allow 3 to 4 ½ minutes, depending how hot the recipe says the pan should be. Since the handles are also made of metal, they also get hot, so a mitt is essential.

Cast-iron pots and pans are ideal for braising comfort-style dishes over low heat, as well as searing foods over high heat on top of the stove and then finishing them in the oven. Throughout this book, I use every cooking technique from searing and sweating foods to simmering and frying—both deep fat and pan-frying—as well as caramelizing. The cookware can also go directly from the stove to the table.

Another friend, Marguerite Thomas, who writes for the Los Angeles Times International Syndicate, adds that the pans are wonderful on an induction cooktop, unlike those made of either copper or aluminum, which do not conduct (or "induce") magnetic energy from the cooktop and thus can't cause metal vessels to heat up. The only place cast-iron doesn't work is in a microwave.

With regards to what can be cooked in cast-iron, I say just about everything. When I was just learning to cook with cast-iron, I remember being told not to use the pans for tomatoes or other acidic foods because the metal can discolor or turn them bitter. Over the years, however, and especially while testing the recipes in this book, my experience has been that if the pan is well seasoned, this isn't a problem. That said, when cooking a lot of tomatoes, where using cast-iron serves no real purpose in the recipe and/or the sauce is made separately anyway, I'd use a non-reactive skillet or pan, such as stainless steel. What I wouldn't do is store cooked foods for a long time in the pots.

Once cast-iron pans are seasoned (see pages xxiii to xxvi) and with minimal care—basically wiping and drying them over low heat, then spreading a thin layer of shortening or even non-stick vegetable spray over them—they improve with use, developing that shiny surface that makes them so good for nonstick cooking without added fat. Their biggest foe is being ignored.

The pans are also an investment in the future and the health of our planet: Long after many expensive pots and pans (especially those with nonstick surfaces which can deteriorate over high heat) have been discarded, your cast-iron cookware will be serviceable and can be passed down to future generations. Even those that have been seriously abused can be cleaned and re-seasoned, and there are tons of gray iron pots and pans in attics and at yard sales waiting to be adopted.

Incidentally, did you ever hear of anyone in your grandparents' generation with anemia? "Iron-poor blood" was pretty rare, since the tiny bit of iron that reacts with food supplies that essential nutrient to stave off the deficiency.

Craving Foods from Yesteryear

As for why we are craving comfort food now, John DeLucie, the chef at The Waverly Inn in New York, writes in his memoir, *The Hunger* (HarperCollins, 2009), "After 9-11, New Yorkers were hankering for a nostalgic take on American dishes from a more innocent time. Nothing too fancy or 'chefy' as the partners liked to say," referring to how he made his mac and cheese exceptional with truffles shaved on top.

"Real" foods—even if somewhat embellished—don't require mental gymnastics to appreciate. Their aromas and tastes can carry us back to more reassuring days shared with family and friends. Like the bite of tea-soaked madeleine that opened the floodgates to Marcel Proust's past, my re-creation of Tamale Pie—a favorite cornbread topped Tex-Mex casserole—instantly transports me back to my childhood in Los Angeles. Similarly, while I've removed the chicken or skirt steak from my Vegetarian Fajitas, those satisfying rolls remain satisfying memories of my youth.

From the earliest days, Americans have used cast-iron skillets to bake desserts like Raspberry-Blackberry Crisp and Ginger-Spice-Topped Peach Cobbler because they are simple and the results are so rewarding. The same is true of the German Apple Pancake or *pfannkuchen* I used to make to the delight of my kids. As for Apple-Cherry Tarte Tatin, the renowned French upside-down fruit tart recalls my years in Paris.

Connections to the Past and Future from around the World

Today the tradition of America as a melting pot continues as new flavors and dishes are introduced with each wave of immigrants. Because of these newcomers, the media, and advances in transportation and technology, we have more diverse ingredients available and we are more open to new preparations. Dishes that once were difficult to re-create are being made with ease across our country.

Yet, for many of us, time remains the biggest challenge to preparing good meals, and I appreciate ways to cut corners without compromising the quality of the food. In some recipes, I use conveniences items that didn't exist until fairly recently. For example, the all-butter puff pastry I buy for the Provençal Onion, Tomato, and Olive Tart and for Tarte Tatin helps me to make these dishes more easily and better; and high-quality purchased pizza dough and sauce put the "easy" in Easy Chicago-Style Pizza. Lest you think that most cast-iron dishes take a lot of time, I suggest you try Crustless Zucchini, Mushroom, and Cheddar Quiche for Two or the amazingly simple Chocolate Omelet Soufflé. It's not only quick to make, it's a decadently delicious dessert.

Through sharing recipes with old and new friends, I realize that we can derive comfort from unfamiliar dishes as well as those we already know, so long as they please our palates and don't seem like work to understand. When I perceive a link to how foods of different cultures are woven into our collective palate, they become more exciting to me.

These days, I enjoy exploring vegetarian dishes like Kale, Chick-peas, Yam, and Couscous Stuffed Bell Peppers. Even friends with hearty appetites find the dish extremely satisfying. These foods are homey and nurturing in tough times. I've also included Posole, a simple stew made with hominy, corn, and tofu, from the Native Americans of our Southwest.

Vegetable lovers (and even those who aren't) will find that cooking in cast iron coaxes flavors that are unachievable and more appealing than those resulting from any other cooking methods. Try Oven-Roasted Asparagus with Macadamia Nuts or Brussels Sprouts with Pistachios.

A Return to Home Cooking

Finally, if the economy has a bright side, it's that this austere climate has brought people back to their kitchens and dining tables. Today we are participating more in our food choices and once again entertaining friends and family at home, often in more relaxed settings. And "the more people cook, the healthier they are," says Michael Pollan, the award-winning author of *In Defense of Food* (Penguin Press, 2009).

I believe many of us want to recapture a sense of community and sharing that may have been lost over time. Cast-iron cooking is both a simple and rewarding way to start, as I hope you discover in this book.

—Joanna Pruess
New York, New York
November, 2013

Cleaning & Seasoning Cast-Iron Cookware

By David G. Smith, a.k.a. The Pan Man™

With proper care, your iron cookware will last forever and will require very little maintenance. If you have acquired a brand new pan, the manufacturer may have stated that it is "pre-seasoned." In most cases, this pre-seasoning is temporary. You will need to build up that seasoned surface. In this brief tutorial, I'll explain how to clean old pans, including rusted pans; how to season pans; and general cleaning and maintenance.

Initial Cleaning

CAUTION: Wear rubber gloves and eye protection while doing this!

Let's begin with an old piece of cast iron that is dirty, cruddy with burned-on food residue, and perhaps also slightly rusted. To initiate the cleaning process, begin by spraying the pan with oven cleaner, putting it in a plastic bag, and tying it shut. The bag will keep the oven cleaner from drying out, so it will continue to work. Leave the pan as it is for two or three days.

Then remove it from the bag, and scrub it with a brush—my favorite is a brass brush I found at the automotive counter of my local hardware store. This brush is marketed for cleaning white wall tires. It is just the right size for doing pans. You can also find brass brushes at the grocery store in the kitchenware aisle or even in your drugstore.

If all the burned on grease doesn't come off on this first try, repeat the process with the bag and the oven cleaner, concentrating the cleaner to the troublesome areas.

For cleaning many pieces at one time, you can prepare a soaking solution of one and a half gallons of water to one (18-ounce) can of lye in a plastic container. Lye, like oven cleaner, is very caustic and will burn you. Always wear rubber gloves.

Mix enough solution in the plastic container to cover the items to be cleaned. Leave the pieces in the soak for about five days; then scrub the pieces. You can use the lye mixture several times. (Be careful not to use oven cleaner or lye on aluminum, finished wooden handles, pans with porcelain or enameled finishes as they will be destroyed.)

Finish the cleaning process as above.

I DO NOT recommend the following methods of cleaning:

- **Open fire:** The intense heat can severely warp or even crack the piece.
- **Self-cleaning oven:** Although this doesn't hold as great a risk as throwing it in a fire, the intense heat of a self-cleaning oven can warp a skillet. There is also a risk of cracking the piece.
- **Sandblasting:** This is the cardinal sin for collectors. Sandblasting destroys the patina making the piece a dull gray color. Most collectors will not buy a piece that has been sandblasted.

To Remove Rust

Buff the pan with a fine wire wheel of an electric drill. Crusted rust can then be dissolved by soaking the piece in a solution of equal amounts of white vinegar and water for a few hours. Don't leave it longer than overnight without checking it. This solution will eventually eat the iron!

It is now important to neutralize and stop the action of the vinegar so it won't continue to attack the iron. To do this, apply the oven cleaner again and let the piece soak overnight. You can also soak the piece overnight in an alkaline solution, such as washing soda, which is available in the cleaning department of most supermarkets and some hardware stores. Scrub the piece in dish detergent and hot water before seasoning.

Seasoning

After removing the burned-on grease, you are ready to season the piece. Preheat the oven to 125°F. This removes any moisture in the oven which could condense on the cold skillet, leaving a very fine gold or rust color.

Heat the piece in the preheated oven for about 15 minutes or until hot. Carefully remove the hot pan and apply shortening all over it. I prefer solid Crisco, but you can also ghee. I don't recommend oil, but it can be used. Solid Crisco will flow right on. Of course, you have to use a hot pad or rag to hold them.

Return the pots to the oven right side up and raise the temperature to 225°F. Leave them in the oven for 30 minutes, then remove and wipe off any pooled shortening, leaving the piece still shining wet. The timing is important here because if you leave them in the oven too long, the shortening begins to thicken.

Return the pieces to the oven for another 30 minutes. Remove and let them cool down for 10 to 15 minutes or until they are very warm but not too hot to work with, then wipe them to a dull shine. If the shiny surface resists wiping, the pan is too cool. The initial seasoning should be accomplished at this point. However, typical of cast-iron cookware, the more you use it (and don't abuse it) the better it will be.

It is generally recommended that you cook fatty foods in the pan the first few times you use it as this adds to the seasoning process. This goes for new pre-seasoned pans as well.

Before adding any fat to the pan when you're cooking, heat the pan for 3 ½ to 4 minutes over medium to high, until hot but not smoking, unless otherwise indicated in the recipe.

Routine Care

CAUTION: DO NOT put cold water in a hot pan! Cold water will crack a hot pan!

DO NOT use detergent to clean a cast-iron pan after cooking with it. That will destroy the seasoning. Instead, put hot water in the pan and bring it to a boil. Let the pan soak for several minutes, then wipe it out with a paper towel. If something sticks, scrape it with a spoon to dislodge it. Do not use a Brillo or other abrasive metal pads to scour the pan as they cut into the seasoned surface.

Next, reheat the pan and apply a fine coating of shortening, oil, or even a non-stick spray, such as Pam. It should just wet the surface and shouldn't run. Wipe off enough of the heated oil to leave the pan with a dull shine. As you use the piece and continue with this maintenance seasoning process, your pan will develop a nice black patina and a stick-free surface.

If you follow these suggestions, you'll be able to pass on your favorite skillets to your children and grandchildren! I know they last—I've been collecting cast iron for more than thirty years and currently buy and sell at www.panman.com. In addition, I coauthored *The Book of Griswold & Wagner* and *The Book of Wagner & Griswold*.

"The secret of good cooking is largely a matter of developing and enhancing the natural food flavors which the Griswold Dutch Oven does so well, because it retains the steam and conserves the natural juices of all foods cooked."

—Aunt Ellen

About Aunt Ellen

> *Write "Aunt Ellen," at the Griswold Kitchen, any time you want advice about recipes, or want more recipes, or want to know more about "Waterless Cooking" or Griswold "Waterless Utensils." The Aunt Ellen service is always free. The Griswold Mfg. Company, Erie, Pa.*

Aunt Ellen was "born" in the 1920s, when Miss M. Etta Moses began fielding letters received at the Griswold Manufacturing Company about the use and care of the brand's cookware utensils.

She soon began offering recipes and advice on cooking with cast-iron, under the pen name "Aunt Ellen." Griswold's commercial cookware lines were founded around that time, and after World War II included complete kitchenware packages, so there was a need for a woman's voice in their ranks.

Aunt Ellen became so well-known that stacks of mail came across her desk every day for her hints and advice. And continued to do so for twenty-five years.

Miss M. Etta Moses died in 1948, after more than fifty years as a Griswold employee.

Her recipes and advice, included throughout this book, are as helpful and as much fun to read as they were nearly a century ago.

CAST IRON

COOKING FOR

VEGETARIANS

LUNCHEON & OTHER NIBBLES

Mom's Mac and Cheese
Serves 8

When I was growing up, my mother made scrumptious macaroni and cheese with creamy sauce, sautéed onions, paprika, and loads of Tillamook or sharp Cheddar cheese. My siblings and I loved it, especially the crunchy-cheesy topping. Mom baked the casserole in the cast-iron Dutch oven she received as a wedding present. I prefer to use a 10-inch skillet.

When I added Parmesan cheese and panko bread crumbs to the topping, my kids and friends attacked that mac with a vengeance, thus it took on the name "macattacaroni." My favorite pasta for this is cellentani, a tubular cork-screw shape that has a ridged surface.

Preheat your oven to 350°F. Bring a large pot of salted water to a boil. Add the pasta and cook until al dente, about 10 minutes; drain and set aside.

Meanwhile, heat a 10-inch Dutch oven or skillet over medium-high heat until hot. Add the oil and onions and cook until they are golden, about 4 minutes.

Add the butter and, when melted, stir in the flour and cook until lightly colored, about 3 minutes, stirring constantly. Whisk in the milk and bring to a boil, stirring until smooth. Reduce the heat and simmer for 10 minutes

INGREDIENTS

½ pound uncooked elbow macaroni, cellentani, or other tubular pasta

1 medium yellow onion, peeled and diced

1 Tablespoon vegetable oil

1 to 2 Tablespoons unsalted butter

3 Tablespoons unbleached all-purpose flour

3 ¼ cups whole milk

4 cups (1 pound) shredded sharp Cheddar cheese

1 teaspoon salt or to taste

1 teaspoon paprika

Freshly ground black pepper

½ cup grated Parmigiano-Reggiano cheese

⅓ cup panko bread crumbs, found in the Asian food section of supermarkets

or until the sauce thickens, stirring occasionally. Add 3 cups of the cheese and stir until it has melted. Stir in the macaroni and season with paprika, salt, and pepper to taste.

Combine the remaining cup of Cheddar, the Parmigiano-Reggiano, and panko crumbs in a bowl. Spoon the mixture over the macaroni and bake for 30 minutes or until the top is golden brown. If it is not browned enough, turn the broiler on and cook for 3 to 4 minutes longer, watching carefully that it doesn't burn. Remove the casserole and cool for 5 minutes before serving.

Note: Try the following mac and cheese additions: diced, canned, or chopped sun-dried tomatoes; a small white truffle thinly shaved and/or white truffle oil.

Provençal Onion, Tomato, and Olive Tart (Pissaladière)

Serves 4 to 6

Pissaladières are popular pizza-like snacks in the south of France. Some of the most delicious are made with puff pastry. Although my version isn't classic, friends love the generous tangle of sautéed onions, sun-dried tomatoes, and olives baked with the flaky crust on top, like a Tarte Tatin (page 75), then flipped before serving. The thin layer of caramel accents the tangy onions. The tart is best eaten soon after baking.

INGREDIENTS

- 1 (14-ounce) package all-butter puff pastry, defrosted according to package directions
- ¾ pound yellow onions, peeled, cut in half lengthwise and thinly sliced crosswise
- 2 Tablespoons olive oil
- 2 Tablespoons white balsamic vinegar
- ½ Tablespoon herbes de Provence
- ½ teaspoon salt
- Freshly ground black pepper
- 3 Tablespoons sugar
- 1 ½ Tablespoons water
- ⅔ cup (3 ounces) sun-dried tomatoes, blotted dry and thinly sliced
- ⅓ cup (2 ounces) pitted oil-cured black olives, chopped

Preheat your oven to 425°F. Unfold the pastry and, using a circular pattern, cut it into an 11-inch round; lay the dough on a cutting board, cover with a towel, and refrigerate for hour.

Meanwhile, heat a 10-inch cast-iron skillet over medium-high heat until hot but not smoking, 3 ½ to 4 minutes. In a large bowl, combine the onions and oil; add them to the skillet and sauté over medium-low heat until they are golden, about 15 minutes, stirring often. Pour in the vinegar, raise the heat to high, and boil until the vinegar evaporates, about 30 seconds, stirring often. Scrape the onions into a bowl, then stir in the herbes de Provence, salt, and a generous amount of pepper.

Wipe out the skillet and heat it over medium-high heat. Add the sugar and water and cook until the sugar melts and turns a rich amber brown, about 5 minutes, rotating the pan to coat it evenly. Remove the skillet from the heat and spoon the onions over the caramel; scatter the tomatoes and olives evenly over the onions and lay the puff pastry on top, tucking the edges into the pan. With a sharp knife, make four or five 1-inch cuts in the top.

Bake in the middle of the oven for 10 minutes; adjust the heat down to 350°F and continue baking until the crust is puffed and golden, about 20 minutes. Remove and let it stand for 5 minutes. Run a knife around the edges of the pan to loosen the pastry, then place a 10-inch plate directly on the pissaladière and flip it out. Replace any ingredients that remain in the pan. With a serrated knife, cut the pissaladière into wedges and serve.

My Favorite Deep-Dish Vegetarian Pizza

Serves 4 as a main course

This substantial deep-dish pizza of broccoli, sun-dried tomatoes, olives, and artichoke hearts is topped with mozzarella and a final shower of fresh basil leaves. To me, this is comfort food. The cheese sprinkled over most of the ingredients prevents the ingredients from burning or drying out. Be sure to let the pizza rest once it comes from the oven; this way, the pizza will easily slide out of the skillet, and you won't burn your mouth.

INGREDIENTS

1 pound pizza dough, defrosted in the refrigerator, if frozen (see the recipe notes on page 10)

2 Tablespoons olive oil

1 small yellow onion, peeled and thinly sliced crosswise

1 cup purchased Italian tomato pasta sauce

2 large cloves garlic, peeled and minced

2 cups small broccoli florets, cooked

½ cup (2 ounces) sun-dried tomatoes in oil, blotted on paper towels and thinly sliced

⅓ cup (2 ounces) pitted oil-cured olives, chopped

1 ½ teaspoons dried oregano, crushed

Pinch of red pepper flakes, crushed (optional)

2 cups (½ pound) shredded low-moisture mozzarella

1 (6.5-ounce) jar marinated and quartered artichoke hearts, drained and blotted on paper towels

2 Tablespoons grated Parmigiano-Reggiano

2 Tablespoons julienned fresh basil leaves

Remove the dough from the refrigerator about 1 hour before starting to prepare the pizza. Preheat your oven to 500°F and position the rack in the lower third of the oven.

Heat a 10-inch cast-iron skillet over medium-high heat until hot but not smoking, 3 ½ to 4 minutes. Add 1 Tablespoon of the oil and the onions and sauté until they are limp and golden brown, about 3 minutes;

remove with a slotted spoon to a bowl. Wipe out the skillet and brush the bottom and sides with oil.

Work the dough into a disc about 12 inches in diameter, pressing from the center outwards with your fingertips and gently stretching it. Lay it in the skillet and gently push it up the sides, taking care not to tear it. If the dough extends over the edges, trim it even with the pan. The sauce will help hold it up.

Ladle on the sauce, spreading it with a spatula to within ½ inch of the edges; add the garlic, onion, broccoli, sun-dried tomatoes, and olives followed by the oregano, pepper flakes, and finally the mozzarella. Bake for 15 minutes; then add the artichoke hearts, sprinkle on the cheese, adjust the heat down to 400°F, and cook until the cheese is bubbling and golden brown, 8 to 10 minutes.

Remove the pizza from the oven and let cool for at least 15 minutes. Then, using a wide metal spatula, slide the pizza onto a cutting board. Sprinkle on the basil and, if desired, brush the crust with the remaining oil, then slice and serve.

Swiss Cheese and Apple Frittata

Serves 4 to 5 as a first course or light main course

When I first started making frittatas, they were usually with sautéed vegetables like zucchini and onions. But after developing the recipes for an article about the flat Italian omelets, I discovered numerous foods took well to the basic technique. For example, apples and cheese are often served together. I combined them with toasted almonds and onions into a savory appetizer or light main course. You can also cut a frittata into squares to serve as an hors d'oeuvre for 12 to 15 guests. In that case, you can make it ahead of time and serve it at room temperature.

INGREDIENTS

- 5 large eggs
- ½ teaspoon water
- 1 teaspoon finely chopped tarragon leaves
- ½ teaspoon salt, or to taste
- ¼ teaspoon ground nutmeg
- ⅛ teaspoon white pepper
- 2 Tablespoons unsalted butter
- 1 teaspoon canola or vegetable oil
- 1 medium yellow onion, peeled and chopped
- 2 medium Granny Smith or other tart green apples, peeled, cored, and chopped fairly fine
- ⅓ cup slivered almonds, toasted in a 350°F oven or toaster oven until lightly browned
- 1 cup (4 ounces) shredded Gruyère or other Swiss cheese
- Chopped flat-leaf parsley, to garnish

In a large bowl, beat the eggs and water together. Stir in the tarragon, salt, nutmeg, and white pepper. Preheat your oven to 350°F.

Heat a 10-inch cast-iron skillet over medium-high heat until hot but not smoking, 3 ½ to 4 minutes. Add 1 Tablespoon of the butter, the oil, and chopped onion, and sauté until the onions are golden, 3 to 4 minutes, stirring occasionally. Add the apples and cook until limp, 3 to 4 minutes. Scrape them into the egg mixture, then add the slivered almonds and mix well.

Melt the remaining 1 Tablespoon of butter over medium-high heat; pour in the egg mixture, shaking to distribute the ingredients evenly. Cook for 1 minute, then sprinkle on the cheese and adjust the heat to low. After 10 minutes, loosen the edges with a metal spatula, gradually working under the entire frittata. Shake the pan to be sure it is detached. Transfer the skillet to the oven and bake until the eggs are set, 4 to 5 minutes. Remove, cut into wedges, and serve with a little parsley on top.

Huevos Rancheros
Serves 4 to 6

The combination of Cheddar cheese, corn, onions, and pickled jalapeños makes Mexican farmer-style eggs a tasty and colorful brunch option. Roasted frying peppers, cut in half lengthwise and laid flat in the skillet to cover the bottom before the eggs are poured in, help you to easily loft out each portion. Serve with refried beans and garnish with avocado slices. Once baked, the dish can stay for at least a half an hour in a slow oven.

INGREDIENTS

2 Tablespoons canola or vegetable oil

1 yellow onion, peeled and diced

2 Tablespoons softened unsalted butter

4 slices firm white bread

4 ounces thinly sliced Swiss cheese, preferably Gruyère or other imported cheese

4 ounces mixed mushrooms, trimmed, wiped, and sliced

Preheat your oven to 400°F. Lay the peppers directly on a gas or electric burner preheated to the hottest setting and roast until the skins are completely charred on all sides, including the ends, turning with tongs. Peppers can also be roasted under a broiler. Transfer them to a paper bag, close the top and let them steam for about 10 minutes to help remove the skin. Using a paring knife or your fingers, scrape off the blackened skin. Cut them in half lengthwise and remove the stem, seeds, and membranes.

Heat a 10-inch cast-iron skillet over medium-high heat until hot but not smoking, 3 ½ to 4 minutes. Add the oil and onion and sauté until it is lightly browned, 3 to 4 minutes, stirring often. Using a slotted spoon, remove it to a large bowl. Add another Tablespoon of oil and lay the peppers in a single layer, skin-side down, covering as much of the bottom as possible.

In a large bowl, beat the eggs and milk until blended. Stir in the cheese, corn, cilantro, jalapeños, and salt and black pepper to taste. Scrape the mixture into the skillet and cook for 1 minute over medium-high heat. Adjust the heat down to medium-low and cook for 10 minutes more.

Transfer the skillet to the middle of the oven, turn the heat down to 325°F, and bake until a knife inserted into the center comes out almost clean, 22 to 25 minutes. Remove and let stand for a few minutes before cutting into wedges. Spoon on some salsa and serve with a sprig of cilantro, a few avocado slices, and some refried beans, if desired.

Note: There are many recipes for fresh and cooked tomato salsa, as well as some terrific prepared products. I often buy chunky tomato salsa and add a pinch of chipotle chile powder for a hint of smoky heat.

Croque Monsieur
Serves 2

In France, when the proverbial ham-and-cheese sandwich is grilled, it rises to new culinary heights and is called a Croque Monsieur. Some versions are dipped in egg before cooking, but I think my vegetarian version is so easy and offers almost instant gratification. I like to turn the sandwiches a couple of times to get those appealing cross-hatch grill marks on the bread.

INGREDIENTS

2 Tablespoons canola or vegetable oil

1 yellow onion, peeled and diced

2 tablespoons softened unsalted butter

4 slices firm white bread

4 ounces thinly sliced Swiss cheese, preferably Gruyère or other imported cheese

4 ounces mixed mushrooms, trimmed, wiped, and sliced

2 Tablespoons softened unsalted butter

4 slices firm white bread

4 ounces thinly sliced Swiss cheese

2 Tablespoons canola or vegetable oil

4 slices, (preferably Gruyère or other imported) cheese

4 ounces mixed mushrooms, trimmed, wiped, and sliced

1 yellow onion, peeled and diced

Dijon mustard

Heat a cast-iron skillet over medium heat. Add oil and onions and sauté until the onion is soft, 3 to 4 minutes. Add the mushrooms and cook until wilted, about 3 minutes.

Heat a cast-iron grill pan or griddle over medium heat until hot but not smoking. Butter one side of each piece of bread. Lay the slices on a cutting board with the buttered sides down. Divide the cheese evenly among the four slices (you may have to fold the slices in half to fit the bread). Place an even amount of onions and mushrooms on each slice, spread each with a generous teaspoon of Dijon mustard, and then put the remaining two cheese-covered slices on top.

Put the sandwiches in the grill pan and cook for 1 minute, pressing lightly with a spatula; then turn and cook the other side for

1 minute. Turn the sandwich back over, cook for 1 minute or until the toast is golden brown; turn again and cook until both sides are golden, rotating them about a quarter turn from where the original grill marks are to finish cooking and create those attractive cross-hatch grill marks. Remove the sandwiches from the grill, cut them into halves, and serve.

Spanish Quesadillas

Makes 8 triangles; serves 4 as an hors d'oeuvre or 1-2 for lunch

Quesadillas are typically Spanish, Mexican, or Southwestern American–style snacks made with white or whole wheat flour tortillas and melted cheese. (In Spanish, the word quesadilla means "little cheesy thing.") Once you've made a couple of quesadilla variations, you'll figure out many other possibilities. For example, these tasty triangles are filled with Spanish ingredients—Manchego cheese and jalapeños— and topped with Spanish smoked paprika.

INGREDIENTS

3 jalapeños

1 cup (4 ounces) shredded Manchego cheese

2 (10-inch) flour tortillas

Olive oil

½ Tablespoon small capers, blotted dry

Pinch of sweet Pimentón de la Vera (see note)

Heat a cast-iron skillet over medium heat. Add the jalapeños and roast until the skins are blackened. Place roasted jalapeños into a plastic bag until cool enough to handle, then remove the skins and chop.

Sprinkle half of the cheese evenly over one tortilla and cover with the jalapeños. Sprinkle on the capers, then cover with the remaining cheese and second tortilla.

Heat a 10-inch cast-iron skillet over medium heat until hot but not smoking, 3 ½ to 4 minutes; brush with a little oil. Put the filled quesadilla in the pan, brush the top with a little oil, and put a small skillet or pan on top and cook until the edges of the tortilla are browned, 2 to 3 minutes. With a wide spatula, flip the tortilla, and cook the other side until lightly browned, about 2 minutes. Remove the quesadilla, sprinkle on the Pimentón de la Vera, and let it stand for 1 minute; then cut into eighths with a pizza cutter or sharp knife, and serve.

Note: Spanish smoked paprika is known as Pimentón de la Vera. There are two varieties: sweet (*dulce*) and hot (*picante*). It is made from dried peppers that are slowly smoked over an oak fire for several weeks to impart the characteristic smoky flavor to many authentic Spanish dishes.

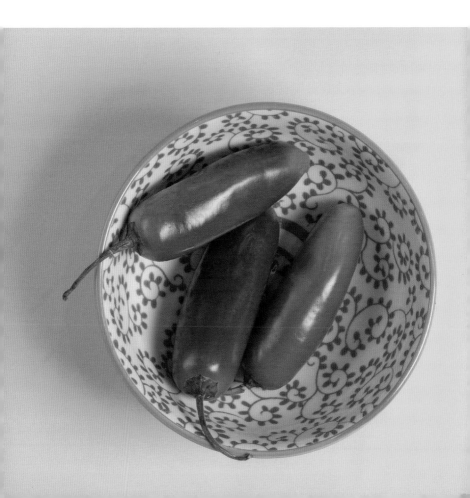

Asian Quesadillas
Makes 8 triangles; serves 4 as an hors d'oeuvre or 1-2 for lunch

Here's another global approach to quesadillas: pan-fried tortillas filled with zesty Chinese-flavored tofu topped with Jack cheese. While cheese isn't typical in Asian foods, I like this fusion of flavors.

INGREDIENTS

Canola or vegetable oil

5 ounces extra firm tofu, drained, cut into ½-inch cubes, and blotted dry on paper towels

3 Tablespoons finely chopped cilantro leaves

3 Tablespoons finely chopped scallion + thinly sliced scallion greens, to garnish

3 canned water chestnuts, finely chopped

3 Tablespoons hoisin sauce

1 ½ teaspoons soy sauce

1 teaspoon minced fresh ginger root

1 teaspoon hot chili oil

1 cup (4 ounces) shredded Monterey Jack or other mild cheese

2 (10-inch) flour tortillas

Heat a 10-inch cast-iron skillet over medium-high heat until hot but not smoking, 3 ½ to 4 minutes, and brush with 2 teaspoons of oil. Add the tofu. Cook until all sides are browned, stirring occasionally, about 5 minutes; stir in the cilantro, scallion, water chestnuts, hoisin, soy sauce, ginger, and chili oil. Scrape the mixture into a bowl and wipe out the skillet.

Heat the skillet over medium heat until hot but not smoking, 3 ½ to 4 minutes; brush with a little oil. Lightly brush one side of the first tortilla with oil and place it oiled-side down in the skillet. Spoon the meat evenly on top of the tortilla; sprinkle on the cheese and top with the second tortilla, lightly brushing the top with oil. Place a small heavy skillet (or pan with a can of food in it) on the quesadilla and cook until nicely browned, 1 to 1 ½ minutes, checking that it doesn't burn.

Turn the quesadilla and cook the other side until the cheese is melted and the tortilla is lightly browned, about 1 to 2 minutes more. Remove, cut into eighths with a pizza cutter or sharp knife, and serve.

VEGETABLES & OTHER SIDES

Mini Cast-Iron Skillet Cornbread
Serves 2 to 4

This toothsome cornbread made in a 6-inch skillet feeds two or four friends, depending on how hungry they are. Coarsely ground cornmeal, chopped jalapeños, and corn kernels add flavor and texture. I serve it with softened butter bumped up with a touch of honey or maple syrup.

A well-seasoned cast-iron skillet is essential for the crisp edges and golden brown crust. To preserve the crunchy texture, turn the bread onto a plate while still hot and leave it bottom-side up or serve it directly from the pan. This recipe is easily doubled. You'll also find those small skillets have a lot of other uses. (See note.)

Preheat your oven to 450°F. Put a 6-inch cast-iron skillet in the oven for 15 minutes to heat. Meanwhile combine the cornmeal, flour, sugar, baking powder, and salt in a bowl. Stir in the corn and jalapeños. In a separate bowl, whisk together the buttermilk, 4 Tablespoons of the butter, and the egg; stir the wet mixture into the dry ingredients until just blended.

Remove the skillet from the oven, brush with the remaining Tablespoon of butter, and spoon in the batter, smoothing the top with a metal spatula. Bake until the top of the cornbread is golden and a toothpick inserted in the center comes out clean, 23 to 25 minutes. Remove, and

INGREDIENTS

- ³⁄₄ cup coarsely ground yellow cornmeal
- ¼ cup unbleached all-purpose flour
- 1 Tablespoon sugar
- 1 teaspoon baking powder
- ½ teaspoon salt
- ½ cup defrosted frozen or canned corn kernels, drained
- 2 Tablespoons chopped pickled jalapeño peppers
- ½ cup buttermilk
- 5 Tablespoons melted unsalted butter
- 1 large egg

let stand on a rack for a few minutes before inverting (or serve the cornbread out of the pan). Serve with softened butter.

Note: Mini cast-iron skillets make appealing individual serving containers. For example, the Chocolate Chunk-Pecan Cookie Sundaes with Salted Caramel Sauce (page 96) are a decadent way to finish your dinner. Or, as Elyse Harney suggests, they are the perfect answer to breakfast for the "me generation." Elyse puts a small skillet on each of her stove's six burners and lets everyone make his or her eggs to their own taste. Some like them up; others prefer them over easy or scrambled, she says.

Sweet and Tangy Glazed Carrots with Cranberries
Serves 4

When honey and vinegar plus a handful of dried cranberries are reduced to glaze young carrots, it becomes a memorable side dish to enjoy for holidays or anytime you want a special vegetable. I like thyme honey because it adds a slightly bitter taste to the complex flavors, but any variety works. These can be made ahead and reheated.

INGREDIENTS

- 1 ½ pounds young carrots, peeled or large carrots cut lengthwise into quarters and in half widthwise
- 1 Tablespoon canola or vegetable oil
- 1 teaspoon salt
- ½ cup good-quality vegetable stock
- 1 Tablespoon unsalted butter
- ¼ cup dried cranberries
- 2 Tablespoons thyme honey or other variety
- 2 Tablespoons sherry or white wine vinegar
- 1 Tablespoon finely chopped flat-leaf parsley

Combine the carrots, oil, and salt in a bowl. Heat a cast-iron skillet large enough to hold the carrots in a single layer over medium heat until just hot, about 3 ½ minutes. Scrape the carrots into the pan oil and cook for 2 minutes, stirring once or twice. Stir in the stock and butter, cover the skillet, reduce the heat to low, and cook for 15 minutes or until the carrots are almost tender when pierced with the tip of a knife.

Remove the lid and stir in the cranberries, honey, and vinegar. Bring to a boil and cook until the liquid reduces to glaze the carrots, about 5 minutes, shaking the pan occasionally. Stir in the parsley and serve.

Glazed Butternut Squash
Serves 4 to 6

Butternut squash, luxuriously glazed with brown sugar, maple syrup, and bourbon, is so delicious, you may find everyone asking for seconds. The touch of minced fresh rosemary adds an exciting counterpoint to the sweet flavors. A few months ago I went looking for butternut squash and discovered that it is now more often sold already peeled and cubed, a welcome convenience.

Toss the squash with the oil, about 1 teaspoon of salt, and pepper to taste. Heat a 10-inch cast-iron skillet over medium-high heat until hot but not smoking, 3 ½ to 4 minutes. Add the squash and cook until lightly browned on all sides, about 5 minutes, turning often.

Add the butter, brown sugar, and maple syrup; bring to a boil, and cook until the sugar is melted, turning to coat the squash. Off the heat, carefully pour in the bourbon (it might flame) and cook until the flames subside. Cover and cook over medium heat until the squash is almost tender, about 10 minutes, then uncover and gently reduce the liquid until it glazes the squash, about 3 minutes more, turning often. Stir in the rosemary, if using, and serve.

Zucchini Pancakes
Serves 6

Many vegetables other than potatoes can be shredded and fried into tasty pancakes. I particularly like this combination of zucchini, scallions, dill, mint, feta, and pine nuts. It reminds me of a pancake-like hors d'oeuvre called mücver *that I've eaten on several occasions in Turkey. Serve the pancakes with a dab of Red Pepper–Yogurt Sauce or simply, as Turks do, with plain yogurt on top, either as a side dish or a nibble before a meal.*

In a colander, toss the zucchini with about ½ Tablespoon of salt and drain for 20 to 25 minutes. Meanwhile, prepare the Red Pepper–Yogurt Sauce, if using, and set aside.

Working in batches, squeeze the zucchini with your hands to remove as much moisture as possible, then transfer it to a kitchen towel or several layers of paper towels and squeeze again. In a bowl, combine the zucchini, eggs, scallions, dill, mint or parsley, about ½ teaspoon of salt, and a generous amount of pepper, and mix well. Stir in the flour, then add the feta, and stir to blend. Just before cooking, stir in the pine nuts.

Preheat your oven to 300°F. Line a baking sheet with paper towels and put it in the oven.

Heat a 12-inch cast-iron skillet or griddle over medium-high heat until hot. Add enough oil to coat the bottom of the pan. Drop the

INGREDIENTS

1 pound zucchini, trimmed and coarsely grated by hand or in a food processor

Coarse or kosher salt

2 large eggs, beaten

1 cup chopped scallions, including most of the green parts

⅓ cup chopped fresh dill or 1 ½ Tablespoons dried dillweed

⅓ cup chopped fresh mint or flat-leaf parsley

Freshly ground black pepper

½ cup unbleached all-purpose flour

½ cup crumbled feta cheese

½ cup pine nuts

Olive oil, for frying

Red Pepper–Yogurt Sauce (page 93)

zucchini mixture by generous soup-spoonfuls into the skillet (about 3 Tablespoons) and flatten with the back of a spatula into 3-inch discs, cooking only as many pancakes as will fit comfortably without crowding. Fry until golden brown, 2 ½ to 3 minutes, then turn and fry the other side for the same length of time. Transfer the pancakes to the baking sheet to keep warm while frying the remaining pancakes. Serve hot.

Brussels Sprouts in Olive Oil with Pistachios
Serves 4

Forget the old-fashioned notion that everyone hates Brussels sprouts. This version—or one similar to it—is served by many of today's best restaurants to great acclaim. The Brussels sprouts are blanched in salted water to keep them bright green, then finished with pistachios.

Bring a pot of salted water to a boil. Add the Brussels sprouts and cook until just tender, about 3 minutes. Drain, rinse under very cold water to stop the cooking, and blot dry on a clean towel.

Add the oil, thyme, Brussels sprouts, and pistachios to a large cast-iron skillet and cook until heated through, turning often. Season to taste with salt and pepper, and serve.

INGREDIENTS

1 pound Brussels sprouts, outer leaves removed, cored and quartered lengthwise

Kosher salt

1 ½ Tablespoons olive or vegetable oil

Leaves from 2 sprigs fresh thyme, chopped

¼ cup (2 ounces) shelled pistachios

Freshly ground black pepper

Oven-Roasted Asparagus with Macadamia Nuts

Serves 4

If you haven't tasted asparagus roasted in the oven in a cast-iron skillet, you're in for a treat. The beautiful green stalks gain a depth of flavor impossible to achieve by simply boiling or steaming. Topped with chopped macadamia nuts and a little lemon zest, they are irresistible.

INGREDIENTS

1 pound medium asparagus, woody ends snapped off

1 Tablespoon extra-virgin olive oil

Coarse sea or kosher salt and freshly ground black pepper

1 Tablespoon unsalted butter

2 Tablespoons chopped macadamia nuts

1 teaspoon grated lemon zest

Preheat your oven to 450°F. Heat a 10-inch cast-iron skillet over medium-high heat until hot but not smoking, 3 ½ to 4 minutes. Add the asparagus, oil, about ½ teaspoon salt, and black pepper to taste, and shake to coat evenly. Place the skillet in the oven and roast until the stalks are bright green and crisp-tender with little char spots, about 10 minutes (or longer if you prefer them softer), shaking the pan occasionally.

Meanwhile, melt the butter in a small skillet over medium heat. Add the macadamias and cook until lightly browned, 2 to 3 minutes, watching that they don't burn. Stir in the lemon zest and keep warm over low heat.

When the asparagus are cooked, pour on the macadamia nuts and butter, turning to coat the stalks evenly, and serve.

Cheesy Stone-Ground Grits
Serves 6

If you haven't tried slowly simmered grits, liberally laced with Cheddar cheese, you're in for a treat. Although instant and quick-cooking grits are easier to find, coarse-ground grits produce an incomparably toothy yet creamy texture and satisfying taste. Given a choice, white grits are preferable to yellow, because they are less starchy, but both are delicious.

Like hominy, grits are a Native American corn product. The dried and processed corn kernels are coarsely ground on a stone mill. In the South, devotees enjoy them at every meal from breakfast straight through dinner and dessert. I've found cooking times for grits from different suppliers can vary from under an hour to 2 hours. Stir the pot frequently, especially the bottom, with a flexible scraper and wait until after you've added the cheese to add salt.

Combine 2 cups of stock and the milk in a 10-inch cast-iron Dutch oven and bring a boil. Add the grits, stirring continuously until blended and smooth. Turn the heat down to low and simmer according to the package directions until the grits are tender, about 1 hour (some brands can take up to 2 hours), stirring frequently with a flexible scraper to prevent the grits from sticking to the bottom of the pan.

INGREDIENTS
2+ cups vegetable stock
2 cups whole milk
1 cup coarse stone-ground grits, preferably white
1 Tablespoon unsalted butter
2 cups (8 ounces) shredded sharp white Cheddar cheese
Salt
Tabasco or other hot sauce (optional)

If the mixture gets thick and starts to dry out, stir in more liquid—water or stock by ¼-cupfuls—until smooth. Once the grits are done, stir in the butter and cheese and cook until melted. Season to taste with salt and Tabasco sauce, if desired, before serving.

Blazin' Baked Beans
Serves 12

If you're a fan of baked beans with a little heat, this simple version—emboldened with chipotle chiles in adobo sauce—will assuredly excite your taste buds.

Put the beans in a large cast-iron Dutch oven with enough water to cover. Bring to a boil and cook for 3 minutes; turn off the heat, cover, and let them stand for 1 hour. Drain, cover again with water, add salt, and bring to a boil for 5 minutes, then reduce the heat to a simmer, cover, and cook for 30 minutes more. Remove from the heat, pour the beans and their liquid into a large bowl, and let them stand in the liquid until cooled.

Meanwhile, preheat your oven to 250°F.

Heat a Dutch oven over medium-high heat until hot. Add the oil and onions and sauté until golden brown, 3 to 4 minutes.

Drain the beans and combine them with the onions, chipotle chiles, mustard, brown sugar, and barbecue sauce. Add enough boiling water to just cover the beans, cover the pot, and bake for 4 hours. Remove the lid for the last 30 minutes of cooking time, or until the liquid is reduced and the beans are very tender. Taste to adjust the seasonings, adding salt if needed. Let them stand for 15 minutes before serving.

MAIN COURSES

Savory Mushroom, Spinach, and Feta Bread Pudding

Serves 6 to 8

This simple-to-make bread pudding makes a sophisticated centerpiece for brunch, lunch, or on a buffet. Serve it with a green salad, if desired.

INGREDIENTS

2 cups whole milk

5 large eggs

1 teaspoon salt

Freshly ground black pepper

8 cups day-old French or Italian bread, roughly torn into 1 ½-inch cubes

3 Tablespoons olive oil

1 large yellow onion, peeled and diced

10 ounces mixed wild mushrooms, such as cremini, shiitake, and oyster, trimmed and sliced

2 large cloves garlic, peeled and minced

1 (10-ounce) package frozen leaf spinach, defrosted and squeezed very dry

6 ounces feta cheese, crumbled

1 Tablespoon finely chopped fresh thyme leaves

Nonstick vegetable spray

¼ cup grated aged Asiago cheese

In a large bowl, beat together the milk, eggs, salt, and black pepper to taste. Stir in the bread cubes, turning to coat evenly, and let them stand until the liquid is absorbed, about 15 minutes.

Meanwhile, preheat the oven to 350°F.

Heat a 10-inch cast-iron skillet over medium-high heat until hot. Add the oil and onions and sauté until golden, about 5 minutes. Stir in the mushrooms, and continue cooking until the mushrooms are wilted, stirring or shaking the pan occasionally. Add the garlic, cook for 1 minute, and then stir in the spinach. Gently fold the mushroom mixture, feta cheese, and thyme into the bread cubes.

Wipe out the pan if necessary. Spray the pan with vegetable spray. Scrape the mixture back into the skillet and bake for 40 minutes.

Sprinkle on the Asiago cheese and continue baking until the top is puffed and golden brown, about 10 minutes. Remove from the oven and let stand for a few minutes before serving.

Moroccan Vegetable Stew with Chermoula

Serves 6 to 8

When I visited Morocco, I sampled many flavorful vegetarian dishes, such as this colorful stew. It is finished with chermoula, a piquant condiment made with herbs and spices that is used throughout North Africa. Serve over couscous and, for added zest, use a tiny amount harissa, a peppery hot Middle Eastern sauce. Typically this dish would be cooked in a tagine, a conical-shaped clay pot.

INGREDIENTS

For the stew:

¼ cup olive oil

1 medium yellow onion, peeled and grated (about ½ cup)

1 teaspoon minced garlic

1 (14-ounce) can diced tomatoes, undrained

1 teaspoon sweet paprika

½ teaspoon ground cumin

½ teaspoon ground ginger

Generous pinch saffron threads

2 cups water

2 cups (about 8 ounces) baby carrots, peeled

2 cups (about 8 ounces) peeled parsnips, cut into ½-inch slices

2 cups (about 8 ounces) peeled butternut squash, cut into ¾-inch cubes

2 cups (about 8 ounces) small turnips, peeled and cut into ½-inch cubes

6 small Yukon gold potatoes, scrubbed and cut in halves or quarters, depending on size

1 cup vegetable stock or 1 additional cup water

12 small boiling onions, peeled

1 medium zucchini, cut in half and then into 1-inch lengths

Salt and freshly ground black pepper

For the chermoula:

¾ cup packed cilantro leaves

¼ cup packed flat-leaf parsley leaves

1 Tablespoon chopped garlic

1 Tablespoon sweet or smoked paprika

1 ½ teaspoons grated fresh gingerroot

2 teaspoons ground cumin

1 teaspoon ground turmeric

1 teaspoon ground coriander

⅛ teaspoon cayenne pepper

1 ½ tablespoons olive oil

1 Tablespoon freshly squeezed lemon juice

½ teaspoon kosher salt

4 to 6 cups cooked couscous, to serve with the stew

Heat a large cast-iron Dutch oven over medium heat until hot. Add the oil, grated onion, and garlic, and sauté until softened but not brown, about 2 minutes. Stir in the tomatoes, paprika, cumin, ginger, and saffron and bring to a gentle boil.

Add the water and carrots and cook until half-way done, about 10 minutes. Add the parsnips, butternut squash, turnips, potatoes, and stock. Lay a circular piece of parchment paper over the vegetables, cover the pan, and boil gently for 10 minutes.

Add the onions and zucchini, recover, and continue cooking until the vegetables are just tender when pierced with the tip of a knife. Season to taste with salt and pepper.

Meanwhile, prepare the chermoula: In a food processor, combine the cilantro, parsley, garlic, paprika, ginger, cumin, turmeric, coriander, and cayenne and pulse until roughly chopped. Add the olive oil, lemon juice, and salt and pulse into a chunky-smooth sauce. Adjust the seasonings to taste. Stir into the stew, and simmer briefly before serving.

Easy Shepherd's Pie
Serves 8

Lovers of this classic comfort dish who prefer not to eat meat can get plenty of protein by substituting lentils. This super easy dish, made with frozen cut-up vegetables, will appeal to all ages.

INGREDIENTS

2 pounds russet potatoes, peeled and cut into 1-inch cubes

⅓ cup whole milk

3 Tablespoons unsalted butter

Freshly ground black pepper

1 cup dry brown lentils, rinsed and sorted

1 bay leaf

2 cups water

3 Tablespoons olive oil

1 yellow onion, peeled and finely diced

4 ounces white mushrooms, wiped and sliced

1 teaspoon minced garlic

3 cups mixed frozen carrots, corn, green beans, and peas, defrosted

1 (14-ounce) can diced tomatoes, drained

¼ cup chopped flat-leaf parsley

1 Tablespoon Worcestershire sauce

1 teaspoon dried oregano

Salt and freshly ground black pepper

Tabasco Sauce (optional)

¼ cup grated imported Parmesan cheese

Preheat your oven to 375°F.

In a large pot, combine the potatoes with enough water to cover. Add salt and bring to a boil. Cook until tender when pierced with the tip of a knife, about 15 minutes. Drain, return to the pan, add the milk and butter, and mash with a potato masher until smooth. Season to taste with salt and pepper, cover, and keep warm.

Meanwhile, in a small saucepan, combine the lentils and bay leaf with 2 cups of water and bring to a boil; reduce the heat and simmer until the lentils are just about tender, 15 to 20 minutes. Take care not to overcook. Drain and set aside. Remove the bay leaf.

Heat a 10- or 11-inch cast-iron skillet over medium heat until hot. Add the oil and onions and sauté until lightly colored, 5 to 6 minutes. Add the mushrooms and cook until wilted, about 3 minutes, stirring frequently. Stir in the garlic and cook for 30 seconds longer.

Return the lentils to the skillet along with the defrosted vegetables, tomatoes, parsley, Worcestershire sauce, and oregano, and mix together. Bring the mixture to a boil over high heat; adjust the heat down to a simmer and cook the vegetables until tender, about 5 minutes, stirring often. Season to taste with salt, pepper, and Tabasco Sauce, if using.

Spoon the potatoes on top of the lentil-vegetable mixture and, using the tines of a fork, make a decorative pattern in them. Drizzle on the Parmesan cheese and run the casserole briefly under the broiler until the top is lightly browned, about 5 minutes, watching that it doesn't burn. Remove, let stand for at least 10 minutes, and serve.

Mexican Mac and Cheese
Serves 6

Classic mac and cheese takes a south-of-the-border turn with the addition of a chipotle in adobo, which imparts a hint of heat, and the crushed tortillas and Cotija cheese used for the topping. It's based on a recipe from chef Ivy Stark, with whom I coauthored the two Dos Caminos cookbooks. Serve with small bowls of sliced scallions, sour cream, sliced black olives, and pickled jalapeños, if you like.

INGREDIENTS

Salt

8 ounces uncooked wagon wheel macaroni

2 Tablespoons unsalted butter

¾ cup finely chopped onion

½ tablespoon minced garlic

1 teaspoon ground cumin

½ teaspoon ground coriander

2 Tablespoons all-purpose flour

2 cups milk

1 chipotle en adobo, minced

½ cup sundried tomatoes, thinly sliced

2 ¼ cups grated sharp Cheddar cheese

1 cup grated Jack cheese

1 ½ cups crushed tortilla chips

1 ⅓ cups freshly grated Cotija cheese

Bring a large pot of salted water to a boil. Add the pasta and cook according to package directions until al dente. Remove, drain, and set aside.

Meanwhile, heat a 10-inch cast-iron skillet over medium heat until hot. Add the butter, onion, garlic, cumin, and coriander, and cook over medium-low heat, stirring often, until the onion is softened, about 7 minutes.

Preheat your oven to 350°F.

Add the flour to the onions and stir continuously for 3 minutes. Whisk in the milk and bring to a boil. Reduce the heat and simmer for 2 minutes. Add the chipotle and tomatoes and cool slightly; add the cheeses and stir until melted. Stir the pasta into the cheese mixture.

In a bowl, toss the tortilla chips and Cotija cheese together and drizzle on top of the macaroni. Bake until the dish is hot and the top is golden brown, 25 to 30 minutes. Remove and let stand for 10 minutes before serving.

Crustless Zucchini, Mushroom, and Gruyère Cheese Quiche for Two

Serves 2

Quiche is a perennial favorite for a hearty breakfast, lunch, or light dinner. This crustless version for two is baked in a 6-inch cast-iron skillet and served straight from the oven. You can substitute any number of savory ingredients, including spinach or broccoli, as well as other kinds of cheeses.

INGREDIENTS

3 large eggs

¼ cup light cream or milk

½ teaspoon Dijon mustard

1 Tablespoon finely chopped fresh basil or flat-leaf parsley

Non-stick vegetable spray

1 ½ Tablespoons olive oil

½ cup (about 2 ounces) thinly sliced zucchini

½ cup thinly sliced yellow onion

¼ pound white mushrooms, wiped, trimmed, and thinly sliced

Salt and freshly ground black pepper

½ cup shredded Gruyère or Swiss cheese

In a bowl, beat together the eggs, cream, mustard, basil or parsley, and salt and pepper to taste.

Preheat the oven to 350°F. Lightly coat a 6-inch cast-iron skillet with non-stick vegetable spray.

Heat the skillet over medium-high heat until hot. Add the oil and zucchini slices in batches, and sauté until lightly browned on both sides, turning once. Using a slotted spoon, transfer the slices to the bowl with the eggs.

Add the onion to the skillet and sauté until golden; combine with the zucchini. Add a little more oil if needed, stir in the mushrooms, and sauté until wilted. Scrape into the bowl with the vegetables, and season with about a ½ teaspoon of salt, or to taste, and pepper. Stir in the cheese.

If needed, wipe out the pan. Spray again with non-stick spray. Scrape the egg mixture into the skillet and transfer to the oven. Bake until a knife inserted in the center comes out clean, about 30 minutes. Remove and serve with a spatula.

Kale, Chickpeas, Yam, Feta, and Couscous Stuffed Peppers

Serves 6

These colorful filled bell pepper halves are bursting with flavor and nutrition. Every meat-eater who has ever tried them has said they were completely satisfying. If you prefer, use quinoa rather than couscous. You can fill the peppers ahead and then bake them just before serving. They also reheat well in a microwave-safe dish. I use a red, orange, and yellow pepper.

INGREDIENTS

2 Tablespoons extra-virgin olive oil, plus extra oil to brush on the peppers and pan

¾ cup finely chopped yellow onion

3 ounces white mushrooms, wiped, trimmed, and sliced

¼ cup finely chopped celery

1 ½ teaspoons minced garlic

½ tablespoon ground cumin

5 ounces kale, rinsed with a little water left on the leaves, stems removed, and chopped (about 6 cups)

1 cup canned chickpeas, rinsed and drained

1 cup peeled and finely diced yams (about 5 ounces)

½ cup dried couscous

1 ½ cups vegetable stock

½ cup drained petite diced tomatoes

½ cup chopped cilantro

6 ounces crumbled feta cheese (about 1 ½ cups)

Salt and freshly ground black pepper

3 large bell peppers, cut in half lengthwise, seeds and membranes removed

Cucumber-Yogurt-Mint Sauce (page 95)

Preheat your oven to 350°F.

Heat a 10-inch cast-iron skillet over medium heat. Add the oil, onion, and celery and sauté until soft, 4 to 5 minutes, stirring often. Add garlic and cumin, and sauté for 30 seconds more. Add the mushrooms and sauté until softened; stir in the kale and cook until softened. Stir in the chickpeas, yams, couscous or quinoa, and stock; cover and bring to a boil. Reduce the heat and simmer until the quinoa is tender, about 5 minutes. Scrape into a large bowl, stir in the tomatoes, cilantro, 1 cup of the cheese, and salt and pepper to taste.

Wipe out the skillet. Brush the outsides of the peppers and the pan with a little oil. Lay the pepper halves in the skillet, cut side up, and spoon about 1 cup of filling into each, mounding it slightly in the center. Cover the pan tightly with aluminum foil and bake for 45 minutes. Uncover, sprinkle on the remaining cheese, and return to the oven until the tops are browned, about 15 minutes more.

Meanwhile, prepare the Cucumber-Yogurt-Mint Sauce (page 95). Remove the skillet from the oven, and let it stand for 5 minutes before transferring the peppers to plates and serving.

Vegetarian Fajitas
Serves 4

My family loves fajitas. They're versatile, easy to make, and appeal to all ages. This robust version includes bell peppers, onions, yellow and green squash, corn, and black beans seasoned with chili powder and minced pickled jalapeños. The filling is sprinkled with Jack cheese before being rolled in tortillas. Fajitas can easily be reheated in a partially covered microwave-safe dish.

Preheat your oven to 350°F. Wrap the tortillas in aluminum foil and heat in the oven until hot, about 15 minutes. Alternatively, once the filling is prepared, lay the tortillas directly on a flame on top of the stove, for a few seconds on each side, until little brown spots appear, turning once.

Heat a 10-inch cast-iron skillet over medium-high heat. Add the oil and onions, and sauté until the onions are soft and lightly colored, about 5 minutes. Add the pepper, zucchini, and yellow squash, and continue cooking until the vegetables are tender and lightly browned, about 15 minutes, stirring often.

INGREDIENTS

8 (8-inch) flour tortillas

2 Tablespoons olive oil

1 large yellow onion, peeled and cut crosswise into ¼-inch slices

1 large red bell pepper, seeds and membranes removed, cut into ¼-inch strips

2 cups julienned zucchini (about 8 ounces)

2 cups julienned yellow squash (about 8 ounces)

1 Tablespoon minced garlic

1 Tablespoon chili powder

¾ cup canned or defrosted frozen corn kernels

½ cup canned black beans, rinsed and drained

2 large scallions, trimmed and thinly sliced

1 Tablespoon minced pickled jalapeños (optional)

Salt and freshly ground black pepper

12 ounces shredded Jack cheese

1 ½ cups purchased tomato salsa

Add the garlic and chili powder and cook for 30 seconds; stir in the corn, black beans, scallions, and pickled jalapeños, if using. Season to taste with salt and pepper. Keep warm.

For each warm tortilla, spoon about ½ cup of the vegetables down the center, sprinkle on the cheese, roll up, and serve with a tablespoon or two of salsa drizzled on top.

DESSERTS

Raspberry-Blackberry Crisp

Serves 4 to 6

I don't like blueberries, which, I know, for many summer fruit lovers is a sin. On the other hand, I adore raspberries and blackberries, so when I make the proverbial summer fruit crisp—that generations of bakers have made in cast-iron skillets—they are the berries I choose. I think you'll find the combination is fabulous!

Preheat your oven to 375°F. Put a baking sheet in the middle of the oven. Lightly butter a 10-inch cast-iron skillet.

In a large bowl, stir the cornstarch and lemon juice together until blended; add the berries and sugar, and gently stir to combine them evenly. Scrape the mixture into the skillet.

In the same bowl, combine the oatmeal, flour, brown sugar, salt, and butter. Using a fork or your fingers, stir the mixture until it is crumbly and blended, and scatter it over the berries. Transfer the skillet to the baking sheet in the oven and bake until the topping is set and the berries are bubbling, about 40 minutes. Remove and cool for at least 15 minutes before serving the crisp from the skillet with vanilla ice cream or whipped cream on top.

INGREDIENTS

Unsalted butter to grease the skillet

1 Tablespoon + 1 teaspoon cornstarch

1 Tablespoon freshly squeezed lemon juice

4 cups mixed fresh blackberries and raspberries

½ to ⅔ cup sugar, depending on how sweet the berries are

⅔ cup quick-cooking oatmeal

⅓ cup unbleached all-purpose flour

⅓ cup firmly packed dark brown sugar

⅛ teaspoon salt

4 Tablespoons unsalted butter, at room temperature

Vanilla ice cream or sweetened whipped cream

Plum Clafoutis
Serves 6

Clafoutis is a classic French dessert—a puffy, custardy, fruit-filled pancake. Most often they are made with cherries, but my favorite fruit for this dish is plums. Serve it warm, straight from the pan either for brunch or dessert. Pfannkuchen (page 79) is another puffy pancake made with apples.

INGREDIENTS

½ cup unbleached all-purpose flour

½ cup + 3 Tablespoons sugar

Pinch of salt

1 cup whole milk

3 large eggs

1 teaspoon almond extract

2 Tablespoons unsalted butter

3 firm, ripe black plums (about 12 ounces), pitted and cut into medium slices

1 Tablespoon plum brandy or cognac Confectioners' sugar

Sweetened whipped cream or crème fraîche, to garnish

Preheat your oven to 425°F. In a large bowl, sift the flour, the ½ cup of sugar, and salt. In a small bowl, blend the milk, eggs, and almond extract together, and then whisk them into the dry ingredients until smooth.

Heat the butter in a 10-inch cast-iron skillet over medium heat until melted and bubbling. Stir in the plums and cook them for 2 minutes, or until almost soft, turning occasionally. Sprinkle on the remaining 3 Tablespoons of sugar, cook until the sugar is melted, then pour in the brandy or cognac and bring to a boil, shaking the pan to spread the fruit evenly.

Turn off the heat, pour the batter over the plums, and transfer the skillet to the oven. Bake until the clafouti is puffy, the edges are richly browned, and a knife inserted in the center comes out clean, about 18 minutes. Remove and let the clafoutis stand for 10 minutes, then sprinkle on some confectioners' sugar, and serve with a dollop of whipped cream or crème fraîche.

Ginger-Spice-Topped Peach Cobbler

Serves 8

Cobblers are among the most popular of Southern desserts. In this simple yet personal version, a ginger-spice batter is poured into the pan and topped by delicately rum-scented peaches. As it bakes, the crust rises to the top and almost covers the fruit. Serve the dessert directly from the skillet with ice cream or whipped cream.

Preheat your oven to 350°F. Put a baking sheet in the middle of the oven.

In a large bowl, stir the rum and cornstarch until smooth.

Add the peaches, sugar, and lemon juice and stir. Set aside.

In a 10-inch cast-iron skillet, heat the butter over medium heat until melted. Meanwhile, in a medium bowl, mix the flour, white and brown sugars, ginger, cinnamon, salt, and cloves. Whisk the milk and melted butter into the dry ingredients, leaving a thin coating of the butter on the bottom of the skillet.

Reheat the skillet over medium heat; pour in the batter and then add the peaches. Put the skillet

INGREDIENTS

Filling:

3 Tablespoons dark rum

2 ½ Tablespoons cornstarch

2 (16-ounce) packages frozen peaches, defrosted

1 cup sugar

2 Tablespoons freshly squeezed lemon juice

Topping:

6 Tablespoons unsalted butter

1 cup self-rising flour

⅓ cup sugar

⅓ cup firmly packed light brown sugar

1 Teaspoon ground ginger

½ teaspoon cinnamon

¼ teaspoon salt

⅛ teaspoon ground clove

1 cup whole milk

Vanilla ice cream or sweetened whipped cream, to garnish

on the baking sheet and bake until the cobbler's top is golden brown and the filling is bubbling, about 45 minutes. Remove from the oven and cool for at least 15 minutes, then serve the cobbler with vanilla ice cream or whipped cream.

Apple-Cherry Tarte Tatin
Serves 8

This famous upside-down tart of caramelized apples and puff pastry was first made by the two Tatin sisters from France's Loire Valley. There are countless versions, including this one in which the thick apple slices are complemented by tangy dried cherries. When I can find Jonagold apples, I use them because they are sweet and juicy with just a touch of tartness. They also hold together while baking.

In a small bowl, combine the cherries with the brandy and set aside. Roll out the puff pastry on a lightly floured surface to a thickness of ⅛ inch. With a sharp knife, cut it into an 11-inch circle and brush off any excess flour. Lay the pastry on a cutting board, cover with a towel, and refrigerate.

Peel and core the apples; slice them in half lengthwise, then cut each half in thirds lengthwise. Put them in a large bowl and drizzle with lemon juice as you cut them to prevent discoloring.

Preheat your oven to 400°F. Put the sugar in a 10-inch cast-iron skillet and drizzle on the water. Turn the heat to high and cook until the sugar melts into a rich, golden amber-colored syrup, 6 to 7 minutes, swirling and shaking the pan often to melt it evenly. Watch that it doesn't burn. Immediately remove the pan from the heat, add the butter (it might bubble up), and stir until it is incorporated. Continue stirring the mixture until the caramel cools, 3 to 4

INGREDIENTS

¼ cup dried cherries

2 Tablespoons apple brandy or Calvados

1 (15-ounce) package all-butter puff pastry, defrosted according to package directions

5 to 6 medium firm, tart-sweet apples, such as Jonagold, Cortland, Northern Spy, Golden Delicious

Juice of 1 to 2 lemons

¾ cup sugar

1 Tablespoon water

4 Tablespoons unsalted butter, cut into small pieces

Crème fraîche or sweetened whipped cream, to garnish

minutes. If the sugar seizes up when you add the butter, return the pan to the heat to re-melt it.

Lay the apple slices on the caramel around the outside of the pan, on their side and each in the same direction with the stem end closest to the pan's edge. Put the remaining apple slices in the center. (You may not need all of the apples.) Drain the cherries and add them around the edges, between each apple slice, and in the middle.

Remove the puff pastry from the refrigerator and lay it over the apples, pushing the edges down the sides of the pan. Cut 3 or 4 small gashes in the surface of the pastry as air vents, then transfer the skillet to the oven and bake for 10 minutes. Reduce the heat to 375°F and bake for 20 minutes longer, or until the crust is golden brown and the syrup is bubbling up the sides.

Remove and cool the tart for about 20 minutes in the pan. Using a plate with a lip that is slightly larger than the skillet, put it upside down over the skillet and, holding them together with one hand, invert the skillet and let the tart slide out onto the plate, rearranging any apples that may have moved. Using a pie server with a sharp edge, cut the tart into slices and serve with a generous dollop of crème fraîche or whipped cream. You can also leave the tart in the pan and reheat it for 15 minutes in a preheated 375°F oven.

German-Style Apple Pancake (Pfannkuchen)

Serves 4

I remember making this German-style apple pancake for my kids as they were growing up. They were always wide-eyed with excitement as I took the puffy pancake from the oven and added the confectioners' sugar and lemon juice that were the final garnishes before we cut it up and devoured it. Don't worry if the pancake collapses. It'll still be delectable.

Preheat your oven to 400°F. Position the rack in the middle of the oven. Heat a 10-inch cast-iron skillet over medium heat until hot, about 3 minutes.

In a bowl, combine the apple slices with 1 Tablespoon of the lemon juice and set aside. In a large bowl, beat together the egg yolks, milk, sugar, cornstarch, salt, and lemon zest. In a separate large bowl, whisk the egg whites into soft peaks. Using a flexible spatula, gently fold the yolks into the whites until just mixed.

Add the butter to the heated skillet. When the butter foams, add the apples, turning to coat them with butter, and then arrange them in a single layer. Pour the egg mixture evenly over the apples. Partially cover, and cook for 10 minutes. Uncover the skillet, transfer it to the oven, and bake for about 15 minutes, or until the bottom of the *pfannkuchen* is nicely browned and it is set in the middle.

Remove, sprinkle with the confectioners' sugar and remaining lemon juice, and serve immediately.

INGREDIENTS

1 large tart-sweet apple, such as Cortland, peeled, cored, and thinly sliced

Juice and grated zest of 1 large lemon

4 large eggs, separated

½ cup whole milk

2 Tablespoons sugar

2 Tablespoons cornstarch

½ teaspoon salt

2 Tablespoons unsalted butter

Confectioners' sugar, to garnish

Tuscan Pineapple Upside-Down Cake
Serves 8

Some years ago while visiting my friend, food writer Nancy Harmon Jenkins, in Tuscany, we had lunch with her neighbor, Mita Antolini, a local farmer. Mita made her "special dessert" in an old wood-burning stove. To my surprise, it turned out to be the best pineapple upside-down cake I'd ever tasted. The cake's texture was unique: kind of firm but light at the same time. I tried to re-create the effect of Italian durum wheat flour by adding a little whole-wheat flour to the batter. It is not especially sweet, so I serve it with sweetened whipped cream or vanilla ice cream.

Preheat your oven to 350°F. Position a rack in the top third of the oven.

In a large bowl, beat together ¾ cup sugar, the egg yolks, lemon zest, ½ cup of the reserved pineapple juice, the brandy, and vanilla until blended. Sift in the flours, baking soda, and salt; mix until smooth. Stir in the melted butter.

Heat the remaining ½ cup of sugar in a 10-inch cast-iron skillet over medium-high heat until the sugar melts and lightly caramelizes, about 5 minutes, rotating the pan often. Immediately remove the pan from the heat and continue to rotate to cool slightly. (The few remaining sugar crystals will melt in the residual heat while you are rotating the pan, so be careful not to over-brown the

INGREDIENTS

¾ cup sugar + ½ cup sugar

3 large eggs, separated

Grated zest of 1 lemon

1 (20-ounce) can sliced pineapple packed in its own juice, drained, juice reserved

2 Tablespoons brandy or dark rum

1 teaspoon vanilla extract

1 ¼ cups unbleached all-purpose flour

¼ cup whole wheat flour

1 ½ teaspoons baking soda

½ teaspoon salt

8 Tablespoons (1 stick) unsalted butter, melted

1 cup chopped pecans or walnuts

Whipped cream or vanilla ice cream, to garnish

sugar while cooking.) Lay enough pineapple slices in the bottom of the skillet to cover (usually 7 or 8 slices), and sprinkle on the chopped nuts.

Beat the egg whites into soft peaks. Mix about a quarter of the whites into the batter; then fold in the remaining whites until blended. Spoon the batter evenly over the pineapple, taking care not to disturb the nuts, and spread with a metal spatula.

Bake in the top third of the oven until the cake is lightly browned on top and the center springs back when gently pressed with a finger, 25 to 27 minutes. Remove the skillet from the oven, run a knife around the inside edges, and carefully invert the cake onto a plate. Cool on a rack, cut into slices, and serve with whipped cream or ice cream.

Chocolate Chunk–Pecan Cookie Sundaes with Salted Caramel Sauce

Serves 12

This dessert is decadence personified: luscious pecan-chocolate chunk cookies topped with great ice cream, and a "to die for" salted caramel sauce. The cookies are baked and served in individual cast-iron skillets. Although the recipe serves 12, bake as many cookies as you have guests and pans, and keep the remaining cookie dough and sauce in the refrigerator in covered containers. Or, freeze individual balls of dough and bake them whenever you want a special dessert. To serve 12, you could also bake one large cookie in a 10-inch cast-iron skillet and bring it to the table while still warm.

INGREDIENTS

- 1 stick (8 Tablespoons) unsalted butter, at room temperature, + butter to grease pans
- ½ cup firmly packed dark brown sugar
- ½ cup sugar
- 1 large egg
- 1 teaspoon pure vanilla extract
- 1 cup + 2 Tablespoons unbleached all-purpose flour
- ½ teaspoon baking soda
- ¼ teaspoon salt
- 1 cup coarsely chopped dark chocolate chunks (about 6 ounces)
- ½ cup coarsely chopped pecans
- Salted Caramel Sauce (page 96)
- Vanilla or chocolate ice cream

Preheat your oven to 350°F. Grease as many 6-inch cast-iron skillets as you will use or a 10-inch skillet with butter.

In a large bowl, cream the butter and sugars until smooth.

Stir in the egg and vanilla. In another bowl, combine the flour, baking soda, and salt. Add the dry ingredients to the butter mixture and stir until smooth. Mix in the chocolate chunks and the pecans.

For each cookie, scoop out a level ¼-cup measure of the dough (or weigh out 2-ounce portions on a kitchen scale) and put the dough in the center of the 6-inch pan.

Repeat until all the pans are filled, then put them in the oven and bake until the cookies are lightly browned, about 13 to 15 minutes. Remove the pans and let them cool until the cookies are warm, not hot.

(Alternatively, put the dough into the 10-inch skillet, flatten into a 1-inch thick disc, and bake at 325°F until done.)

Place a scoop of ice cream on each cookie (or cut the large cookie into 8 to 12 slices while still warm), drizzle on the caramel sauce, and serve.

Aunt Ellen's
Delicious Kitchen-Tested Dishes

✖ ✖

CONFECTION WAFFLES

For tender, delicate Confection Waffles, use one cupful of rice boiled to a mush, and rubbed through a sieve; add two well-beaten egg yolks, two tablespoonfuls of sugar, one-half teaspoonful of salt—and beat until velvety. Measure out one cupful of flour sifted once with two teaspoonfuls of baking powder, and measure out a cup and a half of rich milk and melt one tablespoonful of butter. Add the flour and the milk alternately to the egg and rice mixture, beating hard; whip in half a cupful of finely chopped nut meats; then fold in the stiffly beaten whites of the two eggs, and the melted butter. Cook on hot Waffle Baker, and serve with hard sauce.

✖ ✖

FRENCH MELANGE

Ever eat a bouquet of flowers? French Melange is like that, really! Use two cupfuls of chopped rhubarb (tender stalks that have been put through the coarse blade or your Food Chopper without peeling them). Use two cupfuls of pineapple also chopped, and one cupful of fresh strawberries cut in quarters. Cover with four cupfuls of granulated sugar and let stand for an hour. Then put over the fire in the clean dry Skillet, stir once or twice; cover the Skillet, and let cook slowly over low heat for half an hour. By this time the Melange should begin to thicken. Add a half cupful of shredded almonds or walnuts and tablespoonful of grated orange rind. Leave uncovered and let cook till thick and clear. Stir very little during entire cooking process—distinct bits of fruit should show all through. Pour into glasses dipped in hot water and let cool before covering with paraffin. Serve on nut-buttered bread at tea.

✖ ✖

Chocolate Omelet Soufflé
Serves 4

If you are a chocoholic who loves simple yet intensely rich indulgences, Joe DiMaggio's dessert is a real treat and easy to make.

INGREDIENTS

¼ cup coarsely chopped walnut pieces

1 teaspoon vanilla

8 ounces semisweet chocolate, melted

4 large eggs

⅓ cup heavy cream

3 Tablespoons clarified butter

3 Tablespoons confectioners' sugar

Sweetened whipped cream, to garnish

Preheat your oven to 425°F. Toss the walnuts with the vanilla. Scatter them on a baking sheet lined with aluminum foil and bake in the oven for 5 to 6 minutes, watching that they don't burn.

In a bowl, beat the eggs and cream to blend; add the melted chocolate and beat vigorously until frothy.

Heat a 10-inch cast iron skillet over medium heat until just hot, about 3 minutes; add the butter and walnuts, and cook for 30 seconds. Pour in the egg-chocolate mixture and cook for 1 minute. Transfer the skillet to the oven and bake until slightly firm, 8 to 9 minutes. Remove from the oven, and immediately invert the omelet onto a 10-inch plate. Dust with confectioners' sugar and cut in wedges, serving each portion with a generous dollop of whipped cream.

SAUCES & STOCKS

Red Pepper–Yogurt Sauce
Serves 6

In the jar of an electric blender or food processor, purée the bell pepper, garlic, and salt with the yogurt until smooth. Scrape into a small bowl and stir in the olive oil. Add the mint just before serving.

INGREDIENTS

1 large roasted red bell pepper (from a jar is fine), blotted dry

1 clove garlic, peeled

¼ teaspoon salt

2 Tablespoons Greek-style (thick) plain yogurt

1 Tablespoon extra-virgin olive oil

2 Tablespoons chopped fresh mint leaves

Cucumber-Yogurt-Mint Sauce

Serves 4

In a small bowl, combine the cucumber, yogurt, and salt and pepper to taste. Add the mint. Use this on the stuffed peppers if desired.

INGREDIENTS

1 small cucumber, peeled, seeded, and finely diced

1 cup thick Middle Eastern–style plain yogurt

Salt and freshly ground black pepper

Chopped mint leaves, to garnish

Salted Caramel Sauce
Makes about 2 cups

INGREDIENTS

1 ¼ cups sugar

⅓ cup water

3 Tablespoons light corn syrup

1 cup heavy cream

5 Tablespoons unsalted butter, at room temperature

1 ½ teaspoons coarse sea salt, finely crushe

In a medium saucepan, combine the sugar, water, and corn syrup and bring to a boil over high heat. Cook until the syrup turns a rich amber color, about 6 minutes, swirling the pan and washing down any crystals on the sides of the pan with a wet pastry brush to prevent them from burning. Remove the pan from the heat and whisk in the cream (it will bubble up, so be careful), butter, and salt. Set the sauce aside and serve warm.

Vegetable Stock
Makes about 2 quarts

One of the easiest ways to collect fixings for vegetable stock is to get in the habit of keeping vegetable trimmings including onion skins; carrot, turnip and potato peelings; and those wonderful dark green tops of leeks and celery hearts. Lots of chefs use papery onion skins in their stocks since they add color. The trick is to keep all the fixings in good condition. Unless you gather them within a day or two, it's best to freeze them in a resealable plastic bag, with all the air squeezed out, until you have a sizeable quantity. My vegetable stock differs each time I make it. What follows is a general plan. Don't forget lots of onions and garlic.

INGREDIENTS

1 Tablespoon canola or other vegetable oil

5 large carrots, peeled and coarsely chopped

3 large unpeeled yellow onions, coarsely chopped

3 large stalks celery including leaves, coarsely chopped

2 large leeks, trimmed, rinsed, and split in half lengthwise

2 large cloves garlic, split

Leftover bell peppers, turnips, tomatoes, etc., chopped

2 quarts water

½ cup warm water

4 large sprigs flat-leaf parsley

3 sprigs fresh thyme

1 bay leaf

Salt and black pepper

Preheat your oven to 375°F. Brush a large, flat roasting pan with a little oil.

Scatter the chopped vegetables in the pan, turning to coat them evenly, and roast until they are a rich dark golden brown, turning often, 40 to 55 minutes depending on the size. Be sure they don't burn. Remove the pan from the oven and transfer the vegetables to a deep pot. Add the 2 quarts of water, parsley, thyme, and bay leaf, and bring to a boil.

Meanwhile, stir the warm water into the roasting pan, scraping up the browned cooking bits with a wooden spoon, and add it to the pot. Cover and simmer until the vegetables are very soft, 1 to 1 ½ hours, and then strain through cheesecloth into a clean pot. Season to taste with salt and pepper. Cool and refrigerate until needed. It will keep for 3 to 4 days in the refrigerator. Or freeze for up to 3 months in airtight containers.

"The Secret of Good Cooking is: First, be a critical judge—know excellent cooking from poor cooking; Second, find a fascination in the science, and become thoroughly familiar with 'what, and what not to do'; Third, find a genuine pleasure in the practice—mastering the basic recipes and the operation and control of your Range—and above all, 'THINK.'"

—*Aunt Ellen*

APPENDIX

Cast-Iron FAQs

By David G. Smith

What does it mean to season a pan?

Seasoning is the process used to protect bare cast iron from rusting, provide a non-stick surface for cooking, and prevent food from interacting with the iron of the pan. The process oxidizes the iron to form magnetite, the black oxide of iron (as opposed to rust, the red oxide of iron). Seasoning is a three-step process: First, the cookware needs to be cleaned well to expose the bare metal (using oven cleaner or lye), applying a layer of vegetable fat, and heating the cookware to bond the fat to the metal. Using the cookware continues to season it as foods deposit oils or fats on the pan.

What happens to the fat? Can it get rancid?

When the fats (vegetable shortenings work best) are placed in the hot pan, it saturates the pan's surface. The heat after repeated uses gradually turns the fats to carbon creating the non stick surface—that's why seasoned pans are black. You need to make sure to wipe out the pan well, until it holds only a dull sheen. If you leave any melted fat on the pan, it can turn rancid over a period of time.

Why can't I use detergent on my pan?

Chemicals in detergents are designed to break down oils, so detergents will break down the very fats you want working for you.

What if my pan is "pre-seasoned"?

A pre-seasoned pan is sprayed with oil after it's manufactured, and baked at high temperatures to achieve iron oxidation. The oil seeps into the pores of the metal and the pan is ready to be used, although it's recommended that it should be re-seasoned. A pre-seasoned skillet is black, while an unseasoned skillet is silvery gray.

Could my pan be coated with wax?

Yes, an unseasoned new pan might be sold with a protective coating (wax or shellac). This coating must be removed (typically by scouring) to expose the bare cast iron surface before the pan is seasoned.

Is it ever "too late" for a cast-iron pan?

Unfortunately, yes. If the pan has a crack in it, or is rusted to the point where the surface is pitted—if the rust has actually eaten holes right through the cast iron—you won't be able to get these back to working condition.

Glossary

AL DENTE usually referring to pasta or vegetables that are cooked until just tender yet retaining some "bite."

BASTE to moisten the surface of foods with a liquid or fat while cooking.

BLANCH to partially cook foods in boiling water to set the color, remove an outside skin (such as with nuts), or to soften the texture of vegetables. In many cases, vegetables are immediately plunged into cold water to stop the cooking and retain the color.

BOIL to cook food in rapidly bubbling liquid.

BRAISE a moist-heat method of cooking foods in a covered pan.

BROIL to cook foods under a direct heat source. (Grilling is the same but the heat source is below the food.)

BROTH/STOCK the liquid derived from slowly simmering, herbs and aromatic root vegetables in large quantities of water. The foundation for many dishes.

CHOP to cut into coarse, irregular pieces.

DEGLAZE to stir a liquid into a hot pan that has been used for sautéing or roasting foods, thereby incorporating and dissolving the browned cooking solids that remain in the pan. A good source for pan sauces and juices.

DICE to cut foods into small, uniform cubes.

GRATINÉ to run food under a broiler to add additional color.

JULIENNE to cut foods into thin, matchstick-like strips.

MINCE to chop finely.

POACH to submerge foods in a gently simmering liquid.

PURÉE to turn a solid food into a semi-liquid state.

REDUCE to boil a liquid to reduce the volume and concentrate flavors.

REFRESH to plunge hot food into cold water to arrest the cooking and set the color or to reconstitute, as with dried herbs.

ROAST a dry-heat method of cooking, usually in an uncovered, shallow pan.

ROUX equal parts by weight of flour and fat cooked together to create a thickening agent. It may be cooked to various stages from white to lightly colored to dark brown, depending on its final use.

SAUTÉ to cook foods quickly in a small amount of fat over high heat.

SIMMER the stage just below boil when bubbles just begin to break the surface.

STEAM to cook foods over rapidly boiling water in a covered pan.

SWEAT to soften vegetables in a minimum amount of fat in a covered pan over low heat.

ZEST (V.) to remove the colored outside layer of citrus fruit; (n.) the colorful outside layer of citrus fruit.

About the Contributors

JOANNA PRUESS is an award-winning author who has written extensively on food for the *New York Times Sunday Magazine,* the *Washington Post, Food Arts, Saveur, Food & Wine,* and the Associated Press syndicate. Her most recent cookbooks include *Mod Mex* and *Seduced by Bacon.*

Pruess is well-known in the specialty food business as a consultant, as well as a regular contributor to NASFT's *Specialty Food Magazine* and as a speaker at many shows. She has developed recipes for numerous clients including Bella Cucina Artful Food, Bigelow Tea, Stonewall Kitchen, Sarabeth's Kitchen, More Than Gourmet, Dufour Pastry Kitchens, and Vanns Spices. She founded and was the first director of the Cookingstudio, a cooking school within Kings Super Market in New Jersey, where she had more than 15,000 students in five years.

She and her husband, restaurant critic Bob Lape, reside in the Bronx, New York.

DAVID G. SMITH is a cofounder of the Wagner and Griswold Society, and coauthored *The Book of Griswold & Wagner* and *The Book of Wagner & Griswold.* He was a contributing author to the authoritative kitchenware book, *300 Years of Kitchen Collectibles,* and has had articles published in various antique trade publications. Smith, a judge in upstate New York, has collected cast iron for more than 30 years.

THE GRISWOLD MANUFACTURING COMPANY and THE WAGNER MANUFACTURING COMPANY, which were combined under the leadership of the Wagner brothers in the 1880s, first developed cast-iron, aluminum, and blended-metal cookware. These manufacturers remain a testimony to over a century of dedication to quality and value.

METRIC AND IMPERIAL CONVERSIONS

(These conversions are rounded for convenience)

Ingredient	Cups/Tablespoons/Teaspoons	Ounces	Grams/Milliliters
Butter	1 cup=16 tablespoons= 2 sticks	8 ounces	230 grams
Cream cheese	1 tablespoon	0.5 ounce	14.5 grams
Cheese, shredded	1 cup	4 ounces	110 grams
Cornstarch	1 tablespoon	0.3 ounce	8 grams
Flour, all-purpose	1 cup/1 tablespoon	4.5 ounces/0.3 ounce	125 grams/8 grams
Flour, whole wheat	1 cup	4 ounces	120 grams
Fruit, dried	1 cup	4 ounces	120 grams
Fruits or veggies, chopped	1 cup	5 to 7 ounces	145 to 200 grams
Fruits or veggies, puréed	1 cup	8.5 ounces	245 grams
Honey, maple syrup, or corn syrup	1 tablespoon	.75 ounce	20 grams
Liquids: cream, milk, water, or juice	1 cup	8 fluid ounces	240 milliliters
Oats	1 cup	5.5 ounces	150 grams
Salt	1 teaspoon	0.2 ounces	6 grams
Spices: cinnamon, cloves, ginger, or nutmeg (ground)	1 teaspoon	0.2 ounce	5 milliliters
Sugar, brown, firmly packed	1 cup	7 ounces	200 grams
Sugar, white	1 cup/1 tablespoon	7 ounces/0.5 ounce	200 grams/12.5 grams
Vanilla extract	1 teaspoon	0.2 ounce	4 grams

OVEN TEMPERATURES

Fahrenheit	Celcius	Gas Mark
225°	110°	¼
250°	120°	½
275°	140°	1
300°	150°	2
325°	160°	3
350°	180°	4
375°	190°	5
400°	200°	6
425°	220°	7
450°	230°	8